Return to
PARADISE

Laina Villeneuve

BELLA
BOOKS

2016

Bella Books, Inc.
P.O. Box 10543
Tallahassee, FL 32302

Printed in the United States of America on acid-free paper.

First Bella Books Edition 2016

Editor: Cath Walker
Cover Designer: Judith Fellows

ISBN: 978-1-59493-510-7

Other Bella Books by Laina Villeneuve

Take Only Pictures
The Right Thing Easy
Such Happiness as This

About the Author

Laina Villeneuve thought that growing up with more than a dozen cousins would prepare her for marrying into the Villeneuve family. She was wrong. Her entry into the fold was a call in the wee hours of the morning from the Easter Bunny and his assistant.

Acknowledgments

Just as I started getting to know these characters, my sister and I started having monthly dinners. Thanks Kat for always lying when I asked if I talked about the book too much. Belated thanks for helping me get the right music on my playlist for writing.

My family, both immediate and extended, has a gift for stories and for memory. Thanks for letting me capture some homes, holidays and car history we share.

Thanks again to Citrus colleagues, especially Dr. Salwak whose book *Faith in the Family* planted the seed that began this book. Professor Korn gave me great material for my auto technician. Dr. Peters, thank you for your thoughts on the presidents. Professor Woolum, thanks for your guidance on legal issues. Proffessora McGarry thank you for your insights on the story line and character development. Professor Eisel, get ready for lunch!

A huge thank-you to my fellow Bella writers who offered me advice on how to tighten up both style and story. Blayne Cooper, Rachel Gold and Jaime Clevenger, I'm so fortunate to have met you and been able to talk through stories with you.

Thanks again to my editor Cath Walker who has improved my vocabulary and helped me round off loose ends. The more I talk about editing and revising, the luckier I feel to have been paired with you.

My lovely wife continues to contribute to character and story development, but more importantly, puts up with super long phone conversations and hours spent emailing people to try to create the strongest story possible. I hope the final product is worth the times I slip away to write, revise and edit.

Thanks also to my readers. It means so much to me to know that my stories resonate with you. Few things beat hearing what you think of the finished product!

Dedication

For my mom
I got just the right one

CHAPTER ONE

Madison

"How's Paradise?"

I groaned inwardly at the joke that never got old for anyone except me. One more reason I was glad I only lived in the small northern Californian town for two months of the year. "A fair bit drier than where you are, boss," I responded. The news kept reporting the record snowfall in eastern Oregon where I managed Steve's guest ranch the rest of the year. I wasn't used to him calling during my time off, but I'd anticipated it with the weather. "Are you calling for reinforcements, or are you going to have to push opening day?"

"Yeah, about that." He sighed heavily.

His tone made my stomach drop.

"Steve?" He had always begged me to come back. I had practical experience at almost any job on the ranch and wasn't above pitching in at the corrals, in the kitchen, even with minor repairs, but I also had a degree in business management and ran the place more smoothly than anyone he'd ever had. He routinely took his own vacation while I was at the helm knowing that I ran the place exactly as he did.

"Timmy's wife kicked him out for good."

I'd worked with him before. Steve often pulled his brother-in-law in at the peak of the season when he needed an extra hand. Like me, he could fill any role. *Any* role, my brain reminded me. He could take *my* role. "He's going to be your manager?" I tried to sound neutral, but my throat had constricted making the words squeak.

"I don't have a choice. He's family. I have to help him out. You know we think the world of you. If you're interested in one of the other jobs…"

"No." I set down the heavy biography about Roosevelt's and Taft's presidencies I'd been reading when he called. I am a big-picture person. I do best when I have a lot to juggle. Put me on one task for a season, and I'd be knocking-my-head-against-the-barn bored in a week.

"I'd be happy to write you a letter…"

"Thanks," I said, pressing three fingertips to my forehead. I fanned them from eyebrows to hairline in an attempt to center myself. "I'll let you know if I need it."

"Maybe—"

Pressing my head to my fingers again, I interrupted him. "Thanks for letting me know early." I hit end and set down my phone. Eyes closed, I considered my next move. My savings put me in a position to be choosy about my next job, but the enormity of what was out there and how I would ever find it felt overwhelming. I suppose I was feeling the way people who are dumped feel. There's that old saying about there being more fish in the sea, but I could never figure out how that's supposed to help anyone figure out how to catch one of them. I didn't have any experience dating, but I'd invested all I had in Steve's business. And now I'd been cut loose.

I'd been with Steve long enough to feel like family. I'd thought he considered me family, but real family… Real families complicate everything.

"Madison, honey! You joining us for lunch?"

The smell of bacon hit me the same time as Ruth's voice.

Knowing that she would have returned to the iron skillet on the stove, I descended the stairs to give my answer. "Of course,"

I said, leaning against the lightweight door to the entry hall that could be shut, but never was. It had a simple gold turnlock that sent out a small circular tongue. I flicked it in and out as I looked out the window at the acres of ranch land where I'd lived most of my life.

I heard Bo at the back door, the distinct thud of his work boots before he closed it and then the run of water as he scrubbed up. He'd come into the kitchen still drying his hands with the hand towel, his thin hair askew from his felt Stetson and the quick scrub he gave his face. Ruth hated how he moved that towel. She wouldn't be able to sit down to eat until she returned it to the hook by the sink.

"What's wrong?" He rested his hand on mine.

"Nothing," I said clicking the tongue back inside the door to leave it unlocked.

"Plenty to do out there if you're restless in here," he said, setting the towel down on the kitchen counter.

Ruth frowned at the towel. "Girl's got a right to rest on her vacation." I felt her blue eyes on me, but it was Bo who spoke.

"Just 'cause your body is still doesn't mean your mind isn't spinning." He turned from Ruth to me. "You might as well spill it now before your mouth gets busy with lunch."

I'd always found Ruth to be formal and reserved with me whereas Bo was intuitive to my emotional state. He'd do anything to see that I got what I wanted. That's where the trouble was, I realized. I had to know what I wanted, and what most prominently rattled in my brain was scary. "Steve doesn't need me back," I said frankly as Ruth handed around plates with two pieces of toasted bread for us to turn into BLTs.

With the backs of her wrists, catlike in her movements, Ruth brushed tendrils of gray back from her stunned face. "Excuse me?"

"His brother-in-law needs the job."

She bristled crisply as she made her sandwich. Bo stood mutely when she snatched his plate back without a word to load up his two pieces of bread. "At least he paid you well all those years. You're not hurting for money until you find something else, are you?"

"I'm fine."

"Because if you're not..."

"No. I've got some savings set aside. Now I have to figure out what it means"

"What it means?" Ruth wiped her hands on her apron before shoving Bo's plate into his midsection, forcing him into motion. "Why wouldn't it mean finding another place to manage?"

I delivered my sandwich to the table and returned to the stove to pour two coffees. I set the doctored one by my spot and a steaming black cup in front of Bo.

He nodded his thanks but sat with his forearms on the table on either side of his plate, making up his mind about what to say. "She doesn't have to manage." He turned his bright blue eyes on me. "You don't. You could find your own place, be your own boss. That's what you're thinking, isn't it?" he said, looking pointedly at me before he picked up his sandwich and took a bite big enough that he'd polish off the lot with five more.

As he chewed, Ruth sat with her hands on her lap, her sandwich untouched. "You want to buy a place? If you want your own place, stay here. We're not getting any younger, you know, and we would love to have you here."

"You two are still plenty young, and you've got all the help you need." I bit into my sandwich and looked out the window at their ranch hand's double-wide trailer. I spent a lot of time as a child right there watching out the window, waiting for him to come home. It mattered more to me when I was young and still wanted my father, but he never stopped working. I'd seen him fold a sandwich in half and tuck it in his breast pocket to eat in the saddle. Even when the ranch fed him, like when they did a branding party, he'd stand with his plate. When forced to sit, he inhaled his meal without a single comment and found any reason to excuse himself from the table.

I used to think that he was on the go to get away from me. As someone who had put in five years for an employer, I now considered the possibility that he worked all those hours to make himself indispensable. My father had given Bo and Ruth a good twenty years. I was pretty confident that they would always take care of him, but if they sold where would that put him, or us, if I accepted their offer?

"Madison's in a position to explore her own dreams, not get stuck with a bunch of cattle," Bo said.

"I would miss booking the trips and sharing a piece of beautiful country with people. I'm good with people," I agreed. I'd always been better with people than Steve. Even though I'd never felt like I could truly call Bo and Ruth's place home, or maybe because I always felt that edge of being a guest, I had a knack at making people feel at home on their vacation.

I'd never been entirely home, not where I lived, certainly not where I worked. Not for the first time, the home I didn't really remember came to mind, the one in the background of the faded square pictures my father had from when we lived in Quincy.

My brown eyes rested on Ruth, the woman who raised me. If I'd been theirs, I would have had blue eyes. I hated how often that basic fact of biology reminded me that I was an outsider. With my average height, short brown hair and androgynous build, I was used to being overlooked. Ruth had kept her eye on me for most of my life. It wasn't really fair to her that I didn't think of the ranch as my home, but it wasn't. It was a sanctuary, but it wasn't mine. Suddenly, all I could think about was a place that *could* be.

"You should talk it over with Charlie," Bo said.

I nodded, knowing he was right even though Bo and Ruth's opinion was much more important to me.

CHAPTER TWO

Madison

Hands deep in my coat pockets, I walked the fence line. If I were Charlie, I'd have brought tools in case I found some loose wire, but I wasn't working anything but my mind. Steve's call had opened the entire world to me, yet one property immediately spoke to me. I'd grown up listening to Charlie talk about the place he'd worked up in Quincy. For a while, he talked like he'd go back and make a go of it as owner instead of ranch hand, but over the years the dreams shifted to memories, and then he stopped talking about them altogether.

During my business program at Chico State, I based every project on the property that had once been Hot Rocks Cattle Co. I ran numbers on how many head of cattle I'd need to sell to stay in the black and how long it would take to raise up the numbers, how much capital I'd need to wait out lean years, paying for feed and vaccinations before the cattle ever started earning their keep. I went as far as to find it listed, and month after month when I scrolled through the pictures online, I could hear it calling me. I'd considered telling Charlie about it, but I would have had to initiate the conversation, which has never been my strong suit. By the time I graduated, I was saddled with student loans, not the money to figure out whether my college degree could revitalize an old fallow ranch.

Working for Steve gave me more than the opportunity to pay down the loans and start a nest egg. He kept horses and cattle, but he invested in cabins to rent to guests who wanted a taste of ranch life. Over the years, he found a steadier income from the paying guests and invested in activities that attracted more customers—campfires and cattle runs, trail rides and roping lessons, anything to generate a little more cash.

Bo and Ruth ran a more traditional place, one very much like Hot Rocks, and though they were well-established, I watched them run their numbers in the months leading up to spring sales, always worried about whether they would make it through the winter. With a new door open in front of me, I spun the possibility of turning an old cattle ranch into something like the guest ranch I'd managed for Steve. It wasn't listed anymore, but after sitting on the market for so many years, I crossed my fingers that they had simply taken it off, putting me in a good position to pitch an offer below their asking price.

The sun was sinking over the heifer pasture when Charlie rattled up the drive in his dear old "Love Machine," a faded orange pickup he'd had since before I was born. When he saw me out at the corrals, he gimped over to me instead of his trailer. His hips had never worked right after a cow hooked him in the yards. He drew his brows together, never one for many words.

"Hey Charlie," I said. Hands tucked into his high vest pockets, he waited for me to continue. "Wanted to let you know I'm heading up to Quincy tomorrow."

His gaze left me and traveled over the cattle that were in his charge. Though he didn't chew tobacco anymore, out of habit, he ran his tongue along the inside of his bottom lip. "You want to see her, do you?"

"I want to look at that property you always used to talk about when I was a kid," I said, dodging his question.

His hooded eyes came back to me. Uniformly dark, they were difficult to read. He took off the small-brimmed gray felt hat he wore until blazing hot days forced him to switch to straw.

He slowly turned it in his beat-up hands, a hatband I'd braided him in junior high still circling the crown. I liked him better with the hat on. His cheeks and neck were dark and leathery. I had the same gold undertones and tanned easily, though looking at how constant tanning took a toll on his skin, I was more careful to wear long sleeves and slather on sunscreen. Without the hat, his ghostly white forehead drew my attention away from his eyes. He had hardly any hair left, but he pawed what he had down. "What for?"

"I won't be going back to Steve's. I'd like to run a place, and I don't have any better ideas of where to start looking."

"It didn't make it before."

"I know that." I could make it work. I knew what it was like to be abandoned and was prepared to give the place my all.

"You'd run cattle?"

"I was thinking of outfitting it more like Steve's."

He scratched a hand across his stubbly face. "Old place didn't have buildings for that."

"If the ranch house is big enough, I can start out with lodge rooms." A big fire didn't need anything more than a handful of kindling to get started. I knew how to build a fire from a tiny spark. The spark is the key. Once I got the fire going, I knew I could add the bigger logs that made up my dream.

"You're talking a lot of cash."

"I've been saving some."

He nodded and squinted as if it would give him a better look at the future.

"You don't need my blessing."

"No," I agreed. "The address would be nice though."

He turned without a word and walked ahead of me to the trailer, letting the screen go as he passed through it, unconcerned about whether I was following him or not. I caught it and swept it back open to follow him into the dim space. It was tidy, mostly because he had no clutter, no pictures on the dark wood-paneled walls. On one of the kitchen cupboards, he'd pinned a free calendar. The picture displayed was of a Fourth of July parade in town, a handsome pair of Clydesdales pulling an old-fashioned fire truck, American flags everywhere.

He'd gotten it from a local bank and had forgotten all about it after seven months. It was frozen in a July almost ten years before. Charlie scribbled some notes on a pad of paper. "Don't know the street number, just how to get there." He ripped off the sheet and slid it across the counter, replacing the pen to the pad and turning to the kitchen to make his dinner. "You hungry?"

"Still full from lunch." It was a half-truth which would do. The day had unsettled me, and I didn't feel up to sitting across from my father at the tiny kitchen table watching him try to hide his desire to read the newspaper and struggle to find a way to talk to me.

I couldn't remember eating with my father. As far back as memory went, I'd eaten up at the house with Bo and Ruth. Ruth picked me up from school. It was less of an interruption to her day. At first, I'd hang my backpack by the door and help in the garden or kitchen until my father came to collect me. If he'd ever tried to pull me out and talk to me about my day, I had no recollection of it. No wonder I preferred to spend my time with Ruth and Bo.

The trailer always felt dark. I couldn't understand how the two places could feel so different. Even when I turned on every light, I still couldn't chase away the darkness. I'd had my own small room in the trailer, with my twin bed, bookshelf and desk. Unlike the room I had up at Bo and Ruth's, it never felt like it was mine. Now I realized it was warmth I was reacting to because I could crawl into Ruth's lap and ask her to read a book to me nestled against her chest, something I'd never do with Charlie.

Bo and Ruth had never had any children and welcomed me as if I was their own. For years, I stayed at the house as long as I could, going back to the trailer to sleep down the hall from Charlie, listening to him turn pages late into the night and waking to the sound of the percolator that popped and gurgled before sunup. When school kids started inviting each other for sleepovers, I wanted to be able to do the same, but I didn't want them to see where I lived. That's how I got my room in the main house. Bo sought me out, gently prodding around what was bothering me. I told him about the sleepovers and how I didn't want to have to show my friends the trailer.

The main house sat on a hill shaded by poplars on one side with a generous garden on the other. They had rooms to spare in the large two-story place, inviting with its generous porch and gabled windows. They gave me my pick, and Ruth helped me decorate. We chose the paint color together, and Bo took me shopping for all the supplies and taught me how to cut the edges and roll without splatters. Ruth knew things about dust skirts and what looked nice on the wall, and by the time it was finished, and I could invite the other kids to play, it didn't feel like lying when I said it was my house.

I never considered how Charlie felt when I started sleeping in my bed with the pretty eyelet comforter. The adults must have talked about it when I started asking for sleepovers. Eventually, they weren't sleepovers anymore. All my clothes came up to my room, and I always slept there. Some nights, I looked out to the trailer after I'd turned out the light. More often than not, his truck wasn't parked in front. I'd stand there wondering where he was at my bedtime. If I'd been there, would he have left me by myself?

Now standing in the living room as an adult, it still felt lonely. I don't know that I'd have stopped by to tell him about my road trip had I not needed directions. When I arrived home, I always made sure to say hello and catch up with him, and I always said goodbye before I left, but we were stiff around each other, like distant relatives.

I'd talked about going back to Quincy before. Picking out a dress for a dance, getting my first bra, when I first started my period: there were plenty of times that I thought about my mother. When I tried to talk to Charlie about her, he got even more taciturn. The most he'd ever shared was that she wasn't fit to be a mother, that Ruth was a better mother to me than I could have ever asked for. I knew he said that out of honesty and not to make me feel guilty, but I quickly learned that I wasn't going to get anything more specific out of him. He let me keep the pictures he had of her holding me when I was a newborn and some of me as a toddler. There weren't many. I never found any pictures of a wedding.

My albums were full of either Ruth or Bo holding birthday cakes out to me, or beaming in the background as I opened Christmas presents. Charlie was in plenty of these pictures, but in the background looking like he'd rather be somewhere else.

By the time I was old enough to drive the nearly two hours to Quincy to meet my mother, I had no desire to do so. I'd written to her when I was a kid, but I'd never had a reply. What parent can simply let her child slip away?

I looked at my father. How could they both?

The directions lay on the counter. I picked them up and nodded my thanks. "G'night then Charlie." We didn't hug, and he didn't see me out. I let the screen slam behind me.

CHAPTER THREE

Madison

I'm used to mountain roads, and the stretch up Feather River Canyon is one of the prettiest I know. I left the sweeping pastures of Paradise to follow the curve of the river itself, hairpin turns carved out of rock face on one side and a drop down to the water on the other. As I climbed in elevation over the long drive, I watched for black ice in the shadows that the weak winter sun wouldn't have a chance to thaw.

I never had trouble driving in weather. When I first started working for Steve, he'd ask someone else to run errands if it was raining assuming that nobody from California knew how to drive in the rain. Years went by before my record overrode that assumption. I slowed before curves, accelerating out of them, hardly touching my brakes.

That said, I'd never navigated a narrow mountain road when a tire blew and was completely unprepared for the pull of it. I braked quickly, adrenaline making my skin tingle as I checked the rearview to make sure I wasn't about to be rear-ended. Luckily, I was alone on the road. As I looked for a decent place to pull over to put on the spare, the truck thumped through the next two turns, the rubber thwapping against the pavement. A turnout wouldn't do. I'd be inviting a slow traveler pulling over to plow into me. The river to my right, I had no shoulder.

On the other side of the road, one of the turns had a pocket large enough for my pickup, so I cut across the lane and pulled to a halt facing traffic. I grabbed the tool kit from under the jump seat and retrieved the spare from under the bed of the truck. I assembled the tool to lower the tire, popping out the retaining clip to free it from the cable.

Bo and Ruth had given me the truck in high school, but Charlie had been the one who insisted that if a person owned a car, she should know how to take care of it. We took off the spare and tucked it back away. He taught me how to jump on the wrench to get the lug nuts loose. He showed me how to check my oil and put in wiper fluid, keeping up a running monologue about how mechanics took advantage of people who knew nothing about engines.

I stood the whole time, mesmerized by his words. I never heard him put together so many in such a short time span. I didn't see how learning to change my own oil was going to make me any more knowledgeable and less vulnerable to an unscrupulous mechanic. However, I was happy to spend another afternoon under his tutelage, first at the store learning what supplies I needed, and later under the truck as my hands followed the instructions from the voice I'd so seldom heard.

Now examining the flat, I couldn't make sense of how something with so much tread could look so trashed. I tossed it into the back of the pickup wondering if I should add finding a mechanic to my to-do list in Quincy. I didn't have a choice about finishing the trip up the mountain on the spare but didn't know if it would do to drive the round trip on it. I was about twenty miles outside of Quincy, so if I didn't replace the tire, I was looking at putting about a hundred miles on the spare. Bo would say ask Charlie, but Charlie still refused to own a cell phone, so after I checked out the property I resigned myself to finding a mechanic.

I made the rest of the trip more cautiously, wondering what I was supposed to do if a second tire blew. I took my time, enjoying the whisper quiet of the forest. As I neared town, a small snow berm appeared at the side of the road where the plows had cleared the road, making me grateful I'd had my blowout on more level ground further back down the mountain.

Much of the way up the canyon, I'd been boxed in by sheer mountains and tall evergreens. When the road started to open up a bit, the straightaways longer, the trees thinning out, sometimes interrupted by small meadows blanketed by snow, I relaxed my grip on the wheel. I began to wonder if someone at home should have talked me out of driving up without phoning any of the realtors in the area. Irrational as it now seemed, I just wanted to see the place. The place of my father's dreams called me.

Before I caught sight of the town, I spotted the sign for my turn to Hot Rocks. I found myself alone on the road. Evergreens again towered on both sides. Beyond the dirty snow at the edge of the road, undisturbed white stretched through the forest. Without recent snow, the trees stood in dark contrast, their needles having shed their weight. I passed Charlie's landmarks—a bridge, water still running below, then a long narrow meadow, and finally a dirt drive leading to the property.

I swung around, pointing my truck back the way I'd come, and carefully pulled off the road as much as I dared, wishing I'd had the foresight to borrow Charlie's big old Dodge Power Wagon. I wouldn't have worried about angling his "Love Machine" back out of the unplowed drive like I did my little pickup. I tucked my jeans into my rubber-soled Sorel work boots and shrugged into my coat before I opened the door.

My eyes closed as I took a deep breath of crisp mountain air. I breathed in wood smoke and pine but also the richness of the land, wet under the snow that crunched underfoot. When I stopped, there was silence, not even the whisper of wind in the trees. Without a scarf, my cheeks and ears started to tingle. A very loose padlocked chain held the gate across the drive. It had enough play that I could easily squeeze through and continue over a bridge up the undisturbed snow to the ranch house, my legs and lungs burning.

Charlie had driven these roads for years from the house he and my mother shared in East Quincy. Did the owners have a bunkhouse he could have used had he not been saddled with a family? I'd found a few pictures of him at work, but they never showed the buildings. Black and whites of Charlie driving cattle astride a big bay horse. Charlie kneeling on a calf's shoulder, immobilizing it while another cowboy applied the brand.

I never learned these people's names. Charlie never took me to Hot Rocks with him, and when I'd unearthed the pictures as a teen, he'd quietly tucked them back in the box without a word. In contrast, Bo would have joined me cross-legged on the carpet to reminisce about the horse in the picture or talk about how the sales had been that spring. Maybe it was Charlie's unwillingness to talk about it that built the mystery for me and fueled my desire to return.

The master house came into view, and I stopped at the bottom of the large turnaround drive to take in what a guest would see on arrival. I imagined the wraparound porch would beckon travelers year-round, an escape from the snow or the heat of a summer day. Though I was really more interested in the property, I tromped up to the porch and stomped the snow from my boots, peeking in the dark windows at an empty living room and a few dusty bedrooms. The sight cheered me. The place didn't seem to be waiting for anyone to return after winter.

The back door angled toward the barn and corrals. I couldn't fathom where the cattle would have been kept. The holding pen might have held a few dozen head. Bo's could take a few hundred. I knew from Bo that Charlie had helped him grow his herd, that he'd shipped his heifers up to be bred to the bull at Hot Rocks until he'd become established enough to buy his own. My mind started spinning with the possibilities when something beyond the pens caught my eye.

A small movement. My body tensed as I felt eyes on me. Again I felt how alone I was. Was there cell phone coverage here? How long it would take for someone to track me down were something to happen to me? I relaxed immediately when my eyes finally sorted out the white body against the background of the snow. The huge white horse held my gaze a few ticks before he moved. I caught myself holding my breath, illogically trying not to spook him. Dumbfounded, I stood rooted as he walked to me, his gait as sound as it was slow.

"This your place?" I asked conversationally when he reached me, butting my red-cold hands with his muzzle. I ran my hands over his coarse, dense winter coat, and they welcomed the heat caught under his long yellowed mane. He smelled like home to me, all dusty saltiness. Age revealed itself in his pronounced withers and hollowed-out hind end, but he was clearly being fed, no ribs sticking out as I ran a hand over his barrel. "You're keeping an eye out? I promise I'm legit, on my way to talk to a realtor about the place. You happen to know if it's for sale?"

He swung his head around as if surveying the place with me. I checked the snow. Aside from our tracks, the place was pristine. I hadn't seen any other residences that he could have popped over from and found myself worried about the stray. It didn't feel right to put him in one of the pens if he was due back to his own home, but it didn't feel right to leave him either.

I chewed the inside of my cheek as I stroked the broad expanse of his forehead. He was a good-sized animal, easily sixteen hands, and built for work. "What's your story? I hate to leave you here."

It was impossible that he understood me, but suddenly he was walking again, this time back toward the house and the road I'd trudged up. When I didn't follow, he stopped and looked back at me. Like I said, impossible. "What? You're going to walk me out?" He waited, so I followed. When I reached him, I put my hand on his withers and steadied myself from slipping.

When the trees opened up to the small meadow, and I spotted my truck safe by the side of the road, I realized how privately tucked away the main house was. Even when I turned around for one last look, with the slow curve of the road I could barely make it out. At the gate, I slipped through, pausing once more to pat the big horse.

"You'll be okay?" I fussed.

In answer, he turned and walked away. I shrugged and carefully picked my way over the short bridge to the road, afraid of ice. When I climbed into the cab and looked for my friend, he was nowhere in sight.

I sat in the truck for a moment trying to decide what to prioritize, the tire or the realtor. I mused that what came to mind first probably answered my question. As I rounded the bend to follow the highway through town, I felt like I was driving back in time, grand brick buildings lining both sides of the now one-way street. Following the reduced speed limit, I registered a handful of businesses, an appealing café. A bank and a bookstore. Before I knew it, I was leaving the business area, the buildings more sparse and then suddenly those, too were behind me. I didn't see a reason to stop at the big shopping center on my right and found myself heading up a hill, the familiar evergreens again lining the two-way highway.

A rush of butterflies swept through my belly. I had anticipated being able to turn around and swing back through town and had no idea how I'd do that now, back on a curving hill that did not invite a U-turn. My hands tighter on the steering wheel, I reached the crest of the hill and found another stretch of town on the other side.

The sight of more businesses ahead didn't allay my anxiety. I vowed to stop at the next mechanic I spotted. I coasted down the hill and into the straightaway with two-way traffic. On the left, I recognized the open bay doors of a shop and turned, smiling at the small sign that read "Rainbow Auto." The mechanic was busy with a customer, so I dropped the gearshift to neutral, pulled the hand brake and released the clutch to wait for them to finish.

Waiting in the warmth of my cab, I tucked my hands under my thighs. Though the chill from my hike had faded on the drive into town, the tips of my fingers still tingled. The garage looked more house than business. I pressed my head to the cold driver's side window, staring at the second story perched above the second bay door. The curtains suggested that it was a living space.

A wall of split firewood stacked neatly between posts blocked my view, but somehow I knew that in the summer with the porch cleared of wood, there would be pretty cut glass in the upper half of the front door. I shut my eyes and the image of my young parents standing in that spot flashed in my memory.

I'd seen this house before in a small square photograph.

My father's left arm draped around my mother's shoulder, and an infant me stretched out along his right forearm. He held me as casually as some would hold a football, my face cradled in his hand and my limbs hanging down loosely.

I'd unknowingly come back to the place that I would have grown up in had Charlie stayed with my mom. My body felt icy cold.

I compressed the clutch and started to put the car in reverse, but the mechanic's eyes had found me, and I felt stuck having idled there as long as I had. The customer handed her keys to him, a big guy with a lumberjack beard and ball cap. It struck me that they were the same height, but while he had a heavy bulk to him, broad shoulders under his jean jacket, she was lithe in a well-cut business suit. Styled almost-blond hair framed her face—wispy bangs and sculpted eyebrows—this was a woman who took care with her appearance. She spoke with her hands and easy large smile on her face. Her posture suggested homecoming queen, the girl everyone liked and everyone wanted to be seen with. Having always got her way through school, it made perfect sense that she would continue to use her skills in the adult world.

She continued to stand in the shop when the lumberjack got into her SUV, and I waited for him to pull it onto the blocks, surprised when white lights signaled that he was backing up. He maneuvered around me in the small driveway and disappeared into the traffic behind me. I sat uncomprehending as the homecoming queen approached my truck.

CHAPTER FOUR

Lacey

What the fuck, I thought eyeing the woman in her black truck, not wanting to deal with anything in my business getup. Figures that someone would show up in the five-minute window I had opened up to get Guy's Suburban back to him. She continued to sit there even after he left, forcing me to leave the relative warmth of the shop.

"Can I help you?" I asked her. I squinted into the cab, and she stared at me without speaking. Great, a space cadet. She opened her mouth like she was going to speak but looked back at the house. She seemed lost. "Shop's not technically open, but if it's something simple…" I prompted, cold and ready to get inside and into some warm clothes.

"You live here?"

I turned to look at the house. What the hell did that have to do with anything? "Yes."

"How long?"

"Look, I wasn't planning on working today. I'm obviously not dressed for it. Did you need directions?" My feet were starting to freeze in my pumps, corporate drag for the monthly small business meeting at the Chamber of Commerce.

This got her brown eyes to focus on me instead of the house. Maybe she was high and drawn to my sign. I heard my friend Hope's warnings about putting Rainbow in my business name.

"I…" She stared at the open bay door as if she were trying to remember why she was parked in front. "I got a flat on my way up the canyon. I'm on the spare right now and wanted to make sure it'll get me back home."

"Which tire are we talking?"

"This one." She pointed down at the front driver's side.

I quickly read the information on the tire. "You've got a standard tire there, so you're fine driving on it until you can fix the flat. If you're worried, you can pull up on into the garage. I can check the pressure for you." I stepped back and let her put the truck in gear and pull in ahead of me, noting a small rainbow sticker on the back window. Well, that changed everything. I decided she must be in awe of how bold I dared to be with my signage in a small town.

She had already shut off the engine and was stepping out of the truck to remove the cap from the tire valve, making me feel a little bad about the pothead assumption. I assessed her in a wholly unprofessional manner, admiring the hair so short it stuck up a bit at her crown and would have been boyish on a less feminine face. She moved freely in clothes that had seen real work, the worn barn jacket and heavy jeans tucked into snow boots, and now seeming much more capable than at first glance.

I pulled the air hose over and checked her pressure to the manufacturer's specs on the door, adding a pound before I held my out my hand. Long, slender fingers as feminine as her facial features surrendered the valve cap. I noted with disappointment that she didn't register the brush of my fingertips across hers. "This tire's good to go for a trip down the mountain, though it'd be good to get the one from the set patched up and back on for balance and wear, if it's salvageable and you've got the time."

Stabilizing herself with a hand on her cab, the woman studied my shop as if she hadn't heard me. When her gaze did return to me, she said, "You're not open."

"C'mon," I said, smiling big. "I wouldn't turn away family."

She furrowed her brow, so I pointed to the rainbow on her truck. She looked to her sticker and back to me with a blank expression. Okay, I thought, going back to my original take on her. She might be cute. Too bad she's a brick shy of a load.

"I…" There was the lost look again. "I think I know this place, but not as a garage. It was a house." She patted her pockets as if she could locate the answer in one.

I frowned. I grew up in Quincy, yet I had never seen this woman before. My parents had bought the place when my mom found out she was pregnant with her fifth kid, and we'd been there nearly twenty years. How did she know I'd converted it into a garage? Did she know that we were standing in what had been my bedroom? The humor of poking around in someone's engine or having my hands on the intimate workings of the transmission never grew old for me. I never shared with my local clients that I worked on cars in my former bedroom, but I was tempted to tell her. If she was like most of my friends, though, she wouldn't find it funny. Best to get back to business and move her on her way. "Did you want me to look at the tire to see if it could be patched?"

"Oh, it's long gone," she stated.

I peered in the back of her truck and saw how shredded it was all around the rim. "Oh, yeah. You're pretty much screwed there." Though she hadn't asked for advice, I checked out her rear tires and saw that there was plenty of wear left on them. "Your rear looks fine," I said before I realized what I was saying. For a moment, I hoped she'd take it flirtatiously. It could have led us into a conversation about what she was doing in town and how long she'd be around. Unfortunately, she didn't react to the double entendre. I could easily see her cluelessness getting her snowed on a full set of tires she didn't need. "You could easily get away buying just two new tires. You'll want the new ones up front for the best steering."

"Can't I pair a new one with the spare and carry the old front passenger as my spare?"

Crossing my arms over my chest, I puzzled over her first logical utterance. I liked a person confident enough to speak her mind. "If that tire is in good shape, you could do that. How long have you been driving on the spare?"

"Thirty, forty miles?" she estimated.

"You said you were heading home today?"

"Yes."

I put my hands in my pockets, trying to ward off the chill seeping through my too-thin business jacket. To get my blood moving, I walked to the other side of the truck to eyeball the tread and then came back around to check the coding on the side of her spare. "I wouldn't recommend driving any distance the way you're matched up here." As I got into the details of tires, her attention drifted again, maybe to hold up the cost of tires to the balance in her bank account. More likely, she'd gotten lost in her impossible idea that she knew my house. Whatever it was, I had to snap her out of it. She was dressed for the weather; I was not.

"How long did you say you'd lived here?" she asked in a faraway voice.

"I grew up here," I answered curtly. Enough with the chitchat. At this rate, I'd never get my feet warmed up. I glanced at my watch as discreetly as I could and found I was now running late for my lunch date. "If you wanted that referral," I prompted.

That finally put her into motion. "Sure. That would be helpful."

I grabbed one of my business cards and wrote down the number of a friend who mostly did tires. With the briefest of eye contact, she took the card and slid into her cab. To my relief she immediately turned over the ignition.

"Whatever you do about that tire," I said in parting, "don't get screwed into a full set. You don't need it."

She gave me a thumbs-up as she pulled out of the bay stall, and I felt a pang of sadness. It wasn't every day a cute lesbian in my age range visited what had been my bedroom. I silently wished her well on her journey, hoping she was safe and found herself where she needed to be.

CHAPTER FIVE

Lacey

"Lacey! Over here, girl!" my lunch date Delevasha hollered, like I hadn't spotted her sitting smack in the middle of the nearly empty restaurant. She pointed to the empty seat with a tray waiting in front of it.

I wrapped an arm around her shoulder as I slipped into my seat, grateful to settle into the warmth of the burger joint. "Coach Michaels," I said, toasting her with a fry.

"You're late, and you're still in costume. What gives?" she mumbled around the french fry she'd folded into her mouth. She paused her chewing to give her signature greeting, an expression of concerned sympathy that had grated on me the brief period we'd tried to date. Whether she stood at the door with a birthday bouquet and bottle of wine or met me at the local vet to hold my hand as I had my dog put down, her expression was always the same.

When we were dating, I obsessed about what aura I carried to make her so concerned about my well-being. Her heavy sigh and the way the inside tip of her eyebrows curved up so they pointed toward the ceiling made me paranoid that I was barely holding my life together. Now that we'd been buddies for years, I realized that it had nothing to do with me. She'd similarly sigh her thanks to the busboy who brought our catsup.

"I got held up."

"I told you not to keep cash in your shop."

"As if Annie Oakley comes through Quincy on a regular basis." I took a bite of my burger, glad Della had ordered for me even if it was so she could have her onion rings and swipe some of my fries as well. "You think Annie Oakley was a lesbian?"

Della took a long draw of soda. "What in the world makes you think that? Just because she was a better sharpshooter than most men doesn't mean she favored women. She was married."

"I got held up by a lesbian is all."

Della's hands smacked the table and she raised herself up as if by looking around the restaurant, she could locate her. "Here in town? Where is she?"

"She had tire trouble. I couldn't help. She said she was driving down the canyon tonight."

"So you let her go?" She held out an onion ring which I declined.

"What was I supposed to do? Invent some reason she had to leave her truck with me?"

"Yes! Wiggle some hose or plug or something so the thing wouldn't start. Then tell her that all the rooms in town are booked but your friend Della happens to have room for her."

"We're not that desperate."

"Speak for yourself, sister. It's been a year since I got laid."

"Not a year," I argued. "What about Natasha? You said last Christmas…oh."

"Yeah, like I said, a year, and it was a pity lay for an old lady, the worst kind."

"You're not old," I reminded her. I placed my hand on hers for a moment. I loved her skin, the dark richness of it like soil in fall. Mine was the stark contrast of winter snow unless I had burned to a painful red. My thoughts drifted to the stranger's fingers brushing against mine. I placed my hands back in my lap.

"Let's write that down and see how you feel when *you're* in your thirties. These are my best years, and I might as well be locked away in some tower living here."

"But imagine the glory when you turn your basketball team into champions."

She let her head fall dramatically on her forearms crisscrossed on the tabletop. "We're not in last place this year."

"You think it's because Patty graduated?" I asked, glad we'd directed the conversation away from the last time either of us had been laid. Since we had broken up, I tried to date a woman I'd met in Chico, but I'd ended it when it became clear that she was getting everything she wanted out of the long-distance relationship, but I wasn't. I needed someone who wanted to be with me, day in and day out.

"I've never seen a girl so untalented and driven at the same time. I lost count of the times she fell on her face."

"I've never seen someone trip on the court lines."

Della laughed so hard she choked and waved her hands in front of her face to stop me from saying another word. "You cannot say things like that about my students. Everyone gets a shot, everyone."

"Everyone gets a shot, even if she never makes it in the basket."

"No more." The swat she landed on my shoulder had a hint of seriousness. "This isn't exactly a recruiter's dream here, McAlpine."

"You don't have to tell me," I said.

I was the grandchild recruited to keep an eye on her grandmother once she started to need more help with her errands. You're looking to start your own shop, so do it in Quincy, my parents argued. You can have the old house and pop over to Gran's once a week. Twice a week. After work each day. You don't have any kids, two of my siblings argued. We've got our own families to care for and no energy to spare. I knew about sacrifice too. Grousing about the population that stagnated at fewer than two thousand was one of our favorite topics. That said, there was no way in hell my gran was ever leaving, and her sympathetic ear and rooster-shaped cookie jar always well stocked went a far way to keep me sane.

"Tenure this year, right?" I asked, switching to a safe topic.

"Yep."

"Don't sound so excited. There were only, what, two hundred other people who wanted your job?"

"I'd be a lot more excited if I didn't have to take you as my date to the reception since you let my chance to take a real date drive out of your shop today. I'm never meeting anyone."

"Blazer met Hope," I offered helpfully. "She's your mentor. Why don't you talk to her about it?"

"She scares me," Della said succinctly.

"Scares you?" I said, not wanting to hear yet again the game she played, always measuring herself against others.

Della started ticking off the tasks Dani Blazer handled on the campus. "It's not only how much her students love her. It's the rodeo club. It's being a Senate officer. And now she's working on getting the campus to do the Safe Zone training. And she's got a little one at home. What doesn't she do?"

I pulled a napkin from the dispenser, looking for a way to reroute a discussion we'd had plenty of times. Della's passivity frustrated me. She could be as involved on campus as Dani but preferred to sit back and blow hot air instead of changing anything. I appreciated the way Dani had whipped both the campus and the town into the twenty-first century.

She was a firecracker when she arrived, first making the whole place fall in love with her and then demanding that they continue to treat her with respect when she came out. There were plenty of people in town who suggested that it was her fault that there were any gay people in Quincy at all which was absurd. She was simply the first one who acted like it didn't matter, holding Hope's hand while they walked down Main Street even though it brought pointed stares.

Everything mattered to Della. She believed their colleagues were more comfortable with Dani's being Mexican to her being black. She agonized over the rodeo team's success and the basketball team's losses. I tried to point out how many years

Dani had invested in the school and tried to get Della to spend her energy better, but her self-doubt exhausted me. I set down the napkin and took hold of Della's hands across the table. "She doesn't sit on the sidelines. She's in the game with all she has. You could be too. It's your choice."

"It's my choice on the basketball court, sure, but outside of that it's in someone else's hands." She tipped her chin and flashed her eyes upward. Her face clouded, and with a deep frown on her lips and eyebrows, she pulled her hands from mine. "You don't get to talk about sitting on the sidelines when you let a cute lesbian walk away."

"I never said she was cute." I felt my face flush when I thought again about the stranger's slender fingers.

Della pursed her lips and cocked them to the side. "Mmm hmmmm. Thought so. Details."

"I barely saw her. She wanted me to look at a tire." I picked up the napkin to have something to do with my hands. Della waited, forcing me to admit that even though the stranger was probably well on her way to Chico, she remained in my thoughts, the dichotomy of her slight frame in her worn work clothes and the no-nonsense haircut that was still feminine in the way she swept it to the side. I pulled my thoughts from her face to the one in front of me. Della had been watching as I replayed the meeting, the brush of my fingers across hers.

"Should've pulled a hose and made her stay longer." She gathered our trash to one tray and stacked them.

"Maybe, but we both know that being lesbian in the same town isn't necessarily the ingredients for a relationship."

"You're still sure about that?"

"Still sure." I grabbed our trays and took them to the trashcan. I'd been the one to switch us from meeting for dinner to lunch. After dinner, it was too easy to let the gravitational pull of her bed distract me, but I knew it wasn't fair to sleep with someone I couldn't date. I was okay being friends with Della. A pep talk or gossip exchange once a week, I could do. Beyond that, keeping my own company wasn't so bad.

CHAPTER SIX

Madison

"Well this is certainly exciting, Madison." Ruth beamed her approval across the rough sketch of the property that I'd drawn as I narrated its possibilities.

"I haven't signed anything," I said, feeling a little sick to be moving from thinking about buying property to actually doing it.

"It's a good investment," Bo said. "You have a solid plan. What about the start-up?" he asked, moving into the logistics.

"Not being employed doesn't make me look all that great on paper, but I think I can do ten percent and still have what I need to get the bare bones refurbishing done to open. The place is well situated by a river, so I can offer fishing right away and scope out some hiking trails. Once I have money coming in, I'll be able to take on other projects, the private cabins I want to put beyond the main house."

"Until then, you'll run it more like a bed-and-breakfast?"

"More like a small resort with all of the meals factored in. If I set myself up in the office, there are three bedrooms. One has a private bath, and it doesn't seem like it would be difficult to plumb one more with a half bath. I want enough left in my bank account to take on something like that early. A private bath makes a big difference to a lot of clients." I wanted to remind them that I had experience, that I wasn't going into this cold.

Bo's pale blue eyes settled on me. They always seemed ghostly to me. I saw how they served him during business negotiations. When he settled his glare on a buyer, they knew Bo wasn't budging on price. I knew exactly what he was thinking now. A young single girl was asking for trouble renting out rooms in her home so far from town or any neighbors.

How could I explain that the land called me? It welcomed me as surely as Ruth and Bo had taken me into their home. It stood vacant, waiting for me to make it my own. This was the place that would take away the question of where I belonged.

That thought swung me back around to the auto shop so quickly I lost my bearings and had to rest my hands on the table for a moment. If Charlie had stayed, it could have been me standing in that garage, only it would have been our house. What would the world have looked like from that porch? I once found a picture Charlie had tucked away in his bedside table of us as a brand-new family. Until now, I hadn't realized that I had even registered the house. It was merely in the background. I closed my eyes and saw the place as it was when my parents had it. I had no memory of belonging to that house. I wanted to stand where my parents had as if the house behind me were my home. What would my life look like now if they had stayed there, Charlie's arm around my mom's shoulders?

As Charlie suspected, she was still in town. I'd found her easily in the phone book, but I didn't drive by her place. How many years had it been since she'd lived in the house she'd shared with Charlie and me? Did she ever think about it? I imagined myself growing up with both of my parents. What would it have been like to bring home friends to where you lived with your mom and dad? I wondered if the mechanic's parents were still together.

"How much work do you think the house needs?" Ruth asked.

I shelved the memory of my short talk with the Homecoming Queen and recalled some details from my walk-through. "Quite a bit. Smells like they had a pet that wasn't housebroken. All the carpet's going to need to go, but it's an older place. I'm crossing my fingers that there's a nice wood floor underneath. It's been neglected. Everything needs a fresh coat of paint, but I think a lot of what needs to be done I can do myself."

"Too bad you're not a little closer. I'm a good painter."

"I'm counting on your help with color. And I don't think it's too much for me. Since I'm able to dedicate all my time to it, I should be able to get it looking nice in the next few months."

"I worry about you being lonesome up there in the woods, no friends."

She said nothing about my mom though I knew she knew she still lived in Quincy. That was all my brain needed to flip the mechanic back to the front burner. "I did meet…" As I was about to describe it all, something made me pause. It was strange enough to have spent the entire drive home thinking about her, wondering if she thought I was a whack job, considering whether she'd been flirting with me. She had been flirting, hadn't she?

"You met…" Ruth prompted.

I worried that mentioning her to Ruth and Bo would somehow jinx anything that might come of our chance meeting. The big white horse flashed through my mind. "There was this great white horse the first time I walked the property. I didn't see him with the realtor, but I think he'd be good company."

"So he doesn't come with the land?" Ruth asked.

"When I asked, the realtor said it's the land and buildings, no stock," I answered.

"But you saw this animal on the property," Bo said.

I shrugged. "Maybe there's a fence down between the neighboring property."

"That's something you want to discuss. A neighbor who doesn't maintain the property line can be a real thorn in your side."

"I know."

"You don't need errant stock wandering at will, especially not with the liability they would bring with your guests."

I laughed, picturing the calm, wooly horse as a liability. To me, he was the opposite—a draw. I hadn't expected the realtor to know anything about a horse, but the way she'd frowned and insisted that there had never been an animal when she'd been on the property illogically disappointed me. Eventually, I'd have stock, good bomb-proof riding horses for inexperienced riders. But I couldn't imagine that being among the priorities of setting up my small resort.

"You've factored in insurance? You've talked to a realtor about how much it will take to buy the property, but have you gone through your other costs?"

I sat back feeling the enormity of the task. Though I could get it functioning pretty quickly, it would take a lot of lean years to get it anywhere near the kind of outfit I'd been managing, and even then it would never be the size of Steve's place in Oregon. I reminded myself that I'd never wanted such a big place that I'd have to hire and manage a huge staff. Years stretched in front of me, and I saw myself settling into a rocking chair on the wraparound porch to listen to the sounds of the world tucking itself in to sleep before I turned in to my own bed. All the hard work I put in would be mine to enjoy. Nobody would be able to take that away from me. Whether anyone would be there to enjoy the sunset with me wasn't something I felt I could afford to picture.

For the moment, what I knew was that the place I had my eye on needed a lot of work, needed *me*, and I felt prepared to give myself to the task. I knew how to be frugal, how to keep money in the bank by leaning into the work myself. I smiled at Bo knowing that if I asked, they would put in what I needed to get to twenty percent. If I ever needed anything, they'd be there. All I had to do was ask. But then it wouldn't be mine. "You're not forgetting that I managed Steve's place, are you?" I asked. "I know how much cash I need to cover the mortgage until I have income from guests, and I've got it. Barely, but I can do this."

Bo consulted with Ruth. They didn't say a word, but I saw the look pass between them, his wanting to know if he should push harder and insist that I let them help and her level gaze that told him to leave it. A strange feeling crept into my gut as I realized the level of connection they had with each other. I'd only ever felt that kind of connection with a place. A place I knew solely from the many stories Charlie and Bo told about Hot Rocks. When the two of them reminisced, it felt like they were talking about another land in another time, one that somehow suited me better. As a child, I dreamed about who I would have been if Charlie and I had stayed in Quincy. Now I had the chance to find out.

"We want to be your first guests when you're all set up," Ruth said.

I matched her smile with my own, even though what I'd imagined as my future had started an echo of sadness I'd never felt before. I pushed myself to picture having Ruth and Bo as guests. I could make them proud.

"If you ever get stuck…" she said, not needing to finish the thought.

"I know. And it's not like I'm moving out tomorrow. You're going to have to put up with me through escrow."

"We'll try hard to manage," Bo said, pushing away from the table. He squeezed my shoulder on his way out of the room.

Ruth cleared their dishes, and I carried my own to the kitchen. Setting them down on the counter, an envelope with my name on it caught my eye. I picked it up and raised my eyebrows in question.

Ruth frowned, a mirror of my confusion. I recognized Charlie's neat, deliberate lettering, but it wasn't like him to leave something at the house for me. When I'd been little, I could always count on him to walk up on my birthday with a present, and when I was older a card, always the long narrow ones that simply held cash. This wasn't that familiar shape. I slipped my finger under the lip without consideration, not expecting to find a check tucked inside.

Least of all one with so many zeroes. In a flash, I set it down on the counter and took a step back.

Ruth stepped forward, and I watched her expression change when she looked at the amount he'd penned. A series of emotions flashed over her face. I anticipated her disbelief but was surprised that hurt was among the reactions. Now she looked to me for explanation.

"I don't know," I stammered. "I didn't know he had any money."

"The way he's always worked like a dog, it doesn't surprise me." At my confused look, she asked where I always thought he was at night.

"I thought he had a lady friend he visited."

"Listen to you," she guffawed. "Lady friend. I don't think I've seen Charlie so much as look at a woman as long as I've known him. He's always taken a second, sometimes third job that he can do after the sun goes down here."

All those nights I had watched his trailer, I was convinced he was out with someone. As I got older, I invented all sorts of things about that person. I gave her a husband, kids, something that complicated his being able to stay overnight because his truck was always in the driveway in the morning.

"Is there a note?" Ruth interrupted my thoughts.

Sliding the envelope out from under the check, I peeked inside and found a small slip of paper, something you'd write a midweek grocery list on.

I always meant to buy my own place.—Charlie

I turned it over though I knew the back was blank. Ruth was waiting, but I didn't hand it over. I tucked it and the check back in the envelope and said simply, "He wants me to put it toward the property."

"Well I'll be."

I wished I could go thank him, but I couldn't even imagine how that would go. If Ruth had given me the check, I would have thrown my arms around her. But Charlie wasn't there. He was away on a delivery, and wasn't that the point? Did he think that a huge check equaled us out somehow, made up for the choices he'd made? If he'd been home now, I told myself I would have stormed down and demanded that he explain why we'd left Quincy and why he didn't want me with him in the trailer. Though the amount eased my anxiety about starting up the guest ranch, as I pocketed the check, I still felt angry.

CHAPTER SEVEN

Lacey

I hummed along to the Rolling Stones's "You Can't Always Get What You Want" as I puttered on my 1953 Volkswagen Beetle engine that got my spare time between jobs. I learned to drive on a baby blue version of the same make and model, and the day my dad had sold it to a collector, I vowed to have one for myself even if I had to rebuild it from the inside out.

I spent years scouring junkyards to find authentic parts: a window crank for the passenger door, functional clips for the wind-wings, the turn signal arms that flipped out between the front and rear windows, both chrome bumpers, the gas cap, the rubber accelerator pedal, the steering wheel... The list was never ending.

I'd acquired nearly everything but the missing horn. Jimmy out at Quincy's own salvage yard would call if he ever got one, and Martha at the antique shop next door said she always had her eye out when she was out buying. She'd looked so pleased with herself when she'd come home from a trip with a horn from a late '60s VW that I hated to tell her it wasn't right.

I would have bought it and let it go but realized that wouldn't help me track down the one I longed for. Apologetically, I'd explained how the '53 depicted the water by the castle with three lines that looked like a bowl instead of the two wavy ones on the one she'd found. She'd made me sketch it out, and it touched me that she carried that sketch with her whenever she went, sharing the fervor I had for having every detail right on my restoration.

I grabbed a punch and hammer to bend up the tabs on the flat washer to help lock the crankshaft nut on. At least I thought I was using the hammer on the punch. My knuckle screamed otherwise when I smacked it instead. Dropping the tools, I pinched the throbbing hand between my knees. "Sonofa..." Before I could really let loose, a rusty maroon Chevy Nova nosed into my shop.

Smacking my hand on my thigh, I traded one pain for another.

I steeled myself when the scuffed black heels hit my drive. Shawneen Golden's shapely legs followed, and while I wouldn't call myself a fashion expert, I thought there were rules about what season you could wear a skirt that far above the knee. Or maybe I was thinking about age. While she had to be well into her forties, she dressed like the local high school kids with their low-cut shirts and heavy makeup.

"Shawneen," I said, still rubbing my sore knuckle.

"Honey, this old thing still doesn't start up for me. "Dennis gave me a jump before he went to work...." She tipped her head back filling my shop with her barking laugh when she realized the innuendo. She dabbed at her eyes with her fingertips. "I did not mean to imply...not that it hasn't...but you don't need to hear that."

She smiled at me, and I wondered if her act worked on straight men. It clearly worked on her boyfriend Dennis. I gave her a tight smile and tried to get to business. "That's a brand-new battery." I knew because I'd replaced it myself. I opened the door to check her light to see if she'd drained the battery by leaving the dome light on.

Hand on hip, she leveled her eyes at me. "Dennis already checked. I didn't leave the door open. He said what we need to do is put in a switch, so I can turn off the battery when I'm not driving. He'd do it himself, but…" She turned practiced pleading eyes on me.

I held up my hand. Dennis raised my hackles. He had his own version of fixing things that had more to do with what was on hand or what he knew how to do than what was right for the vehicle. He'd wired the glove box shut instead of tracking down a new clasp, and had installed a button on the dash to turn the headlights on and off when they'd stopped working on the turn signal stalk. "Stop," I said. "Please do not let Dennis do work on this car. Something is draining the battery. I'll figure it out. You need a ride?"

"You're a doll." With a big smile, she stepped close and squeezed my arm. Even with all the grease from the shop, her cloying perfume would linger on my clothes, and I'd be smelling it all day. She'd dropped hints that she knew I dated women, and though she had a boyfriend, she behaved like it was her flirting that got her favors from me. However, I was happy to give customers a lift when they lived or worked close, and Shawneen waited tables just down the street at the Chinese restaurant.

I locked up the shop, leaving my *be right back* sign up, and slid into the little red Nissan two-door my folks had passed on to me when I started driving. "It shouldn't take long to find the problem. I'll give you a call."

"Do you think you'll be able to fix it today?" she asked hopefully.

It was just past noon. I had a pretty good idea of what was wrong with the car and was confident I'd have it back to her, but I knew that if she was only beginning her shift, she wouldn't be off until after I closed up shop for the day. Not wanting to volunteer to deliver the car, I addressed her question directly. "You've got a parasitic drain. It's not the dome light, so I bet it's your trunk or glove box light that's the culprit. If I'm right, I'll have her up this afternoon."

"Maybe I can get Val to swing me by on my break."

I knew her boss wasn't going to give both his staff breaks at the same time. I tried not to grind my teeth. "I could probably drive it down when I'm finished with it."

"Oh, that would be super. Tell me whatever you want on the menu. I'll get you whatever you want." Again her voice dipped suggestively.

You walked right into that trap, I scolded myself as I slowed in front of the restaurant.

She opened the door and then swung pouty honey-brown eyes to me. "It's slushy."

I did clench my teeth at that, but I still backed up and pulled up right next to the sidewalk in front of the place, so she wouldn't have to get her inappropriate footwear wet. Unbelievable. I hated it when she angled to trade my labor for food. If I didn't count on the repeat business from locals, I would never have put up with it. I have to admit, too, that the way she treated my friends, Hope and Dani, bothered me. She'd been a real bitch when the couple came out, and I was going the killing-her-with-kindness route to teach her that none of us were any threat.

She leaned back into the car letting all the heat out of my little sedan. "Thanks doll. See you back here in a bit." She tossed her hair and strutted inside.

I wanted to pound my head on the steering wheel but eased off the brakes instead, rolling back out to the main drag. When I got back to my shop, I opened my bay door again and ran my hand along the Nova's trunk. I had to admit that even though she'd treated it like crap, I still loved it and cared for it the same as I did the VW.

I was sure Shawneen had history with the old tank, and I appreciated someone who stuck with a finicky car instead of tossing it curbside. I bet she'd never climbed into the front seat of anyone else's car mistaking it for her own. Some of my other customers had cars so ubiquitous that they told me stories about approaching a car that looked identical to theirs, puzzling over why their keys didn't work until they realized their car was parked three spots over.

I released the hood latch and attached the ammeter to the negative battery cable to see how many amps were being drawn from the battery when the car was turned off. As I predicted, something was drawing power. I wanted to explain to Dennis that the trick to diagnosing the culprit is to pull the fuses until the meter shows a reduced reading. For the inexperienced, the process could take a while, but with experience comes wisdom, suggesting the glove box and trunk lights as the most likely candidates.

Closer to the engine, I suspected, disconnecting the glove box light. The meter swung down, confirming my choice. The parasitic drain on the car I could fix. I couldn't help wondering if there was any way to fix the drain the vehicle's owner had on me.

CHAPTER EIGHT

Madison

I had no good excuse to offer the realtor for being an hour early. No storms or roadwork warranted giving myself such a large buffer. Reluctant to reveal how anxious I was to call the property my own, I retraced my first trip through town a month ago, ending up at Rainbow Auto again.

Idling in the center divider, I realized how idiotic it would look to approach the Homecoming Queen with a question about my truck that I'd had to leave down in Paradise. I'd driven that truck for six years, and it had never failed to turn over, until this morning. Charlie kept the keys to his "Love Machine" up on the sun visor, so I'd used it to try to jump-start my pickup only to find that the battery wasn't the problem. Fearing that the dead engine was a bad omen, I simply drove Charlie's truck up here instead. He had taken the ranch truck on a long haul and wouldn't miss his old Dodge.

Roaring up the canyon in the same truck Charlie had used to take me away from Quincy tied me up inside. I'd only been four years old, too young to have any memory of sitting between my mother and father. Still, I imagined my smaller self moving my knees to the side every time I pushed the gearshift into fourth. Did we drive anywhere as a family? Were there times they'd been happy or had they hurled insults inside the cab? I talked to the old truck as if it could provide the memories I lacked.

I knew it remembered them loving. One of the few times I've seen Charlie's teeth was in the blushing smile he couldn't stop when I forced him to tell me why he called the old truck the "Love Machine." My beet-red face made him laugh harder than I'd ever heard. *I tried to warn you, kid.* I felt his hand on my shoulder. I felt him with me in the cab.

So when had they soured? I rested both my forearms on the table-like big wheel on the straightaways wondering about my mother's side of the story. Charlie had never wanted to talk about it beyond our being with Bo and Ruth as a blessing I should appreciate.

I overshot the auto shop and found myself parked in front of an antique shop. I didn't mind browsing and was relieved to find the store open. The door triggered a mechanical buzz, and a woman's voice from the back invited me to look around. She kept her shop blazingly warm and bright. Shelves were lined with teapots and other fine china. The glass countertop housed jewelry, and next to the register, she had organized silver cutlery in cardboard holders. None of this interested me.

Tools are my draw. An old awl, manual drills and boxy c-clamps, wood planes, handsaws and tiny knobby hammers, chisels, files and screwdrivers. I easily lost myself in the far corner. In shallow fruit boxes, the proprietor had gathered household hardware. One box held all sorts of door handles, metal, porcelain and crystal. Some were paired on a spindle, some lone cool orbs. Some were even attached to their plates and lock cartridge. In the box, one knob had looked brown, but when I picked it up out of the shadows I discovered a beautiful red and black swirl pattern. Without thought, I polished it on my shirt, appreciating the shine of it and the cool smoothness in my palm. The owner's voice startled me.

"That's marble. Nice one. I'd bet early 1900s." The owner of the store had emerged from the back, her white hair neatly braided and pinned up. She dusted her hands on her full-length skirt before pulling her glasses from her head to balance on the bridge of her nose. She reached for the knob to appraise it. "I wish I could say I had a key for it…" She paused and assessed me with the same intensity. "Doesn't mean you couldn't get it working. Take it apart, grease it up and get the parts in place, spend an afternoon with a box of skeleton keys to find one that works."

I smiled without a word and received it back from her. Self-conscious, I placed it back in the bin and willed her to leave me on my own. Instead, she stood at the small opening that would have allowed me back into the main room of the store.

"Visiting?" she asked simply.

"I'm…um…looking at a property," I said, unwilling to lie even though her presence was making me uncomfortably hot. She wore shirtsleeves, but I still wore my jacket. The space felt too crowded to shrug out of it.

"An older place? In need of refurbishing?" she asked, a gleam in her eye.

"It's in good shape. I may be doing some remodeling." I took a step back, wondering how I'd ever get past her, wishing for once I had a watch I could glance at pointedly to get me on my way.

She surprised me by stepping aside to pick up the marble doorknob.

"Thank you," I said, seeing enough space to duck through behind her.

She stopped me with a hand on my shoulder. The other held the door handle toward me. Confused, I accepted it. "I don't have a place for this."

"Doesn't matter. It's yours. Couldn't you hear it?" She tipped her head toward it, and listened so intently, I almost believed it could communicate with her.

I still heard nothing, but I liked the weight in my hand. I looked for a price. "How much?"

She batted away my words. "I said it's yours. If you find that the place you buy needs antique fixtures, I'll expect to see you back." With that, she shooed me out of her way and settled in behind the glass counters.

I didn't know the etiquette. It didn't seem like she expected me to buy something. The marble had grown warm in my hand, and I realized how tense I felt. The warmth of the stone calmed me, and maybe it was the way the woman had put it, that the knob spoke to me, but I had the feeling that it would actually be fine to simply walk out of the store with it.

"Thank you, again," I said, creeping to the front door.

"I hope it opens up wonderful things for you, dear." She smiled warmly.

I blinked out into the bright snowy day and climbed into the cab of the Dodge. The knob seemed to smile at me from the passenger seat as if ready for an adventure. I steered out onto the road, my childhood home flashing in the rearview for an instant. Something caught my eye. I craned my neck back to look through the cab, and saw the Homecoming Queen standing in front of the house, both hands shading her eyes, watching me as I drove away.

CHAPTER NINE

Lacey

It couldn't be, I thought watching the old Dodge pull away from Martha's shop. But vehicles stick with me, especially old ones. I turned tail back to my shop and pulled a cigar box down from the windowsill. I'd discovered it when I was a kid. One summer, we rearranged the furniture in my room, and I found a small door cut into the bottom of the wall. My room was right next to the downstairs bathroom, and the door revealed the pipes for the tub. Tucked inside, I'd found the box.

I'd opened it, of course. I'd lined up the little treasures someone had gathered: an odd assortment of tiny animals. A tiny green plastic penguin, his black eyes nearly rubbed off and scratches on his white belly, a white rubber dolphin, a glass bird and a few toy squirrels that had once been fuzzy but now had shiny spots and ratty tails. The box also had several stones, some smooth river rocks, an impressive chunk of rose quartz and a crystal. On top was what I was looking for—a single faded photograph, confirming that I'd seen that old orange Dodge before. It was shining new in the photograph. A young couple rested against the truck, the cowboy with his arms spread wide, hands along the length of the bed, his woman leaning against him, her head bent toward the baby in her arms.

I would have sworn that the spacey woman with the flat tire from last week had just climbed into the cab of that same truck. What was she doing with the truck in the photograph? I frowned and replaced the items in the box, latching it shut. A wave of heat swept through me when I realized the woman Della was sure I'd let get away was back in town.

Hearing tires on the drive, I shelved the box and stilled Della's voice in my head screaming at me to jump in my car and track down the Dodge Power Wagon and its driver. Brenna Nelson pulled up in her Ford Bronco. She and my sister went way back, back to when she was the one getting in trouble with police, not the one issuing tickets. I had to thank my siblings, both for being more popular than I'd ever been in school and for calling all of their friends to recommend me when I'd turned my hobby into a career.

"Mornin' Brenna."

"Hey Lace," she called out the window. "Where do you want this?"

"Right in the bay," I said, waving her in. The brake replacement was my first order of business for the day.

"How's Chrystal?" she asked. Though Brenna had been my client for years, she still felt more comfortable talking about my sister. Though age had lessened the difference between us, I knew she still thought of me as Chrystal's pesky little sister.

"She's fine. She says now that the littlest is in kindergarten, she finally has a few minutes in her day when she remembers who she is."

"Her asshole boyfriend still around?"

The asshole boyfriend who was around more to make babies than take care of them was the reason Brenna didn't get her information straight from Chrystal. Chrystal couldn't hear anything negative about Norm, and Brenna wasn't the kind to pretend that she approved of how he treated her. "He's still in Chico, but in his own place."

"That's a step."

The rattle of Gabe Owens's diesel flatbed saved me from having to comment about my sister's choice in men and made me wonder, again, whether something was brewing between Gabe and Brenna. Brenna had pulled out her phone, and I greeted Gabe with a handshake. I noticed that Brenna had stepped away from the two of us though Gabe's smile shone on us both.

"How's your Beetle coming along?" he asked.

"I'm all done with the welding on the frame. Paint comes next, and then I'm ready to get the engine in." I was indebted to him for helping me haul my VW bug over from Reno on that flatbed. I'd worked on that rig as well as all the vehicles out at his family's mule ranch.

"I can't wait to see you zipping around town in it. What are you going to do, green?"

"Baby blue," I said, remembering my father's Beetle. There was no question in my mind.

"That'll look sweet. You need help getting the frame to the body shop?"

"I'm about ready for that. Thanks." My older siblings had hung out with him plenty during school, and they all vowed that college was going to lead them far, far away from Quincy. Now he was back to living with his folks on the ranch. Rumors suggested he'd take over the reins when his father was ready since his older sister, Kristine, had made good on her promise to get out of town.

"How's Kristine?" I asked because I loved seeing how his face lit up and because I knew no one else in town ever asked how she was doing. She'd been pretty quiet about being lesbian when she lived in Quincy. Her moving away to the Northcoast made it easier for most people to ignore that she'd married Gloria, but reminded me again that her main reason behind leaving was her desire to have it all—career and family.

"Real busy. Eliza and Caemon are always on the move and rarely in the same direction."

I laughed. I spent enough time around my nieces and nephews to know what that meant.

"Guess I'd better get busy on the Bronco," I said, realizing that I'd lost track of Brenna while Gabe and I chatted. I hadn't noticed that she'd finished her text and scanned the shop for her. I found her in the passenger seat of Gabe's rig. I rested my hands on my hips. "Something going on between you two?"

He glanced at his rig. "Maybe." A grin spread across his face.

"Chrystal's going to hear about this," I said, inclining my head toward his rig.

"I figured." He crossed his arms across his chest.

"Am I being played? Is this just you being the good guy you are?"

"I hope not. Let me know what Chrystal thinks." He tipped his hat and strode to his rig.

I stood there watching another tailgate disappear down Highway 89. Brenna Nelson and Gabe Owens. I had trouble putting someone as gregarious as Gabe with someone as cool as Brenna, but maybe his warmth would soften her a bit. People had been talking about whether he'd ever find someone, especially after they all assumed he and Dani Blazer were an item after she moved into the little house on his parents' property. There was quite a bit of upset in the community when people discovered it was Hope Fielding she was seeing, not Gabe.

I'd be really happy for Gabe if it turned out that the lift Brenna had asked for meant something *was* cooking between them. I pulled out my cell and keyed my sister's number. "What do you make of this?" I asked, laying out what I'd observed. Keeping my sister in the loop was a requirement of the referrals she sent my way.

CHAPTER TEN

Madison

If I never signed another sheet of paper in my life, it would be too soon. I stared at the escrow agent's bored face as she summarized each page of the loan docs. To her, it was routine, the numbers she read inconsequential. For me, they were heart-palpitating. I tried not to think about how much small print filled the pages and pushed the former owner's failure as far away from myself as I could.

I can make it work, I told myself every time I penned my name. Somehow that confidence felt tied to my giant white friend I looked forward to seeing. The realtor had dismissed my query about the gelding as an impossibility, but he already felt like he was mine.

Signing the papers had taken longer than I'd thought. By the time I drove down the mountain, Ruth and Bo would have already finished dinner. I'd grab something in town.

"For here or to go?" the cheery teen making the best of a terrible uniform asked me at the counter of the mom-and-pop burger place by the high school. She'd matched her bright shade of lipstick to the red stripe in the shirt and wore the matching cap at a jaunty angle.

It hadn't occurred to me that I had another place to eat until she asked the question, and when I realized I did, I stood taller. "To go," I answered Amy, reading her askew nametag. I was all of a sudden eager to have my first meal on what was soon to be my own land.

"Eager to split town so soon again?" came a familiar voice from behind me.

The Homecoming Queen. Being new to town, I assumed I wouldn't recognize anyone, so I hadn't bothered to look back.

"No."

"So you're not leaving, but you ordered to go."

"Hey Lacey," Amy interrupted. "Did you forget something?"

"No. I came for dinner."

"Weren't you here with Coach Michaels for lunch?"

"Now I'm here for a salad." Lacey turned as if trying to end Amy's questions.

My brow furrowed as I processed Amy's information. Lacey, a fitting name for The Homecoming Queen, was doing something outside of her norm. Her decision to stop for dinner had clearly been spontaneous. Remembering her in my rearview mirror as I drove away from her shop, I would have put money on the orange truck parked out front being what spurred the decision.

"For here?" Amy continued.

"To go," Lacey snapped, confirming my suspicion. Her eyes returned to me, and she repunctuated her question by raising her eyebrows.

I savored the idea that someone had purposely stopped to talk to me. I was used to being overlooked, not noticed. I thought about the events of the day, the reason I'd taken Charlie's distinctive truck, her seeing me in it, and my decision to stop for dinner instead of heading straight down the mountain. Everything had set me up to let this woman know she could expect to see me around, so I came clean. I answered, "I'm eating at my place."

"*Your* place?" Her surprise spiked the pitch in the middle of *your*, giving it a triangular shape.

"*My* place," I said, hearing the pride in my voice. "I signed papers today."

"You recently got a job here?" she asked. Right hand on left bicep, she rested her chin in her left hand. One finger lazily edged her lower lip as she openly assessed me.

"The place I bought out on Spanish Creek will be my job," I supplied. I tried not to fidget under her attention. Had I not met her in her shop, I would never have given her a second glance. Her perfect complexion and care she took to style her hair screamed cool-kid crowd to me, the kind in which I'd never felt comfortable. The contrasting oil-stained cuticles intrigued me. If I kept my eyes on her hands, I could imagine having a conversation with her. Otherwise, she would have intimidated me.

When I risked looking up, she'd inclined her perfect face forward, encouraging me to say more. I considered telling her about my property, but absurdly worried that if I shared that much, she'd insist on driving out with me, and tonight all I wanted was to soak it in on my own. Amy provided my way out by sliding my bag and drink across the counter. "Don't want dinner to get cold," I said, fishing out a hot fry before exiting the building, using my hip to open the door to the cold.

I settled the food next to me and cranked the engine, gassing it to a steady idle. It was cranky as an old man, loud and complaining but reliable and tough. I'd learned not to rush when I drove it. I was about to put it into reverse when I felt The Homecoming Queen's eyes on me. She shouldered the burger joint's door open and crunched through the snow up to my truck, motioning me to roll down the window. I complied.

"This is the second time we've met, and I still don't know your name," she said.

"Madison Carter," I said, extending my hand through the window. I liked the way she held it. As I expected, her hand in mine felt as much like home as the property had the first time I'd walked through.

"I'm Lacey McAlpine. Welcome to town." Her eyes were busy on my face in a way I was sure her mind was busy on what she wasn't saying.

"Thanks," I said, taken aback by their intensity. An invitation to eat our to-go orders together on my front porch perched on the tip of my tongue, but I couldn't bring myself to voice it. It couldn't be that easy, could it?

"I wanted to say that you know where to find me if you need anything. Moving's a bitch."

I hadn't expected such kindness from a stranger, and it flooded my system. I felt my face flush, and I turned hoping to hide it.

"Sorry."

"No. It's okay." I risked glancing back, hoping she'd take the redness in my cheeks to mean that the truck had a good heater. "I appreciate it."

"Your dinner's getting cold," she noted.

"It is." Her words brought back the puzzle of where the big white horse on my property was getting his food. I wanted to find him there again to be able to tell him I'd bought the place and that I'd bring some nice alfalfa. "I should go," I said, inexplicably feeling like I had to leave that instant to find him.

Lacey took a step back, disappointed. "Hope to see you around."

"Me too," I said, honestly.

For the second time that day, I caught sight of her in my rearview. A woman like that would be difficult to drive away from in the morning. I rolled through town, cautious of the speed limit. Why would someone that attractive take the time to track down my truck?

Once I rounded the corner and exited the main drag, I took in the mountain backdrop. My timing was opposite of what Charlie's would have been. He'd have been driving out this way to work as the sun crept to peek over the ridge instead of at his back.

Did he watch his wife from the rearview as he left in the morning, or would she stay in bed as he dressed in the dark?

I'd never asked about their daily rituals. I knew that Ruth cooked breakfast for Bo before she got herself ready for the day. I knew that she never ate dinner without him, even if it meant reheating it hours later. I saw very clearly the differences between the couples and knew for sure that Charlie had left a dark and quiet house in the morning and guessed that it was the same way when he returned.

I looked out the same window Charlie had on his way home from work. I wanted to believe that the headlights had swung into the drive to land on my mom standing on the front porch waiting with me propped on her hip. I wanted my past to include the jubilant reunion of a family each day but intuited that his evenings were nothing like my musings.

With a deep sigh, I made the final turns to my new place, confident that Charlie's rig could make it over the snow built up by the road. My headlights swept over the trees, dusk closing in more tightly in the wooded area than out on the highway. As I straightened out, they came to rest on a white figure standing right where I'd left him last time.

I whooped, jumping from the cab with my cold dinner in my hand. I wished I had an apple or carrot for him, but he didn't seem to care. He strode down the road to meet me at the gate. When he reached me, he dipped his head for me to rub. "Hey buddy. You don't know how glad I am to see you! Where's the best place for a picnic dinner?"

He turned and, like the first time I'd been on the property, I took a hold of his mane to steady my steps as we made our way up to the house. My house. A smile spread across my face. I ate quickly. Without the sun, cold seeped in around me. I spread out my dinner on the porch but stood by the horse for warmth. As if he understood, he wrapped me in the curve of his neck.

I imagined the peace this quiet place could bring to those who needed to stop. I hoped that I could create something that felt immediately like home.

"Anything you can tell me about a woman named Lacey?"

He rubbed his head along my body, shoulder to calf.

"That's an enthusiastic endorsement. She doesn't intimidate you?"

He shook his mane.

"I might need your help there." That comment elicited no movement, so I got busy on my greasy dinner, ready to drive home and start packing. His warmth surrounded me like a cozy den. "Do you forage on your own, or is there someone missing you? Is there a corral somewhere that you've figured out how to escape? You know Houdini was an escape artist. How about that for a name?" I gathered my trash and wrapped my arms around his neck. "You'll be here when I've got my keys and I'm back with some alfalfa and a sack of carrots, right? You're in this with me?"

Houdini didn't answer one way or another, and he didn't walk me to the truck. He wandered toward the pasture where I'd first seen him. As quickly as I could, I picked my way back down to the truck, shivering without his warmth.

CHAPTER ELEVEN

Madison

The week I moved in, I considered calling Lacey. She'd been so nice to offer her help, but I never followed through. It didn't feel right to ask a stranger to lug boxes into the garage. I talked about it endlessly with Houdini. Most of the time he dozed, alternating his resting leg, the picture of patience as I explained that I worried about Lacey seeing the house so run down. The tilt of his ears made me consider meeting up with her in town, but there was the possibility of running into my mom. I knew that my mother could be any one of the people I encountered anytime I drove into town. I couldn't ignore the fact that the size of the place guaranteed that I'd run into her eventually. If I were to pass by her, would I know her instinctually and immediately?

I carried in my head the images of her as a woman my age holding the infant me in her arms. I tried to imagine what twenty years would have done to her features like the computer images on milk bottles that guess at a grown child's appearance. Too many women had shoulder-length brown hair. Too many matched her stature. She'd nestled into the crook of Charlie's shoulder whereas I stood an inch above.

Trips to town exhausted me with false recognition. Even trips to the hardware store or lumberyard did a number on my heart though my rational brain tried to calm my nerves by arguing how unlikely it would be to find her there. Knowing that she'd waitressed when she was with Charlie, I avoided the restaurants in town, picking up dinners from the grocery store instead.

I couldn't stop thinking about Lacey's house in East Quincy and how it could have been mine. Could have been *ours*. I'd passed it a few times on errands, always wishing I had a reason to stop and soak it in. At the beginning of this adventure, it hadn't occurred to me to look for where I'd lived as a child. But now that I knew where it was, my curiosity called to be satisfied. About a quarter mile past the shop, I had spotted a Chinese place on the opposite side of the highway. I couldn't imagine my mother working there, so at the end of the week, I decided to treat myself.

Immediately after I pulled in, a beat-up maroon sedan slid into the parking space next to me. Not expecting Lacey but remembering how she'd snuck up behind me at the burger joint, I glanced in the driver's direction.

We both stopped.

"Fancy meeting you here, Madison."

I smiled at that, hearing my name on her lips. She remembered.

"When did you get back?" She didn't pocket her car keys, and I kept my focus on her fingers wrapped around them. Her hands I could talk to.

"Monday."

"You've been here all week."

Her tone made me feel like apologizing, but I didn't. I couldn't explain my need to get the place together on my own, but I knew it was what I needed. "Getting settled."

"I could have helped. Shop's listed."

"I know." I took a breath. There were so many times I could have let her know I was in town. I didn't know her well enough to explain that my mind was a tangle of my past in Quincy. While it was fun to read something into the fact that our paths kept crossing, I still couldn't shake the question of whether I was being led to her or her house. But here she stood again unaware of my thoughts, waiting for me to offer something. "You want to grab dinner with me now?"

Lacey hesitated. "I could eat."

I couldn't think of another reason she would drive across the highway but opened the door for her and followed her as she walked to a booth that offered a view of her shop, my parents' old place. I set the book I'd planned to read on the table and slid in opposite her.

"When you say settling in, somehow I don't get a picture of you moving a bunch of furniture by yourself."

"No. I don't have any furniture yet. I'm living in the place bare bones while I fix it up."

My guard was completely down when the waitress approached our table.

"Lacey honey!" she exclaimed. "Did you figure out what that weird knocking was?"

Lacey's eyes distracted me for a moment. I didn't know her well enough to read the emotion in her expression as she produced a golf ball, which she then extended to our waitress.

Following the gesture, I glanced up at the waitress into eyes framed by long bangs that curled over her finely plucked eyebrows. Her curls, dyed a uniform brown many shades darker than mine, were pulled back in a clip to frame her face. Though she looked much younger than I'd expected, I was certain I was looking at my mother.

I looked down to the crooked nametag clipped to her breast pocket hoping that it would read anything other than "Shawneen." My ears rang from the blood buzzing through my body making everything sound far away. It felt as if I was seeing the scene from a distance, like I was a balloon floating up into the sky. Eventually the people below would disappear, wouldn't they?

Lacey handed the car keys to Shawneen who tucked them into the pocket of her apron. The ball she kept in her hand. "Why are you giving me this?"

"It was bouncing back and forth under that bench seat Dennis replaced in the back."

"Isn't that funny?" she said, handing the ball back to Lacey. "If it was only a golf ball, then the offer of a meal…"

Lacey's gaze shifted between Shawneen and me, and I could see now that my mother tested her patience. "Of course there's no charge for the Nova. I was just planning on delivering the keys, but I ran into a friend who invited me to join her."

Mentioning me forced me back to reality. Shawneen barely looked at me as she extended a menu. When I was young, I'd often imagined finding her. If we went to the county fair or rodeo, I scanned the crowd waiting for her to see me. Back then, I thought she'd be looking for me, and when she found me, she would immediately know me and throw her arms around me. During my first week sharing a town with her again, all I had thought about was whether I'd know her, not what I'd say. My mouth was so dry I couldn't have spoken even if she'd given me time. A stranger to her, I watched her lips as she delivered the specials.

When she stopped, she put her hand on her hip, impatient about something that had passed between her and Lacey that I didn't quite understand. "You need a minute?"

I nodded. I needed so much more than that.

I'd wanted her to recognize that I had her high brows but conceded that since I didn't shape mine as she did that she could easily miss the feature. If she didn't recognize herself in me, couldn't she at least have seen Charlie? I was only a few years younger than he'd been when we'd left. Would she even recognize him after all these years? Didn't she ever look for her daughter in the customers she served, thinking that I might someday come looking for her, or had she once but had stopped somewhere along the way? Most shattering was the realization that perhaps she never gave me a second thought. She just didn't care at all.

I blinked back tears and looked for the spiciest thing offered, something that would give me an excuse for watery eyes.

"Unbelievable." Lacey and I both had our eyes on the menu.

"You work on her car?"

"Yeah, I do a lot of work on it, and she's always offering me a dinner to take care of her bill."

I looked at the prices and couldn't imagine any work that would make Lacey come out ahead. "I can see why you'd be reluctant to accept that offer." The car Lacey had brought back looked so old, I wondered if Shawneen had bought it new when I was a kid. Had she ever carefully buckled me into its backseat?

"Shawneen's a piece of work," she muttered.

My mother's name sliced through me like ice water. I didn't know what to say, especially when she returned to take our order. She was all efficiency repeating the dishes without writing them down as she collected the menus.

"Are you okay?" Lacey asked.

"Sure," I said although I was anything but. Lacey excused herself to use the restroom, and I looked down the street at the house I could have grown up in. Was that why Shawneen chose to work here? Did she spend her days imagining what life she could have had if Charlie and I had stayed with her?

"Are you sure you're okay?" Lacey asked, startling me a little when she scooted back in the booth across from me. She sat very still with the expression she'd worn the day I drove into her shop. I had to stop thinking about Shawneen.

"Sorry. I'm beat. All week I've been washing and sanding walls to get ready to paint."

"You said the place you bought is going to be your work too."

"I did."

"Care to elaborate?"

"I have a big ranch house that I'm turning into a rustic mountain getaway."

"Is all the work you have to do cosmetic, or will there be some remodeling? Whatever you need, I probably know the right person for the job. The contractor who helped me extend my shop was great."

I talked easily about the dirty walls and carpet that made up most of my planned work until Shawneen delivered our food. I kept my eyes down, only chancing a look at her as she walked away. When I looked back to Lacey, she was studying me. Without a word, we ate our meals. As I'd intended, mine was spicy enough to make my eyes water and nose run.

"Have you thought about keeping horses? Mountain getaway makes me think of riding."

"Eventually, I'd like to be able to offer that, but that's way down the line."

"I think you'd like my friend Dani. She's a relative newcomer too. Feather River College hired her five years ago to get the rodeo program going."

I nodded in interest, grateful for her ability to carry the conversation with my mind so occupied with Shawneen.

"Her wife, Hope, owns Cup of Joy, the little diner in Quincy proper."

Her use of the pronoun *her* with wife captured my complete attention. I'd eaten at the diner a few times and searched my memories for the woman she described. "Does she waitress? Long dark hair?"

"No. She manages the place for her family, and these days she's not at the diner so much since her daughter was born."

I choked on the bite I'd been swallowing and coughed an embarrassingly long time. I downed my glass of water trying to drown the cough, and Lacey pushed her glass in my direction when that didn't work.

"That's about how the town took it too. She'd already floored everyone coming out, but people got over that pretty quick. Everyone loves Dani, so it's like they couldn't blame her for falling too. It's hard not to with her Texas drawl. Theirs is a great romance." She paused and sighed, her chopsticks in midair. I'd started to wonder if she was jealous, if she'd been interested in Dani. As if she realized how she sounded, she redirected the conversation, pointing to my book. "Are you reading a great romance?"

I laughed. "You could say that: the country's great romance with Teddy Roosevelt," I said, pushing Doris Kearns Goodwin's *The Bully Pulpit* toward her.

"Weighty."

"Power is a mighty aphrodisiac."

"It's all about politics?" she asked. Though her expression feigned interest, her tone conveyed how boring she considered the subject.

"I've gotten background on Roosevelt's and Taft's childhoods and their wives. You'd be surprised by what a romantic Roosevelt was. He wooed his first wife, Alice, fiercely and thought he'd never marry again."

"But he did?"

"To a childhood friend. She'd always loved him."

"So she waited for him even though he married someone else?"

I frowned at the book. "I don't really have her perspective. She was disappointed when he moved away. He went to college, met Alice, and that was that."

Lacey sat back and hmphed.

"What?"

"Clearly, he didn't deserve her. If the person I loved broke my heart marrying someone else, that'd be it."

"Even if fate brought you back together again?"

"Even then." Lacey placed her napkin next to her plate. "Someone breaks my heart, I'm done."

Shawneen returned to fill our water glasses and leave the bill. I felt Lacey's eyes on me as I avoided eye contact with the waitress. Carrying on as if Shawneen had never been there, I said. "You don't believe in fate?"

To stall, she rearranged her hair, the stylish cut framing her face. "No. That presumes that things are not in your control. It means accepting that there is some supernatural power dictating your life. That holds no appeal to me. You should be talking to Hope. She says her relationship with Dani is Fate."

Fate. I heard the capital in the way she overenunciated the way people uncomfortable with God seem to falter on the word.

How would she react if I were to share how I felt like fate had called me home to her shop across the street? "But you don't... believe that someone can rekindle an old flame?" I pushed, my eyes flicking back toward the kitchen.

Our conversation had me thinking about why I'd always thought about returning to the ranch in Quincy. I'd thought it would make me feel closer to Charlie and would give me the chance to get to know my mother as an adult. There's supposed to be a bond between mother and daughter, something that would make her more likely to talk about what had happened with her and Charlie. I thought there would be an intuition between us. Something special. Her failure to recognize me had already shaken that dream.

She looked at me and then glanced in the direction of the kitchen before looking back to me, a furrow on her brow. "No." She laughed as if such a thought was absurd. "Because what does that mean about Roosevelt's friend's life while she's without him? She was on hold for all of those years pining away for someone who was living, really living? That sounds like such a waste to me."

"Ah." I shifted my plate to the side and collected my book. I'd pay the check at the counter.

"Hey!" She quickly grabbed her coat and followed me. "I didn't mean to offend you."

"I'm not offended," I said, counting out bills to hand to a bored Shawneen. My heart pounded as she made change. Standing directly in front of her, I still didn't even warrant her attention, let alone her recognition, and I suddenly had to get away from her.

"Let me get dinner. I feel like an a-hole for upsetting you."

"You didn't upset me." I insisted pushing out into the cold. I felt better for leaving the building, the cold numbing me like ice pushed against a bruised knee.

"I know we don't know each other well, but you seem upset."

"I've got a lot to do. Did you want a lift back to your shop?" I wanted away from the restaurant, away from Shawneen. I needed space to think. She accepted, and I thought of the flat tire that had led me to her. Pulling into her drive, I remembered too vividly how she'd looked at me like I was a wacko when I'd sat outside her garage, stunned to be home.

I took in the height of her eyebrows, shaped in a way that would have made Shawneen proud, and was glad I hadn't mentioned her to Ruth, so I wouldn't have to explain that I couldn't hang out with her. Seeing my mom had made me want to crawl into a dark, quiet place.

"Thanks again for dinner," I said, meaning it. It would have been so much harder to sit through the meal alone. Now I knew to avoid the Chinese place.

"You're welcome," she said in a professional tone suited for clients. Probably those she hoped she didn't have to deal with again anytime soon.

CHAPTER TWELVE

Madison

"What do you think?" I tapped my teeth with my thumbnail trying to visualize a master suite carved out of the massive garage. "If Lacey can turn a bedroom into a garage, surely we can make a bedroom out of one."

Houdini said nothing.

I reached over and rubbed around his eyes. He dropped his head, relaxed, not even looking at the space and how the mud sink meant it wouldn't be difficult to plumb another bathroom. "I could call her to get her contractor's number. It would be foolish to look one up on my own, wouldn't it? When she trusts the one she worked with?"

I paced out the room design adding to the never-ending list of what I needed to turn the ranch house into something rentable. Houdini seemed to think that the white walls were clean enough and the carpet in good shape, but I couldn't wait to get the old shag pulled up. Pulling up a corner in one closet confirmed my hunch that the original floorboards still had their integrity and were simply waiting to be sanded and refinished.

Ruth would help me make bright rag rugs both for the rustic look and for protecting feet from the cold in the winter months. In the summer, the smooth floors would help keep the rooms cool.

Feeling the tears that lay so close to the surface since I'd seen Shawneen, I stepped out into the cold, inviting it to numb me. Houdini followed me and hung his big head over my shoulder. I leaned into him, giving in and sobbing until I had to catch my breath, hands on my knees, my eyes and nose raw from my tears and the cold mountain air. I gasped for breath, reminding myself that I'd anticipated her not knowing me. But it hurt more than I'd ever imagined. I'd always thought that having Ruth and Bo in my life had immunized me from any hurt Shawneen could cause, but I'd been wrong.

I'd spent so many years feeling detached from my mother and whatever had happened between her and Charlie. In the week that I'd been back, I had foolishly let the idea that moving here might open up a relationship that hadn't been available to me as a child. That fantasy had hinged on instant recognition. Now that I'd faced her and had that bubble burst, I felt an anger I'd never experienced before. It radiated from me begging for an exit.

I grabbed a crowbar from my box of tools and carried it to the largest bedroom. I wedged the blade under the carpet where I had started in the closet and caught the tackboard that held it down, pushing until I heard the whine of nails pulling free and the splintering of brittle wooden tack strip. The whole perimeter of the long closet, I lit into the work, blessedly distracted by it.

Panting from exertion, I bent to rip back the carpet but caught myself. No need to be both foolish and angry, I returned to the garage to retrieve my heavy leather work gloves and a trash can to haul loads out to the rented Dumpster.

"I wrote to her, you know," I snapped at Houdini who was napping in the garage, not that it felt much warmer in there. "And I know Charlie sent them. We addressed the envelopes together. Put postage on them. And she never wrote back."

I carried the trash can into the room. Kneeling, I pulled up the shag feeling like I was skinning Cookie Monster. Nails and wood I tossed into the trash can. The blue carpet I folded back underneath me. Grit and loose fabric still obscured the wood, so I tromped back to the garage for a broom and dustpan.

"So why am I so angry? She never wrote back. I should expect nothing. That's what you're thinking." I waited for a reaction but Houdini's ears remained relaxed, forcing me to admit that I was talking to myself. I grabbed a box cutter and left him but not the lingering question. What did I expect from a woman I hadn't seen for twenty years?

Careful not to nick the floor, I cut the carpet I had freed and briskly swept out the closet. Was I angry with Charlie for not sending her pictures and updates? If he had, she would have recognized me. She would have swept me into her arms and told me how much she wanted me. I wanted to know if she'd missed me. No. She hadn't. She'd never written. If she'd missed me, she would have found me. Charlie already knew that. It's why he'd asked if I was wanting to see her. Did Ruth and Bo know as well? I hadn't spoken to any of them about Shawneen, but I wonder if all three saw Shawneen living in town as part of my motivation for buying Hot Rocks. I didn't want any of them to know that I'd held on to the hope that finding her would make me feel complete. If it didn't work out, it would be my hurt alone.

And where had that landed me? Even more alone. Besides my family, the only friends I had were those I worked with, and I'd left them all in Oregon. I had no one, I realized, not one person I could use as a sounding board for the tangle of ideas pushing around inside my head.

There was Lacey. A whoosh of recognition washed through me as I replayed her expression when her eyes landed on me in the restaurant. She'd been glad to see me until the subject of fate came up. I felt a spark in her presence and would have liked to spend more time with her, but I didn't get the sense that I could talk to her about how the mountain town had called me home.

The mess swept away, I still couldn't tell what shape the floors were in. Once again I returned to the garage for a construction lamp. The reward of my labor tipped the corner of my lip into a smile. "Hello beautiful," I said, squatting to examine the wood. The way it had easily given up the nails and its rich tone suggested it was fir. I couldn't wait to get more of the carpet up and see it in the natural light. The thick shag had saved the floor from a good deal of wear and tear for which I was grateful. I stood, my muscles protesting.

Cautious not to fill it to the point where I wouldn't be able to lift it, I dragged the trash can out to the Dumpster. Come to think of it, I didn't know when trash day was or whether they even came up to the house. The enormity of what I didn't know along with how much there was to do settled on me, and I sank to the floor, brushing off my work clothes.

Houdini clomped over, sneezing in my cloud of dust, adding a layer of snot to my filth. "Thanks. That's really helpful." I rested my elbows on my knees, chin in my hands, my thoughts returning to Lacey. I'd thought we could be friends, and without that, I felt even more alone.

"It's a good thing you're here." I hated that I was choking up yet again. Impossibly, Houdini turned and walked to the space I hoped to turn into a bedroom. "That's not the project right now. We're focusing on the existing rooms first, remember?"

He answered by snuffing around the floor, like a bloodhound picking up a scent.

"Even if you think that should be first up, I don't have Lacey's number. Even if I did have her number, I don't feel like calling her right now. She can keep her attitude in East Quincy. We don't need it or her over here." Now that I had stopped working, I felt chilled and would have appreciated Houdini's warmth. Again, as if wanting to drive home his own point, he left the garage. His gait turned to trot and then a canter echoing through the woods on my property.

"Some friend you are," I growled, picking myself up and returning to my huge carpet-removal project.

CHAPTER THIRTEEN

Lacey

Singing along to the blaring radio, I grunted and pushed at the stubborn bolt. I wanted to get the brake job finished up, so I could get back to the book I was supposed to have finished for the lesbo book club Della had roped me into. I blushed thinking about the erotica she had picked for this month's meeting. Dani and Hope had been reading books together for years when Dani invited Della into their circle. I'd joined in during the brief period Della and I tried to be a couple and enjoyed it too much to give it up even though many of the books fell into a category I knew Della selected to drive home the point of how alone we were.

Hearing footsteps, I rolled out from underneath the '66 Mustang only to find my shop empty. I rolled a bit further out to check the driveway. No cars. I frowned. Was I so self-conscious about what I was reading that I imagined people watching me?

I'd no sooner repositioned my wrench than I heard the sound again. This time, I froze and felt fear creep up my spine. Someone was waiting until I was blind to them to move around in my shop. I found my longest wrench as quietly as possible. I wrapped my fingers around the cool handle imagining how I would describe the sound to the police. The intruder had a distinct footfall that sounded more like a clop rather than a creep. My heartbeat competed with the sound, making it difficult to keep track of where he was, but then I was certain the feet approached from the passenger side of the car.

The hooves were so incongruous that I tried to sit up before sliding out, smacking my head smartly on the car's undercarriage. Hand to head, I rolled out and tried sitting up again.

A huge horse met my bewildered gaze. I stood slowly, not wanting to spook it. Edging toward my phone on the counter, I tried to make small talk. "You having engine trouble? Did your rig break down on the road?"

His bright expression followed me as I inched to my phone and punched in a number.

"Howdy." Dani's Texan drawl graced my ear. "You enjoyin' the book?"

I could see her eyebrows waggling and bowed my head even though she couldn't see me. "It could have a touch more plot, but listen, I didn't call about the book. I want to know what to do with this horse that wandered into my bay."

"Horse?"

"Yes. A rather large white one. He's on the other side of my brake job, and I don't know what to do with him."

"Could he have thrown his rider?" Dani asked.

"There's not a thing on him."

"No halter, no bridle?"

"Not a stitch."

"Weird. What do you want me to do?"

"I thought you could come fetch him," I suggested.

"What am I going to do with a big white horse? It's not one of mine, and it doesn't sound like anything we've got at the college."

"Maybe you could take it to your barn and put up a found horse poster or something. I can't keep it here."

"As much as I'd like to help you, I've got Joy this afternoon, and she's napping. Hope says you never wake a sleeping toddler. You could try Gabe. He'd be willing to help, I'm sure."

"That's a good idea. Thanks." I looked down to end the call and dial Gabe. When I looked back up, my bay was empty.

"Gabe here," Gabe answered as he always did. "Hello?"

"Sorry Gabe. It's Lacey. I…I had a horse."

"Had?"

"Had. It's gone now." I walked to the open bay door and looked up and down the street. No horse. I hadn't heard him clopping out of my shop. He'd simply disappeared.

"You okay over there?" he asked, concerned.

"Fine. Sorry to bother you."

"No bother. I was going to call you about the little front loader I've got out here. Something's up with the transmission. I take my foot off the accelerator and it keeps going. Kristine told me it's done that before and to take advantage of it."

"How does one take advantage of a transmission that keeps a tractor moving without pressure on the accelerator?"

"She said that it makes gates easier, that you jump off, open the gate, let it drive through and shut the gate after it passes."

I pinched the bridge of my nose. "Please tell me you didn't try this."

"Just once. I've been meaning to fix the feeder it busted apart when I couldn't catch the damn thing after I shut the gate."

I laughed remembering Dani's description of Gabe's chicken-like run. "At least you're only destroying your own property, or were you kind of hoping for an excuse for a certain patrol officer to stop by."

"Oh, she doesn't need an excuse."

"It's about time you found someone."

"Someone into dudes. Seems like the whole town's full of lesbians."

His comment made me think of Madison and how much I wished things had gone differently at dinner. Why had I let her comment about fate rile me like it did? Why'd I have to open my trap and let everything in my head spill right out? How hard would it have been to lie and say *sure, I believe in Fate.* Better yet, something romantic like *Fate must have brought you here.* Why had I let it freeze up the conversation? "Well I'm glad she's into you," I said, coming back to the conversation. "You want me to head over to your place this weekend to have a look at the transmission?"

"I could throw it on the flatbed."

"Don't worry about it. I'll be out to see my gran anyway." She lived down the road from Gabe. We saw quite a bit of each other now that he was planting some of her fields with hay.

"How's she doing?"

"Amazing. She might be doing a smaller garden, but it doesn't mean she isn't working all day long. I hope I take after her when I get older."

"None of us is getting any younger."

"And there's still work to do," I agreed, signing off. I held the phone to my chest as I walked around my shop looking for evidence of the horse I knew I'd seen. *Too damn weird*, I thought shaking my head. Feeling uneasy, I lay back down on my creeper and got back to work. Distracted, I threw in the towel around four. I hadn't promised the car back the same day and didn't feel right working on something so important when my mind was so clearly somewhere else.

Once I'd cleaned up, I curled up on the couch with a throw, a cup of cocoa and Della's book pick that had so much sex that I didn't know how I was going to be able to look at Hope and Dani. Della was still hoping to get me hot and bothered enough to shelve my reservations and have a little fun in the sack.

And Madison...I was going to have to divulge to the group that she'd bought a place in Quincy and was fair game. The thought felt crass, and I tossed the book away, frustrated, exactly as Della wanted me to be. Despite feeling like there was some potential for a spark with Madison, I'd decided to steer clear of her after our dinner. Something about the way she watched Shawneen and then avoided looking at her suggested some kind of history there. Knowing Shawneen, there was probably some nasty backstory that I'd be better off leaving alone.

Still, I was restless. I pulled out my phone. "Hey Gran," I said, picturing her on the kitchen landline that had a twisted mess of a cord that, if untangled, gave her access to the whole room as she talked. These days, she simply stood absurdly close to the base instead of fighting with the cord.

"Lacey dear," she answered warmly.

"I hope I didn't drag you across the house."

"Oh, no. I was right here fixing some dinner."

"Oh," I said, disappointed.

"What's wrong, dear?" she asked, catching my tone.

"I was going to offer to bring something out."

"You don't have to do that. I can manage on my own."

"I know you can, Gran."

"Oh, I see."

I could feel her smiling through the phone. "What?"

"You'd like some company. Come on out. I can stretch what I started for two."

"No, no. I was going to take care of you."

"Then I'll let you do the dishes."

"Deal." I smiled. "I'll be there in ten."

An early dinner with my grandmother was exactly what I needed to take my mind off stray horses, ex-girlfriends and airheaded newcomers until my seven o'clock book club.

CHAPTER FOURTEEN

Lacey

When I decided to open my own business, I hadn't understood how very much I hate billing. I'm stubborn about pulling my hands out of the engine, hate fighting with the computer, and absolutely despise sending out repeat invoices. My ringing phone offered a welcome distraction, but before I could even get a good look at the number on my screen, it went dark. I frowned at it and then back at my computer screen and Shawneen's overdue bill. The next time I did any work on the car, I'd make her pick it up at the shop, so she couldn't consider a free dinner wiping her balance away.

The phone rang again, and a local number flashed on the screen. "Rainbow Auto," I answered. My brain tried to decipher the muffled jumble of sounds on the other end. "Hello," I tried again, wondering if someone had dialed the number by mistake. It almost sounded like the phone was under a pile of papers the owner was rustling through. I clicked off and hit print. Holding the bill, I debated writing a personal message to Shawneen, wondering if that might guilt her into settling her debt more quickly.

When the same number rang a third time, I was tempted to ignore it. Annoyed, I picked it up. "Yes?" I barked.

Silence. And then, "Lacey?"

"Who is this?"

"Sorry. It's Madison?"

I closed my eyes to try to expunge my negative attitude, but the way she turned a statement into a question added to my already short fuse. "How can I help you?"

The muffled sounds I'd heard from the second call returned and I heard a distant "Get! Go on now!" before her voice returned at normal register. "I'm so sorry. I don't know what's wrong with Houdini. I keep trying to call you to get the number of your contractor, and he's gone wild, knocking the phone out of my hand."

"Houdini?"

"My horse."

"Of course your horse is named Houdini." I was back to pinching the bridge of my nose.

"He's my escape artist," Madison explained.

"Is this horse white?"

"Yeah. Why?"

"I think we're acquainted," I said, recalling the story of his surprise visit the day before.

"That's impossible," Madison said. "Must be some other white horse because my place is way out by the airport off Spanish Creek Road. We're nowhere near your shop."

Her answer disappointed me. As improbable as it sounded, it would have provided an explanation I could give Dani. Like Gabe, she seemed concerned when I showed up to book club saying the horse had disappeared. She'd glanced ever so briefly at Hope, and I could see them assessing whether I was spending too much time on my own. I am good on my own, I thought, not someone who has to be dating to feel complete. "You called for a number."

"I did, if it's handy."

I rolled the shop chair over to the file cabinet. "Ready?"

"Ready," she said, repeating the number after I'd read it to her. "Thank you."

"Anytime," I said. Should I simply say goodbye? Was that rude? She hadn't said anything, and the silence extended between us. "How's it going at your place?"

"Keeping myself busy. There's a lot of work to do before I'm ready for guests. I can't seem to go a day without having to run to the lumberyard or hardware store, but it's good for me to get out and talk to someone besides Houdini. Someone who says stuff back even if it's 'You sure you can handle that belt sander by yourself?'"

"Belt sander?"

"Refinishing the floors. They're fir."

"You have fur floors?" I saw a variety of pelts stitched together to cover her floors.

"I have no idea if they've been refinished before and fir is such a soft wood that I don't want to risk damaging it with a drum sander."

"You have *fir* floors," I said, finally following.

"That's what I said. I should get back to it. Thanks for the number."

"You bet."

"Bye."

I stared at my phone trying to balance how normal Madison sounded talking about sanding floors with the spacey girl who let a horse knock her phone out of her hand. *Not your circus, not your monkey*, my mother's catch phrase came back to me.

As soon as I set down my phone, the screen lit up again. Shawneen. I groaned, wishing I could so easily apply the circus/monkey comment to her. I took the call.

"Lacey honey, you are not going to believe my day."

Certain whatever had ruined hers was about to ruin mine, I prompted her. "What's up, Shawneen."

"It would be easier if you drove out here. Can you drive out to my place? I...I can't get the door to the Nova shut, and Dennis is already at work, and..."

And it would be too much to pay for roadside assistance, especially when you've got a technician who loves your car. I tipped the phone away from my mouth as I exhaled, trying to let go of how the car's owner annoyed me. Find the bright side.

Find the bright side. In person, I could demand she settle her outstanding bill. "Be there in about ten." I grabbed my coat and a small box of tools and headed over the hill, through Quincy proper and beyond the turnoff for the community college, and Spanish Creek Road which didn't grab my attention or curiosity one bit.

I zoomed by without one thought about the possibility of finding Madison's place. Just because she said she lived off Spanish Creek didn't mean her property was on the main road. There were plenty of side roads, and even if she was right on Spanish Creek, those houses sat so far back, there was no telling whether I'd see her black truck, if she was driving that one and not the familiar orange Dodge from the picture in the treasure box.

See, I didn't think about it at all on my way out to the mobile home place. I pulled up next to the Nova, and at the sound of my car door, she emerged from the long box. She and Dennis had done nothing to make it look like a more permanent home. Others on the lot added planters or awnings. Instead of hiding the difference between Shawneen's place and those around her, the snow accentuated how little Shawneen did to make the place hers.

She whipped a scarf around her neck and walked to the driver's side. I grabbed my tools and joined her, kind of thankful she wasn't going to pretend I was a friend doing a favor. I stopped short as I rounded the vehicle.

"Shawneen," I gasped.

"I know. But with the two of us, do you think you could get it shut?"

The door was bent open almost ninety degrees, firmly wedged in the waist-high snow piled to the side of the drive. I set down my tools and approached the vehicle. "What in the world?"

"I usually back in, but last night, I was too wasted to drive. Dennis parked it for me. This morning, it was all froze over. I couldn't see worth shit, so I opened the door to steer."

"And when the door got stuck in the berm?"

"How the hell was I supposed to know it was stuck? I was moving. Then I wasn't. I figured it was the hill and gunned it. Damn door nearly pulled me out of the car."

Palm to forehead, I tried to find a way out of her mess. I climbed behind the wheel and turned over the engine. Once it purred, I cut the wheel hard away from the berm, leaned out to get a hold on the door and inched forward. I hoped that once we got the door disengaged from the snow, we could push it back to the frame. I left the car in park and motioned for Shawneen to join me on the outside of the door. We pushed together, and it moved an inch. I grabbed a tarp and tossed it on the ground.

"Help me out here." I patted the tarp next to me. Shawneen stared at me like I was hitting myself on the head with a hammer. "Come on. We've got more strength in our legs." Reluctantly, she joined me and put her booted feet to the door. We pushed again and got another two inches, but she'd bent the hinges beyond where they'd ever let the door nestle to the car's frame again. "Shit."

Shawneen looked at her watch. Pointedly.

"What?" I barked.

"I've got to get to work. I was going to say on the phone, but you'd already hung up."

Forcing myself to keep my happy face on, I said, "We can't leave your car here. It needs to be in a garage until you get a new door on there."

"I thought as much." Shawneen's voice had a sharpness I didn't appreciate. Before my feathers fully ruffled, her face and posture softened. I braced myself for what I knew would come next. "Couldn't you take it back to your shop, sugar? Obviously, I can't keep it here. It's perfect. I'll take your car back over to East Quincy, and you can get mine out of the elements." Her hand slid down my arm, squeezing above the elbow. Uncomfortable, I clamped my teeth. I hated that she assumed she could get whatever she wanted from me and knew it was my own doing. I had failed to establish boundaries with her when she first brought the Nova to me. She knew I wanted to help the Nova. Even now, my mind was spinning on how to fix her door.

"The keys are in the ignition," I said.

"Perfect. You let me know when the Nova's ready."

"Oh no. You can park my car at the shop and leave the keys on the visor. I can give the Nova a spot in my garage until you're current on your bill. Then we can address what needs to be done with the door."

The breath she puffed out lifted her bangs for a moment. "Fine."

After she disappeared in my car, I considered who might be able to help me with the door. I couldn't drive any distance with it stuck out like a broken wing. I'd have to get the door off the hinges. Being so close to Spanish Creek Road, I could have asked Madison to help me wrestle the door from its frame, but I didn't want to send her a message that I was trying to find ways to hang out with her. I needed at least one competent person to hold the door while I got the bolts off. I tried Gabe and got his voice mail. Shit. What had I gotten myself into? Hope answered and said she would have helped but was covering one of her waitstaff's shift. She saved me the trouble of calling Dani reminding me that she had Senate. I hit Della's number.

"You can't flake on the game tonight. You know my girls count on every face in the stand," she said.

"I know. I'm not flaking. I'm asking for help."

"With?"

"I've got this door that I need to pull off a car."

"Right now?"

"Preferably."

"Can't right now. I'm on my way to Senate. Getting in the game, you know?"

"Look at you! That's great, Della!"

"Too bad you don't have the spacey chick's number. Could've been a cute way to get to know each other a little better."

I would never admit to her that Madison had come to mind first. I hesitated a second too long.

"Girl, you have her number, don't you?"

"She called for my contractor's number."

"And?"

"And nothing. I gave it to her."

"So that number is just sitting there in your phone waiting for you to share it with your friend Della?"

"What are you going to say when you call?" And did I mind sharing? I had to admit that the fleeting idea of watching them hit it off stung.

"Remember me from Cup of Joy?" Della practiced. "Hope introduced us, but it seemed too forward to ask for your number right then."

"You didn't tell me about that."

"And you tell me everything?"

I still couldn't forget the way I'd felt when Madison's fingers brushed mine in my shop.

"Thought so." I heard Della's satisfied smile.

"So you've met her?"

"I just said that."

"And?" I prompted.

"And what?"

"You thought she was hot?" Why did I say that?

"No, I'm asking for her number, so I can tell her that *you* want to ask her out." Della's sarcasm hung heavily.

"How are you going to explain that you have her number?" I stomped my feet, starting to get cold in the snow. As fun as it was to hear Della be more lighthearted, I wasn't sure how I'd feel if they hit it off.

"Easy. I tell her my terrible friend Lacey promised to come to the basketball game and flaked but had the bright idea of giving the newcomer to town a chance to socialize and take her place."

"But I didn't flake on you. I'm planning on coming."

"Not if the hottie is coming. Last thing I need is you sitting in the stands making moves on her."

"I'm not putting any moves on her."

"Your loss. What's her number?"

"I'll text it to you. Text me if she says yes, and I'll skip."

"Sorry I couldn't help with the car," Della said a little too cheerfully.

"No you're not. But thanks anyway," I grumbled.

Out of options, I scavenged wood from their winter supply to support the door while I worked on the bolts. As I wrestled them into submission, I kept my eye on the neighbors' places, half-hoping that someone would come to my rescue. By the time I swung the door into the trunk and leaned against the car, victorious, I was overheated, every joint hurt and every muscle had turned to jelly.

When I hit the highway, freezing cold air struck my sweaty body and set my teeth to chattering. I cranked up the heat and pointed all the vents at me. In *my* car, I had an emergency blanket. Load of good that did me.

A mile from town, a line of cars at a standstill stumped me. There is no traffic in Quincy. Not in the dead of winter, not even at the lunch rush which was hours gone. I slowed and stuck my head out of the car's frame.

"You have got to be kidding me." I unbuckled my belt and slid out of the car, gimping down the line of cars to where Officer Nelson stood waving her hands at an immobile horse. I passed a dozen cars held up in the road. Most had their windows shut to the cold, but a few were hollering at the officer and included me when I hobbled by.

"Get that thing out of the way!"

"This is absurd!"

"That your horse, Lacey? Get it out of here!"

"Isn't this supposed to scare them off?" Brenna asked, waving her hat at the horse which appeared to be napping right smack in the middle of the two lanes.

The hollering made me feel guilty even though it wasn't my animal. "How am I supposed to know? Did you call Gabe?"

"Why would I call Gabe?" she snapped.

The way Gabe had talked about her, I was sure they were together, but her reaction sent me into a quick backpedal. "Because he's good with horses."

Lips set in a hard line, she challenged me to add more. I caved. "I called him when this guy," I motioned to the sleeping horse, "was in my shop."

"Well, that explains one thing."

"What's that?"

"Why Gabe said, 'Not funny' and hung up on me."

Ah, so maybe there was more than she was letting on. I started to smile and saw there was no humor in her face. "Oh."

"How is it a horse that was in your shop in East Quincy is now blocking my street?" Here I was trying to help, and even she blamed me.

"It's Madison's horse."

"Madison?" Her dark eyes bore into me.

"She's new to town. She said Houdini is hers."

Hearing his name, the horse's head snapped up, his eyes alert. Inexplicably, he ambled off the road to rest his head on my chest.

"Madison's horse?" Brenna stepped into the street and motioned for the cars to pass.

"Keep that thing corralled," someone hollered.

Others stared angrily at me as they crawled past Brenna and me.

"Apparently. I'm pretty sure. Do you want me to call her?"

"First move that thing you're driving. Is that Shawneen's car? You want to explain why you're driving without a door, missy?"

"No, I really don't," I said, utterly finished with my already bad day.

"Of course you don't. Do you..." She let her head fall forward. She'd put her hat back on, so I couldn't see her face. "Does she have anything in there we can put on the horse?"

"Let me see." As I walked to the car, Houdini followed along like a well-trained dog. I climbed in to pull to the shoulder, and he kept walking. "Wait up!" I hollered once I'd parked. Brenna was already running toward him, her hands on her heavy black belt. I glanced around to see if there was anything I could use to catch the horse, but when I looked back to the road, Houdini had moved into a trot. Brenna stopped running, and the horse angled to the shoulder, sailed over the fence and stretched out into a beautiful gallop.

Brenna turned around, hands on hips. Before she could move, I jumped back into the Nova and threw it into gear, in no mood to explain.

CHAPTER FIFTEEN

Lacey

Bent halfway into an engine, the gentle bump against my hip would have caught me off guard a week ago. He'd come into the shop as quietly as he had left my shop the time before. I hadn't even heard his hooves on the concrete. I set down my wrench and wiped my hands on the red rag I hung from my belt.

"Why am I not surprised to see you here again?" I tried to sound annoyed, but his standing there made me think of Madison. What had I said unnecessary at dinner? Something about how believing in fate means accepting that some power out of your control dictates your life. I had no control over this horse, and here he was dictating my thoughts, preventing me from writing off his owner.

He set his wide forehead on my hip and started rubbing.

"I'm sure Madison would be happy to serve as your scratching post. You need an oil change? A tire rotation? I'm your gal, but I don't do horses." He continued to pump his head up and down as I pulled out my phone and scrolled through my calls to find Madison's number. She answered out of breath. "Hey Madison. It's Lacey."

"Lacey! I've been meaning to call you to say thanks for passing on my number to Della. I caught the home game. It was great!"

"Glad that worked out," I said. I was sure Della would be very receptive to Madison's ideas about Fate. "Question: you hard at work?"

"Dragging the last of the carpet out, yeah. Why?"

"Because I'd be hard at work, too, if your horse pal would leave me alone."

"Houdini?"

The way she said it, I could tell she expected him to show up at her side. Resting my hand on his neck, I waited for her to realize he wasn't with her.

"He was just here."

"And then, poof, he's all the way over here in East Quincy? He's not even breathing hard or sweaty." I examined the horse. The way he'd flown over the field when he took off from Brenna and me, I thought he was a young horse, but on closer inspection, he looked ancient. How long would it have taken him to cross the six or so miles between my place and Madison's?

"He's probably in the barn," Madison said.

I waited for her to find that he wasn't.

"He isn't." She sounded suitably befuddled.

"So you'll come get him, right?" I prompted.

"With what? I don't have a horse trailer."

"And yet you have a horse."

"He came with the property. I'm not ready to have stock yet."

"Well what am I supposed to do with him? Teach him how to fix a timing belt?" I briefly thought about offering to call Gabe, but he'd never believe me.

"Okay." She sounded distracted. "I'll...I'll be over as soon as I can."

I slipped the phone back into my pocket and turned to the horse. "Might as well get some work done, don't you think? C'mon. I'll catch you up to where we are." Again deep in engine, narrating my progress, I heard tires on the drive. "There's your mom," I said, emerging to an empty shop. I blinked several times trying to make him reappear. Madison strode into the shop dressed as she always was in work pants, heavy boots and coat. If I hadn't been expecting her, her ball cap might have made me guess I was dealing with a teenaged boy. She looked around expectantly.

I held up my hands guiltily.

"Did you tie him up out back?" she asked, skipping pleasantries.

"He's gone," I admitted.

"Gone," she said, incredulous.

"We were working on the timing belt. He was chewing on my pocket." I held it up for her to see, but there were no teeth marks, no wetness to back up my claim.

"You didn't think to put something on him?"

"Like what?" I asked, exasperated. "The old timing belt? Maybe you should leave something on him instead of letting him wander around naked."

"I'm not letting him wander around naked. Like I told you, he's not wandering around."

"Then how do you explain the horse that was in my shop? How do you explain how he held up traffic on Highway 89 yesterday?"

"My horse wasn't on the road."

"Call the police department if you don't believe me. That horse gets around."

"Clearly." Madison waved her arms about to indicate the empty garage. "My horse is not around here." As she scanned the garage, the door-less Nova stopped her cold. "What are you doing with Shawneen's car?" She pressed her fingertips to her forehead like she was trying to calm down some kind of chaos in her head.

"Do you know Shawneen?" She'd had a similar reaction when I mentioned her at the restaurant, and the way she said her name suggested a connection between them.

Dani's huge rig saved her from answering. She pulled up right to the open bay door and rolled down the window, country music pouring out. "One sec?" I asked.

"I've got Joy with me, and we're happy with the song on the radio," she replied.

I turned back to Madison. "I've got to grab a book inside. I'll be right back." I still wanted the answer to my question, and she certainly didn't look like she was going anywhere. She hadn't acknowledged the truck behind her and stood with her arms hugged around her shoulders, still staring at the car. I almost reached out to touch her but knew Dani was reading me, and the more I gave her, the deeper the inquisition would be the next time I saw her.

In no time at all, I returned with the book I'd promised her at our last book club. "Like I said, the protagonist isn't gay, but she's from Texas, and I couldn't help thinking about you the whole time I read it."

"*Nowhere But Home*," she read the book's title and flipped it over to skim the back.

"And I bet Hope will love the cooking she does. That was my favorite part."

"Thanks." She set the book down on the passenger seat. "Is that the woman you and Della were talking about?"

"It is." I kept my answers short to give Dani less to work with. The woman missed nothing.

"Hmmm. What'd she do to Shawneen's car?"

I'd been wondering where Madison had gone. Sure enough, she was sitting in the driver's seat of Shawneen's Nova. "Shawneen did that to the door herself," I said, hoping she wouldn't ask me to elaborate then and there.

"I think you'd better come to supper soon to fill us in."

"Name the night."

With a thumbs-up, Dani backed out of the drive and waved as she headed out. I took a deep breath, itching to find out what Madison's deal was but also disappointed. I've read enough romances to recognize the character pining for an old flame. In my eyes Shawneen was a little old for her, but there had clearly been something between them. Maybe that was why she had such an investment in fated things working out. I eased into the passenger seat and carefully shut the door. Madison held the wheel with faraway look on her face that tempered any interest I might have otherwise explored.

"What happened to the door?" Madison asked.

"Shawneen about tore it off trying to back up with the door open. It got stuck in a berm. If I had it my way, Dennis would be the one making a trip down the hill to find a new door, but…"

"Dennis?"

"Shawneen's boyfriend."

"Her boyfriend," she repeated. "Do they…do they have any kids?"

Oh, man did I want out of that car. How many more ways could Shawneen make my life difficult? Why was I stuck feeding information about her personal life to…I didn't even know who. Wanting to clear that up, I asked how she knew Shawneen.

"She's…" Madison finally looked at me, those chocolate-brown eyes taking me in, measuring me, weighing how much to trust me. Her eyes welled. "She's my mother. I don't know her. My father…" She took her time searching for the right words. "My father…"

"Raised you?" I asked. I hated seeing her struggle and felt terrible for the assumptions I'd had about her, that she was a dopey pothead or someone who would get lost in the fantasy of an old unattainable love.

"No," she answered, surprising me again. "He moved me away when I was little. Moved me away from this house."

We sat there together, my mind reeling and her thoughts who knew where. Though I barely knew her, I reached out and lay my hand on her shoulder. With just a handful of words, I had a picture of a very broken soul. What did it mean that her father had moved her away but not raised her? Who did?

My mind continued spinning on her strange family dynamic. Her father. Something clicked, and I jumped from the car and reached for the treasure box stowed on my workbench shelf.

I knew what was inside. Did she? I knew where the little treasures fit in my childhood, but not in hers. Sensing they belonged to her, I carried the box back to the car and slid it across the vinyl bench seat.

She placed her hand on the lid, tracing the pattern barely visible on the old tin box. Her thumbs moved to push the lid open, but she hesitated, looking my way for permission.

"Go ahead," I said softly. "I think it was yours."

Carefully, she rocked the lid off the box. She lifted out the picture first, wonder on her face.

"That's your father, isn't it? It's got to be, and you were driving that truck the day you told me you'd bought property here."

"That's me," she said, her fingers touching the baby in the photograph." She slowly examined the rest of the contents, the animal figurines, the rocks. "How in the world do you have this?"

"It was in the wall. I found it when I was a kid. You must have squirreled it away."

"I don't remember doing that."

"I was about eight when I found it. My bed had always covered up the door to the bathroom plumbing—probably on purpose. I wanted to rearrange my room, and I found the door. I found this."

"I was only four when we left."

"Perfect place for a four-year-old to stow her most important things." I picked up the penguin. "Sorry they're so worn. I might have played with them a little."

"They were my friends."

The way she said it felt like they'd been her only ones. "They were good ones." The way she pursed her lips and drew her eyebrows together, I wondered if she was holding in tears. "They should have gone with you."

"Yeah."

I hardly heard her and could imagine all she was reliving. Imagining her thoughts pushed me back to my childhood. "The swan used to pull the little girl in this tin boat," I remembered out loud.

"How?"

"My mom gave me thread. She used to take pictures of the little worlds I created. I loved all the little rocks. Do you remember where you got them?"

She frowned at the polished stones in her hand. "Someone must have given them to me."

"Unless you stole 'em." The minute the words left my mouth, I worried I'd overstepped, but her face lit up.

"What makes you think I stole them!"

"It's the quiet ones you have to watch out for."

We sat there side by side in her mother's car, in what had been her old home. In her bedroom. In mine. We could have been two young girls sitting Indian-style on the carpeted bedroom floor telling secrets and laying the foundation for a first crush. I'd scoped her out, written her off as an airhead but only then began to discover who she was.

CHAPTER SIXTEEN

Madison

Lacey let me keep the box. I picked up the phone to call Ruth and set it down without dialing. A thought went through my head to call Charlie and ask him if he knew about the contents. Would he even know about the box, would Shawneen? Or had it been my secret?

Covered in a fine layer of sawdust after hours of crawling on my knees along baseboards I'd had to reposition after pulling out carpet, I was no closer to an answer about the box, mostly because I was still thinking about Lacey. I turned the memory of sitting next to her in the front seat of my mom's car over and over in my mind as I had spun a smooth flat rock from the box around in my palm. I smiled again at the image of us on opposite sides of the car like two teenagers on a first date afraid to touch. Was she seeing anyone? Did local teens have a place for parking? Would she accept if I asked her on a date? I longed to hear more about what she thought about me.

Could I really have stolen some of these things? I tried to imagine where Shawneen would have taken me. A friend's house?

A garden store? Would I have been the kid who pocketed little treasures? I remembered how Lacey's eyes had sparkled when I'd asked her why she thought I had thieving potential. I liked being able to push a little and have her push back. That was the dance I missed from working at Steve's guest ranch. I read people well, and took great satisfaction in pegging the guests who needed a little nudge toward adventure. Just by herself, Lacey made me feel giddy, and I realized that I had no idea where that feeling was leading me.

Needing some fresh air, I dusted off as best I could and went out to the back porch to stretch and appreciate how warm midday was with the season changing. Spring was setting up house, unwrapping everything she'd put away last year and polishing it up for all to admire.

I closed my eyes remembering the way Lacey's laugh and touch had warmed me. At my feigned hurt about her suggestion of thievery, she'd rested her hand on my arm to reassure me. That simple gesture awakened me. I can't think of any other way to say it. When I looked up at her and met her gaze, I saw her for the first time. She was still homecoming-queen beautiful, but she wasn't a superior member of the upper class making me feel like a peasant. The way she'd listened to me made me think of her as the loyal friend she must have been in high school. She'd be the person people voted for because she was genuine. Her beauty would have stemmed from her willingness to state her own mind even if it didn't match popular opinion.

Here I thought Quincy was a place I'd find myself. Instead I found myself in the position to afford the vision I'd had of enjoying the sunset with someone. Too much had happened to edge me toward Lacey to ignore the possibility of sharing with someone. I was tempted to tell Lacey that the flat tire and the box she'd found were perfect examples of why I thought my path was predetermined but tucked it away not wanting to disturb what was taking hold between us.

In private, I reexamined what it felt like to be with her, excitement shivering up my spine and through my thighs. My body wanted her hands on my skin. Not used to such distracting thoughts, I surrendered to getting no more work done and let my mind wander over what it would be like to call Lacey simply because I wanted to see her again.

Houdini approached the porch, materializing from the forest as he sometimes did. I'd tried to keep him in one of the barn's box stalls when I first moved to the property, but I never found him there in the morning, so I'd taken to tossing a flake of alfalfa into a feeder in the pasture. It disappeared, and most days, the horse checked in on me like he was doing now.

"Have you really been hanging out in her shop?" I asked, rubbing his broad forehead, searching for a legitimate reason to call Lacey. Nothing was wrong with my truck, and I had no need for any more local information. "I can't just call her and say 'Let's hang out.'" Houdini shook his head and neck and surveyed the property as he often did. He turned away from me and started walking.

I followed him, hoping our destination took us to a sunny patch. In the shade of the evergreens that lined my drive, I wrapped my arms around myself for warmth and imagined a stranded motorist who would require a good mechanic. Instead of heading for the road, though, Houdini veered off our drive beyond the trees and stood by the wire fence. "What?" I asked throwing up my arms. "Lacey doesn't fix fences, and that one looks fine to me."

He butted the fence with his muzzle, and I reluctantly left the firmer ground of the drive to pick my way through the slush of melting snow. The fence, I realized up close, had a simple gate held by loops of wire at the top and bottom.

"So? I don't want to go tromping around a soggy field." He refused to budge, so I opened the gate for him, happy to watch him gallop out across the open space. The snow had melted to reveal patches of brown vegetation. The brown wasn't random though. Watching Houdini's hooves on the ground, I recognized clear rows. Had someone plowed the field?

Houdini trotted back to me. "Someone planted this field?" I asked, stroking his face. He rewarded me by stretching his neck toward the sky. He gave the ridiculous horse smile, his upper lip tweaked up from his long yellowed teeth.

"But I don't think I have a tractor." I headed back up to the barn thinking that I must've missed something on the walk-through with the realtor. Halfway up the drive, I stopped dead in my tracks. "A tractor!" A huge smile burst across my face as I pulled my cell from my pocket and found Lacey's number.

"Madison," she said. I swore I heard a smile behind her greeting. "Everything okay?" she added when I couldn't immediately find my words.

"Yes. Sorry. I called to see what you know about tractors."

"Tractors?"

"Well, tractor. Singular. I'm going to need one to plow a field I have here, but I really have no idea what I need or where to start looking."

"How big of a field are you talking?"

"Not big. It's a small pasture down by the road. Although I'm sure it would be handy to have a tractor to clean up the corrals. It's got to be old though."

"Authentic," she said, following my train of thought with ease.

"Exactly." I couldn't help but smile.

"There might be some listed in the recycler. They might need a bit of love to get them back in business, but I might know a good technician who could help with that."

"You might?" I asked. Was she flirting with me?

"It would help if I saw how big of an area we're talking about."

I scanned my property from Lacey's perspective. It wasn't near ready for opening, and I worried about whether it would look good to her. Houdini still stood by the pasture. As if he'd been listening in on the conversation and was again frustrated with my slowness, he stamped his foot. Here was the opportunity to spend time with Lacey that I'd wanted. "Let me give you the address."

"I've got a pen. Shoot."

She read it back to me and asked if she should stop by after she closed up her shop at five.

"That sounds great," I replied. "Thank you."

"I haven't done anything yet," she said, an undercurrent of mischief in her voice.

I held the phone to my chest, knowing she had already done so much.

CHAPTER SEVENTEEN

Lacey

The one upside of Shawneen's Nova taking up space in my shop was that it forced me to get the rebuilt engine back into my now-perfect baby blue Bug, so I could move it outside when I needed the shop. I still had some interior work to do, but it felt great to be rattling down the road in it.

She was standing in the drive waiting and waved as I slowed and turned. I pulled to the side to avoid blocking the driveway and held up a thumb. Madison mirrored the gesture, so I cut the rattling engine. It felt a little strange to be with her again. It wasn't like we'd had a date, but sitting parked in her mom's car had changed things for me. When I'd given Della her number, I'd had no interest in Madison. Or had I? Now I found myself very much interested and in the awkward place of wondering whether Della felt the same way.

"I figured I'd catch you at the road since the field's right here," she said in greeting.

Grateful she directed us right to business, I surveyed Madison's property, trying to recall how she'd described her place at the Chinese restaurant. "You said you would maybe have a few horses, not a full-on dude ranch, right?" I asked. With frost still on the ground and the sun an hour away from setting, the chill sent a shiver through me. It had nothing to do with the woman who stood next to me.

Her feet wide-set, she placed one hand on her hip and the other behind her head, her elbows pointing out like sails on a ship, one up high and one down low. I would've liked to peek inside her head to see what she was envisaging. Whatever it was, she wasn't ready to put it into words. She answered simply, "No, not a full-on ranch."

"Because you could put a few nice-looking horses down here in the pasture. They'd keep the grass down and would catch your attention on the approach."

"You don't think I could put a crop in here?"

"Oh, you could, but what does that have to do with your angle? Unless you're using the rows as some sort of meditation walk or offering to let them to pitch in and live the life of a farmer for a few days, I don't see how it would add to the appeal. Mind if I look at the rest of the place?"

"Not at all."

I followed her over a short bridge, our boots loud on the gravel. Her arms crossed high on her chest across a bright yellow plaid flannel made her look as nervous as I felt. The pasture in question lay on the left and the driveway to the right disappeared into the pines that also ran the western length of the field. She'd called me. Did that mean that she had been thinking about me?

"You seen Della?" I asked. It didn't hurt to see if they'd hit it off.

"Your coach friend? No. Why? Was there another home game?"

"Oh, no. I was just wondering."

"But you didn't ask her?"

We walked side by side our eyes studiously focused up ahead. "I see her at games, and sometimes we do lunch, but since…we're not dating anymore…I tend to not just call her." My stomach tense, I waited for her to say something.

We stopped at the top of the drive to catch our breath. "It was nice of her to invite me to the game, and she did ask if I wanted to hang out afterward." She glanced at me, and my heart raced as I waited for what she had to say. "I told her that I'm pushing like crazy to get my place open by spring and that I don't really have time for anything else."

Was she telling me the same thing, or was she telling me she'd brushed Della off? "Does she know about Shawneen?"

"No." Her answer came fast. "We barely talked. I was just grateful for her giving me a reason to stop working. Sometimes I forget to." She turned to look at the house that was taking up so much of her time.

It sat facing east, and it was easy to imagine guests enjoying a sunrise from the front porch of the large rustic home. "How many guests can you accommodate?"

"Once I finish remodeling, I'll have four rooms. Plus I have space behind the main house to put in some cabins eventually."

"Tucked in between the trees to make them more private."

She tapped her temple and smiled impishly. I could see how that smile would distract people from realizing how much their vacation was costing. A weathered barn sat across a small yard. "Is Houdini put up for the night?"

"I tried to keep him in the barn, but I never found him there in the morning, so I gave up on that. He visits when he wants to."

"But isn't around today?"

"Nope. I thought he might be hanging out with you."

That teasing smile again. I couldn't help but mirror it as we walked over to the barn. She pulled open the doors, and in the fading light, I saw neat stalls, an empty hayloft and plenty of room for a small tractor. Later, I'd think about how the moment had been ripe for a first kiss. But right then, I was still unsure about where we stood, knowing only how appealing it was to be watching someone realizing a vision. I liked to think I could help her with that, which tipped us back to the business of why she'd called me. We walked back out into the last of the evening sun, shadows stretching long in the small corral adjacent to the barn.

"You've got plenty of room for horses up here next to the barn, so I get why you wouldn't pasture them below. I really think you should consider a garden down there instead of a crop. My gran grows a lot of the vegetables Hope uses at Cup of Joy, and I could see you doing the same thing here, pulling people in with the draw of eating what grows right on the property. Customers get really excited about it at Hope's restaurant. Think of how psyched people would be to eat what they had harvested themselves."

"You think people would be happy to work on their vacation?"

"I'm certainly not an expert on vacations. I don't take them because I get bored not doing anything, and I feel guilty for not working. But, say I found a place that had old engines to tinker with during the day. I'd be happy because I'd feel productive, and as a bonus, I might even learn something I could bring home. Think of the stuff you could teach people about crops, how to rotate them, what foods are compatible."

"You sure know a lot about gardening for a mechanic."

I tried unsuccessfully to bite back the annoyance I felt at her choice of words.

"What?" Madison asked.

"I'm an auto technician."

Madison crossed her hands over her chest. "I've always said mechanic."

"Well," I hedged, remembering how speaking my mind about rekindling old loves had pushed Madison away. Though I'd be disappointed to shut down the budding camaraderie, I decided I didn't have the energy to not be myself. "You've always been wrong."

"Really?" Madison sounded curious instead of offended.

"Really. It's like calling a massage therapist a masseuse."

Madison looked away.

"You say masseuse?"

"I have on occasion. What's wrong with that?"

"It's like calling a flight attendant a stewardess. We have professional titles."

"I never knew."

"Now you do," I said lightly. I liked that she didn't trip over herself with apologies like Della would have. Instead, she accepted my point. I put my hands in my pockets. Spring evenings still cooled quickly which reminded me of the hour and how I'd been derailed from our discussion about the field. I gestured to the open space. "And here you have the perfect opportunity to teach people how roses love garlic."

"Roses love garlic?"

"It's called companion planting, and my gran is the local expert. She's expecting me for dinner, and I know she'd be happy to put another plate on the table if you'd care to ask her about your plot."

Madison put her hands on her boyish hips and tilted her chin. "You're inviting me to dinner?"

"Sure." Would she see that as an invitation for a date? She didn't say yes right away, and I wanted to ask if my thoughts on fate continued to tip the scale out of my favor. Worried that she'd taken it the wrong way, I added, "Wouldn't you like to talk gardening with my gran?"

"It's only an introduction, then."

I puzzled at her challenge. Did she want it to be more? "And an effort to make up for horning in on your dinner at the Chinese place."

"I am interested in talking to your grandmother about what I could do with that field. Is she on my side of the valley or yours?"

"Mine," I said, wounded that her tone remained formal after I'd extended an olive branch. I wished I'd asked her to clarify whether she didn't have time for just Della, or for anyone at all. I wanted her to want to spend more time with me.

"I'll grab my coat and keys and follow you."

The breath I hadn't realized I was holding slipped out. "So you accept my apology?"

"No," she said, walking back toward her place.

I jogged to catch up to her, surprised by her answer. "No?"

"You didn't say you were sorry, and saying your gran would

be happy to put another plate on the table doesn't sound like an apology to me."

Her good points gave me pause. I realized I *hadn't*, in fact, apologized. "I feel bad about the way that dinner ended."

"That's a start," she said. "Still not an apology, but I don't want your grandmother's hard work to go to waste, so we can get back to that if you ask me out on a date."

Her words zinged right through me. So she wasn't so busy she wasn't considering dating at all. "Why aren't *you* asking me?"

"I wouldn't want to spoil your surprise."

She left me by her truck with the rainbow sticker while she grabbed her coat and keys, and I spent those few minutes considering how I was supposed to surprise her when she already *knew* I'd be asking her on a date. I kicked the tire that had prompted her to stop at my shop back in January. My shop which had been her home. My garage that had been her childhood bedroom as well as mine. Was that Fate?

I thought back to our exchange. I wasn't sorry for voicing my opinion on stories that reinforce the idea of returning to long-lost loves. I was sorry that my ideas and assumptions about why she was in Quincy had pushed her away. I felt guilty for how I'd misread her attention on Shawneen. When she emerged from the house I couldn't meet her eyes.

She gave me a lift back to my Bug in her truck. The short distance down the drive didn't give me much time to shape the apology, but I had to say something before I got out. "I'm sorry that I laughed at you when you asked if I believed in Fate."

"I'm sorry I took it so personally. Ruth always says that it's as harmful to take offense as it is to give it."

"Ruth?" I asked. She'd said the name like I should be able to place it.

"The woman who raised me."

"I'd like to hear more about her."

"I'll tell you sometime, but you said dinner was waiting."

She had me there. The questions that flooded my mind would have to wait. I tucked them away, looking forward to the time I could ask Madison on a real date where we could talk in private, but equally excited to be introducing her to my gran.

CHAPTER EIGHTEEN

Lacey

The silver Subaru in my gran's drive startled me. Six months ago, I would have expected it, but my little brother had recently moved to Reno. I couldn't imagine what he was doing back and swore under my breath that he'd better behave with my unexpected guest.

"Cal!" I hollered, poking my head inside the door. I hadn't seen that my gran was standing right inside the kitchen.

"Good lord, girl." My gran stepped back, her hand over her heart.

"Sorry Gran. Where's Cal?" He was one to ambush, and I didn't want to risk him pouncing on Madison.

Cal answered as he exited the bathroom down the hall. "Cleaning up."

"What are you doing here?"

"An old client of mine in Portola guilted me into coming over. I called Gran and said if she'd make her honey-ham, I'd drive down here after."

"You never said!" I admonished my gran. If I'd known he'd be in town, I wouldn't have suggested bringing Madison over.

"Don't yell at an old lady's forgetfulness, especially when you're just as much to blame." Her gaze shifted behind me.

"Oh, I'm sorry Madison. This is my grandma, Karen Wheeler, and my brother, Cal. Gran, I hope it's okay I invited Madison to talk gardening."

"One of my favorite topics. It's a pleasure to meet you, Madison. Come in. Come in. Lacey, honey, take her coat. I've about got dinner on the table. Your friend here can help me with that and Cal, let's use the good china, shall we?" she said, setting us all into motion.

After depositing Madison's coat, I returned to the kitchen where Gran was already getting the dimensions of Madison's field. I grabbed a pitcher of tea from the fridge to take to the kitchen table on the other side of Grandma's stove and met Cal carrying the nice dishes from the dining room which currently held hundreds of starts for the garden. "Want to trade an oil change for a massage? I'm not driving home until tomorrow."

"I don't need a massage."

"Is someone helping you out for *free*?" he whispered, looking over at Madison who was headed our way with a bowl of peas.

"No," I smacked him soundly to shut him up and then turned to accept the bowl from Madison. "I forgot to mention that Gran would probably set you to work."

"It's fine." Instead of returning to the kitchen, she stood watching us. Cal had reached to rub the sting of the first hit which would have earned him another if we hadn't been under Madison's scrutiny.

He smiled brightly at her, his close-cropped beard framing his braces-perfect teeth. Cal's a good-looking guy. He went to college on a football scholarship and had a lot of attention from the ladies. Recovering from a career-ending knee injury, he'd developed an interest for sports medicine that led to him learning massage therapy. The youngest of my four siblings, he's the tallest as well as the biggest shit-disturber. He always felt the need to catch up for the pranks my two oldest brothers pulled before he was born. "So are you two..."

Not liking the gleam in his eye, I interrupted him before he could cause any mischief. "We're going to talk to Gran about her tractor. Madison's got a plot of land on her place out at Spanish Creek Road that I am trying to convince her to farm on a small scale. She called me about buying a tractor, but for the size of the place, we could truck Gran's tractor over."

"What's this about my tractor?"

"The piece of land Madison has is about the same as what you garden here with Hope. I was going to ask to borrow it."

Madison interrupted, "I was asking for help finding a tractor to buy."

"Well that's silly." Gran set a basket of sliced bread on the table. "Cal, fetch the ham. The work you've put into that old thing Lacey, I'd say it's yours anyway. If you can find a way to get it to Madison's place, there's no reason to spend good money on another. Are we ready to eat?"

I pointed Madison to the seat between Gran and me at the round table, so that I could keep my eye on Cal. He let me know he knew my intent by squeezing the hell out of my hand during grace.

"It's very kind of you to offer the tractor." Madison picked up the conversation again once everyone was served. "But with all the finishing touches I have to do with the house, I probably won't get to a garden this year. When I called Lacey today, I was sure that finding something in my budget was going to take much longer."

"Planting season's just begun, and my Scout helpers are always asking for more community assistance hours. I'm sure they would be happy to help at your place."

Madison was uncomfortable with the offer. I could tell by her rigid posture, but I couldn't figure out why she'd shy from it. "What do you grow?" Her question soundly redirected the conversation away from her as Gran discussed her vegetables.

"You're a rancher?" Cal inserted, bringing attention back to her.

"I'm opening a small resort this summer," she answered.

"You've worked a resort before?" He sounded doubtful.

I nudged Cal under the table in warning. "The gardening was my idea. I tossed it out as an angle she might be able to exploit. A way to stand out from the competition."

"Gardening makes way more sense than putting rainbow in your business name."

He smirked at me, so I did more than nudge him that time.

"Calvin." Gran said, snapping his attention away from me. Madison eyed the two of us again as he not so subtly rubbed his shin.

"I was only noting that gardening seems to cast a wider net. But it also takes a lot of hours. There are other angles, like making a wellness retreat. Hire a massage therapist..." he said leadingly.

Madison and I shared a smile when she figured out why the word masseuse irked me.

"What?" Cal grumped. "I think that's a better idea. Gran, what would you rather do on vacation, get a massage or garden." Before she could respond, he held up his hand to stop her. "You're the wrong person to ask. I'll ask Trevor."

"Cal, we're eating," Gran warned.

"You're right. I'll shoot him a text." Since his eyes were already on his phone, he didn't see Gran's disappointment. "There. I went ahead and sent it to everyone." He looked pleased with himself. "So are you starting this resort on your own? Or do you have a partner?"

"I'm on my own," Madison answered.

"Yeah, that's good. Be your own boss."

I laughed. "All this advice from the guy who closed his own wellness shop and went to work for someone in Reno."

"There are things I miss about the shop," he countered. His phone chirped, and he checked it. "Trevor is with me," he said with great satisfaction.

"That only evens it up since we know Gran votes for a garden."

The phone chirped again. "Ha! Chrystal is with me."

"Let me see that." I grabbed the phone and saw that Chrystal had, indeed, said she'd prefer a massage. "Chrystal is our sister. No surprise in her wanting a massage. She's never been a big fan of the outdoors."

Gran cut in. "That's the truth. Whenever I had all you little ones out here, I couldn't keep Lacey or the boys inside, but Chrystal was always curled up with a book. Shall we put the electronics away?" Gran asked, inclining her head ever so slightly toward Madison.

"Sorry to be rude," I apologized, poking Cal in the chest with his phone since he'd been the one who started texting. As soon as he tucked it in his back pocket, it chirped again. Cal froze.

"It's okay," Madison said. "Is that another sibling?"

"The last. Bennett is our oldest brother."

"What's his vote?" Madison asked.

"I'll put it on silent after this, promise." Cal glanced at the screen and frowned.

"I suppose that means Benny is with us." Gran's eyes twinkled. Even though the texting bothered her, I knew she was pleased to have another grandchild on her side. "Not that it's our place to dictate what Madison does with her land. But if you do decide on a garden, I'd love to help. I may look old and move slowly, but I get a lot of work done."

"Thank you," Madison said. "And thank you for feeding me tonight. It's been a long time since I had a meal as nice as this."

"Aren't you kind. Your folks raised you right," Gran said pointedly.

Madison blushed and tried to hide it by looking down at her plate. Totally missing her reaction, Cal pushed.

"Where's your family?" he asked.

"Paradise," Madison said. "They run cattle."

She delivered the words to her food, and I thought about how she said her father hadn't raised her and had mentioned a woman named Ruth. My clumsy and clueless brother had no idea how sensitive the topic was for her, so I blocked any other questions with my own about dessert. Madison's eyes thanked me. I would've liked to have squeezed her hand but didn't want to risk making her uncomfortable. I bused her plate, ordering Cal to grab Gran's, so he wouldn't get any ideas about prodding further into Madison's business. "No more grilling," I said as we slipped dishes into the sink.

"C'mon. She's cute. Don't you want to know more about her?"

"Yes, *I* want to know more about her. On my own. That's for me to find out, not you."

"But she's single and into girls? Because if she's into guys…"

"Shut it, Cal."

CHAPTER NINETEEN

Lacey

I sat in my car outside Dani and Hope's trying to wipe off what was surely a giveaway grin. Since I was late, they were bound to be full of questions, and I wanted a minute to run through the call with Madison. We'd chatted on the phone a few times after the dinner with my gran. I'd kept things light for a week, calling to ask about her place or the garden or making sure she knew where Houdini was. That way, when I finally did call to ask her out, it was indeed a surprise for her. Before I had to come clean with the group, I wanted a moment to linger on the smile I heard in her voice when I finally asked her to have dinner with me. I knew Della was going to be upset.

Gabe pulled up at his parents' place across the yard, so I pushed open my own door and waved to him. We climbed different sets of stairs, his to the two-story main house where he lived with his parents, and mine to the two-bedroom place they had originally built for him. He'd never taken up residence, which prompted Hope to suggest they rent it to Dani three years ago when she moved to Quincy to start teaching at the local college. After they married, Hope moved in.

I found a sign taped to the door: *Joy's asleep. Come on in.* Inside, Hope and Dani were cuddled together on the couch, and Della sat in the rocking chair. Dani had pulled one of the kitchen chairs into the living room for me. After delivering hugs and kisses on the cheek to all three, I settled into my spot. "What've I missed?"

"That's what we want to know." Hope smiled. She had her blond hair in a loose ponytail and was wearing sweats and one of Dani's flannel shirts. We'd been the same year in school, but I only ever knew her as the Mormon girl, superconservative and quiet. When I moved back to Quincy after college and ran into her at her diner, Cup of Joy, I'd barely recognized the woman she'd blossomed into. Had that confident elegance not been a product of the woman she was dating, I could have asked her out.

My stomach flip-flopped at the reminder that I had asked Madison out on a proper date, bringing the smile I'd been trying to hide front and center.

"The woman from the shop, I knew it," Dani said.

"You two hooked up?" Della set down her drink with a force that betrayed her emotion. "When I got her number, you said you weren't interested."

"I wasn't. And you said that you don't always tell me everything, so I'm doing the same."

"But then I *did* tell you I was asking her out."

I looked at Dani and Hope apologetically. "But it was only to the game."

"She said she was crazy busy. *I* was giving her some space."

"Last time you said you thought she had some weird thing for Shawneen?" Hope interrupted.

I appreciated her effort to shut down the conversation and tried to figure out what I could say to get everyone to drop it. Since Shawneen didn't know who Madison was, I didn't feel like I could explain exactly why it didn't worry me anymore. It was Madison's business after all. I tried for simple, hoping nobody would ask any follow-up questions. "She doesn't."

"And you know this…" Dani's wheels were turning. "That day I picked up the book, she was sitting in Shawneen's car…"

"Speaking of books, thanks for waiting for me to talk about how great Dani's pick was. I wasn't sure about the supernatural element, but it definitely made the book more layered," I said, hoping they'd accept my redirect.

I was still lost in my thoughts about The Date, trying to figure out the perfect thing to serve, what to wear, how much to clean up my place. Had Della and I not had a past, I would have asked her advice. The group would happily change the topic of the evening from the book to my dating life. A month ago, I'd been okay with how we'd drifted into something more like a therapy session exploring why things had gone so badly at the Chinese restaurant. But now it seemed like there might be something between Madison and me, and book club was definitely not the place to discuss it.

"Not enough sex," Della quipped. She hadn't really accepted that I wanted to change the topic. I knew she was thinking I'd blown her chance to get laid. "So have you slept with Spacey yet?"

I groaned inwardly wondering how much fun they'd had rhyming Lacey with Spacey in my absence and regretted that I'd spun Madison's questioning my ideas about destiny as her lacking sophistication. Nonetheless, I ignored her attempt to bait me. "That's what I liked about the book. There's so much more story."

"Completely unbelievable. I'm surprised you didn't throw it across the room when she started in with the ghosts."

Della had no tolerance for inconsistency in anything. If I didn't believe in ghosts in real life, I shouldn't like them in fiction either. "All I'm saying is I enjoyed a novel plot. If we never read another story about a woman returning home to rekindle things with her high school love, it will be too soon."

Hope agreed, noting that it seemed like every author explored that story at least once. As the group remembered similar stories, I slipped into my own thoughts, remembering how I'd believed Madison had returned because of a romantic connection to Shawneen. I didn't know about her first love yet, or any of her romantic history, if in fact she had one. There was so much about her that I didn't know and was looking forward to finding out.

"Someone's spaced out in her own romance." Della didn't let me stay caught in my own musings for long. "Why didn't you ask her to come with you tonight?"

The tone of her voice made me wonder if I'd ever be able to attend with Madison. "Sure. First date in front of the firing squad. There's nothing wrong with that idea."

"Sounds like someone's got a guilty conscience." Della puffed out her chest and sat taller, ready to fight.

She had me there. "Look, I…"

"She'd be very welcome," Hope broke in softly.

Hope's tone invited me to take a breath before I said more. She's one of those people who has amazing wait time that saves them from saying something they later regret. While I appreciated her attempt, I still felt protective of Madison. "I doubt she'd be interested. She's reading a pretty serious political tome right now. Somehow, I'm guessing romance isn't her genre."

Dani smiled. "It wasn't Hope's either. Remember when you discovered my bookshelf? What was the first one I gave you?"

"*Roller Coaster*. You thought I'd like all the details about food."

With that, they were off on another tangent recalling their favorites. Dani winked at me, and it hit me that in this circle, all of us had multiple siblings. Madison had talked about her parents but had never mentioned brothers or sisters. I was willing to bet that at her dinner table people took turns speaking and didn't banter the way we all were used to.

Although my siblings and I picked at each other, we were as close as puppies in a litter, and we behaved like that too, readily pouncing on each other in a mostly playful way, all of us feeding off the others' energy. Madison had only met one brother. How would she have fared with all four of my siblings, the various spouses and eight nieces and nephews?

I admired the way Hope and Dani had so quickly defused the tension. Neither Della nor I had that in us. We both knew how to make ourselves heard, but neither knew how to listen. I had no patience for her insecurity, and she didn't like the way I called her out on it. She'd argued that we could work it out, but I didn't think a relationship should take that much work.

I couldn't help comparing how Madison challenged me for saying I'd apologized when I hadn't. Della would have accused me and made me defensive whereas Madison's words made me stop and think, an action with which I seriously lacked experience.

CHAPTER TWENTY

Lacey

I could've closed the shop early. Could have closed the bay doors and turned around the *Open* sign an hour ago when I started getting particularly antsy. None of my regulars had a vehicle to pick up, and I didn't expect anyone. My business-woman practicality kept me puttering in the shop until five sharp. It had argued that I didn't even need the half hour I'd given myself to shower and change before Madison came over at five thirty. I didn't need extra time to obsess about how to fix my hair or whether the faded jeans and soft plum shirt I'd picked out were the right choice.

Five minutes before I closed, an old Honda Civic wagon I didn't recognize slowed and, though I willed it to keep going, swung into my drive. *Please be asking for directions.* Barely into my second year of opening Rainbow Auto, I really shouldn't be willing any business away, but glancing at the clock, I felt my control over the evening slip.

"Can I help you?" I asked when the driver, a young woman with shoulder-length brown hair and heavy bangs, stepped out.

"I don't know. You're probably going to laugh at me for stopping, but all of a sudden there's this weird smell coming from my dash."

I propped my broom and walked to the driver's side. I ducked my head in but could only smell the evergreen air freshener she had hanging from the dash. "Was there smoke?"

"No, only the smell."

"Look, I'm about to close. If you could get a ride and let me keep it overnight, I can take a look at it first thing in the morning."

She looked crestfallen. "My aunt and uncle live in Chester. They're expecting me tonight, and I can't ask them to drive forty-five minutes to get me."

And she was worried the car would break down on the last leg of her journey. Great. I couldn't send her on her way with fingers crossed and not spend the rest of the night worrying about what might happen. I took my *be right back* sign and hung it on the front door on the off-chance Madison arrived before I was back with a diagnosis. On my way back over to the Civic, I closed the bay doors. "Let's see if we can't get the car to make the weird smell for me."

"Thank you so much," she gushed. "Do you want to drive?"

"No. You drive. You know the Safeway over the hill?"

"Yeah."

"We'll turn around there."

As we drove toward Quincy, I examined the dash and took deep breaths, wondering what could produce the smell she described as something between burning plastic and melting feathers. She made the left into the market parking lot and shot me an apologetic look. "It really was making a weird smell."

"I believe you, but there's not much I can do if it's stopped. There's nothing wrong with the motor. You've got power. Nothing different in the brakes?"

"They feel like they always do," she answered.

The trip there and back only took seven minutes, and I was thinking if I skipped washing my hair, I'd still be fine as long as Madison wasn't the kind to arrive early. That was factoring in having the young Civic owner popping the hood to let me check the hoses and connections. I had not anticipated Shawneen. When I saw her standing on my front porch, I almost told the driver to keep going, but how would I even begin to explain? Helpless, I sat trapped as the driver pulled up at my shop again.

"Pop the hood, and I'll do a quick check underneath. Seems like you should be fine to get to Chester though."

"I'm so sorry. You were about to close up, weren't you?"

"Don't worry about it," I said. With Shawneen there, I wasn't likely to get a shower at all and wondered if I reeked of the shop from my pores or whether changing my clothes would suffice.

"Lacey honey," Shawneen said, scuttling over to the car when she saw me get out.

"Did Dennis find a new door for the Nova?"

"He said I don't need a new door. He borrowed a welder and said he's sure he can use the wench on his Jeep to pull it closed."

"The wench?" I repeated, trying not to laugh as I pictured Shawneen holding the door handle and him pulling on her ankles.

She nodded making it even harder to resist laughing. "Once it's shut, he said we can weld it in place. It'll cost less than a new door."

Had she still been Shawneen-the-parasitic-drain, I might have handed over the keys to the Nova, but now she was Madison's mother. I hadn't figured out how that factored in, and I still wanted to check the Civic's hoses and connections, and… I glanced at my watch. There was no way I'd be able to clear out these customers before Madison arrived. Surprisingly, the Nova shifted up to the top priority. I simply couldn't let Shawneen's imbecile boyfriend get his hands on it and weld the door shut when all it needed was a new one from a junkyard.

"Hold on a minute, can you?" It wasn't like Dennis was waiting, and I didn't see her driving it without the door. I wanted to at least get the Civic taken care of and figure out a way to move Shawneen along. Trying my best not to let her rush me, I poked and prodded in the Civic's engine so with a clear conscience I could send its driver off to Chester. Of course, while my head was under the hood, Madison arrived.

My frustration spiked when I heard her truck. I hated that our first date was beginning with my shop full of people. This was the first time she hadn't arrived in her work clothes, and I had to be professional and keep my focus. Of course since Shawneen was there, it got worse.

"Shop's closed, honey," Shawneen said as Madison approached the Civic.

Madison stopped short, and I flushed at Shawneen's presumption to handle my shop. "Hey Ma…" I stopped myself before I said her full name. If I addressed her as Madison, Shawneen would have to realize who she was. Wouldn't she? How could she miss that they shared the same high cheeks and wide mouth? "I'm almost finished here."

"That's fine." Madison glanced in Shawneen's direction but otherwise didn't engage her.

I apologized to the young woman for not being able to help more and after she left, stood between Madison and Shawneen. If Madison had been to my house before, I would have asked her if she'd like to wait inside, but given that this was her first time, that felt even more awkward than standing between her and the woman who'd given birth to her and hadn't seen her for twenty years *and* didn't even recognize her… In any other situation, I'd introduce the two, but, unable to do that, I trusted that Madison would understand as I continued my conversation with Shawneen.

"Listen, if you let Dennis weld the door shut, you'll ruin that car. It's a safety issue. Her engine and frame have years left. Plus, think about what it means for you. You don't want to be crawling over the console for years. All you need is a new door off a junker. You could even find a video on how to change out doors on the Internet and do it yourselves."

"But wouldn't we need a new door?"

"True," I admitted. "I didn't have any luck finding anything in town, but there are bigger salvage yards in Chico or Reno."

"My father uses the place in Chico," Madison said as if she was testing Shawneen. I wanted to throttle her for the way she blinked at Madison in surprise like she'd simply forgotten about her.

Madison held Shawneen's gaze. What I'd first taken for her being slow made so much more sense to me now that I had insight into her past. It seemed like she was challenging Shawneen to see her. Quietly, she added, "He used to live here in Quincy and would drive down the canyon for parts."

Shawneen scrunched her mouth to the side before she laughed. "Dennis would never go to all that effort."

"I'm going down the canyon next week. I could take a look. I have a truck, so it would be easy to toss a door in the back if I find one."

"Depends on how much it is," Shawneen said, the flirtatious tone she sometimes used on me creeping into her voice. I don't know what bothered me more, that she was using it on her daughter, unknowingly, but still...or that she completely overlooked Madison's generosity.

I wanted to shout at her, make her see who was in front of her and ask how much more damage she could do. It took everything I had to keep the words in my mouth. I had to say something, so I told her to give me a week to see if I could track down a door. I wanted her gone so badly, I was tempted to drop my argument and let her have the Nova back to do as she wished. Dennis pulled up in his battered flatbed.

"Let me see what he thinks," Shawneen said. "How much do you think it'll cost?"

"Somewhere between fifty and a hundred for the door. You can YouTube a video and replace it yourselves, or I'd do it for a hundred and fifty."

Lips pressed in a firm line, she sauntered over to the car to consult with Dennis through the window. I tried my best to keep my eyes averted from the sight of her rear stuck out at an unattractive angle, but Madison was the most logical place to look, and it pained me to see her discomfort.

Shawneen finally stood and sang out, "If it's any more than a hundred to pick up the door, no deal. Call me!" She scuttled around to the passenger side, and they disappeared, Dennis gesturing something between a salute and a wave as he backed out of the drive.

I was finally able to give Madison my full attention. She had her hands shoved deep into the pockets of thickly woven charcoal cords and let out a deep breath when I finally turned to her. "I'm so sorry. What a terrible way to start a date."

"'S'okay. It's not like I have much to hold it up against."

I didn't see how that could be possible. "You haven't had many girlfriends? Or boyfriends," I added to let her know it wouldn't bother me if she'd dated guys.

"I went to a few dances in high school. Homecoming. Prom. But only because I didn't want Ruth and Bo to worry about me, not because I was interested. Beyond that..." She smiled timidly.

"This is a *first* first date?" I asked, a wave of anxiety washing through me. She nodded, not looking nervous despite the admission. I followed her lead. "Well, then. Let's get it started. I'll ask that you ignore the fact that your date needs a quick costume change. I'll see if I can't get the cat to keep you company."

CHAPTER TWENTY-ONE

Madison

Lacey led me past a tidy den to the kitchen. "Can I get you anything to drink?"

I was glad we'd moved past the incident with Shawneen. It had rattled me, but I had moved back to Quincy in part to figure out why Charlie had left, so I was going to have to drop the bomb of who I was to her sometime. "Whatever is fine."

She poured red wine into two glasses. We clinked, and she took a long drink. I sipped mine, knowing if I had much more before eating, I wouldn't be good for anything. Lacey shut her eyes, and I imagined the rush of warmth that so much alcohol would whoosh through my body. When she opened her eyes again, she rolled out some kinks in her neck and smiled. "Better already." She set down her glass. "Midnight's likely to be lazing in a patch of sunlight somewhere. Feel free to look for her if I take too long."

"Take your time," I said, and she disappeared at the end of the hallway to the right.

The kitchen had been remodeled. I'd memorized every detail of the few childhood pictures I had, most of which were outside. There were a few of me covered in spaghetti sauce in my high chair. The floor had been oak in need of refinishing. Now it was a rich brown tile that complemented granite countertops.

The window above the kitchen sink opened to a full greenhouse. Inside were many colorful orchids as well as some trays of vegetable starts. The dining room and kitchen were open plan, with a large table that matched an ornate hutch. Sliding glass doors gave a view of the backyard beyond a generous deck. As Lacey predicted, I found a short-haired black cat dozing in a patch of sun by the sliding glass doors. It glanced at me before resting back with its eyes closed. At my approach, it stretched out and purred.

I lowered myself fully to the floor next to her and looked out the window. Had I been allowed to play in the backyard? Did Shawneen sit on the porch or explore with me? Would Shawneen watch me from the kitchen window as she made dinner? Was Charlie ever home by then? I tried to imagine what my life would have been like if the three of us had remained in the house.

Lacey's footfall pounded down the hallway. Had I ever walked with such purpose, it would have rattled everything in Charlie's trailer or called much too much attention to me in Bo and Ruth's place.

"So you found Midnight?" Lacey stood above me in worn hip-hugging jeans and a plum long-sleeved shirt that accentuated her very feminine curves.

I stood and took in how relaxed she seemed. "You were popular in high school, weren't you?"

She took my hand. "I had friends. Why?" she asked with a confused grin.

"I can feel how loud this house was. I feel like I can hear you and your brothers slamming this door and your mom reminding you to slow down."

"The worst was summertime with the screen door. Someone was always running right into it. Without fail, my mom would say 'don't run through a screen door. You'll strain yourself!'"

I laughed at the joke but stilled when she put her hand to my face.

"Hi."

The simple gesture and word made my heart pound fiercely in my chest. "Hi," I managed shakily.

"There's something I have to do before I'll be safe to cook dinner."

"Okay," I answered, suddenly panicky about the impression our first kiss would make. I was pretty sure when she invited me over that we'd kiss, at least I'd hoped we would, but I wasn't expecting it to happen right from the...

Her sweet soft lips halted all thought. She brought her other hand up and cradled my face, and together they worked like blinders, limiting my focus to only what was in front of me. Her silky warm lips were my whole world and ignited a sparkler within me. My skin felt like the sparks that fly from the wand, and if you've ever held one of the wands, you know how the end glows red hot and races downward. Lacey's kiss did that to me too, and just like a kid whose sparkler has burned down, the moment the kiss ended, I wanted another.

When she pulled away, her fingers stayed on my cheeks and felt like the afterimage you can see when you close your eyes and your retina remembers. My skin glowed hot like that wherever her fingers rested. "All week I've been thinking about how I should have done that in your barn," she said softly.

"I thought you were interested in Houdini," I said, still amazed that someone like Lacey wanted to kiss me.

"I'll have to be more clear in the future," she said.

I bit my lip and blinked away from her intense stare.

"But first dinner."

As she pulled ingredients from the refrigerator, I found myself back at the sink looking at the greenhouse.

"My dad put that in for my mom. The orchids are some she left behind."

"You've been here a long time, haven't you?"

"I practically grew up here. We moved in just before Cal was born. He's the baby."

"Did you know anything about..." I left the thought unfinished.

"It had been empty for a while when my parents bought it. After I found out you lived here, I called them. My mom said that the realtor was relieved to have an offer. It had been on the market for months."

How long had Shawneen lived in the big house alone after Charlie and I left? That much space with one person must have felt oppressive. The silence started to feel weighted, and I worried that Lacey was thinking I was mad at her family for buying the place. Her parents had obviously filled it with joy. I could feel that. It wouldn't have been the same for a small family of three or for Shawneen on her own. Of course, Lacey lived in it alone too, but she'd converted much of the space for her shop.

"Aren't your brothers or sister mad you got the house?"

My question eased the awkwardness. "Are you kidding me?" Lacey answered lightly. "None of them wanted it. Once Cal graduated, my dad applied to various firehouses down in Chico because my mom was itching to live close to Chrystal once she started providing grandbabies. Anyway, my dad hoped to sell this place, but it wasn't moving. He said I'd be doing him a favor if I'd use it."

"None of your family stayed in Quincy?"

"Cal only recently moved. Trevor is relatively close in Chester, but has his own family to take care of, so I hardly ever see him. Bennett's up in Washington State, so he's the one I see the least. With Gran still here, most of the time we all round up at her place around the holidays."

I tried to imagine what it would have been like to grow up with four siblings. Then I added in the spouses and children she'd mentioned so far. "How does everyone fit?"

"The kids don't stay still long, and Chrystal's man is out of the picture. Like I said, Bennett hardly ever makes it back. We usually max out at a dozen."

"It must get so loud."

"When we kids got too rambunctious, my mom would grab the nozzle from the sink and start spraying people to get our attention."

"Inside?" The idea completely shocked me.

"Oh, yeah!" Lacey's eyes sparkled. "Shut us up real quick. But then we'd be screaming to get away from her!"

"What would your dad do?" I tried my best to imagine the kind of family she described.

"Get a mop."

She cooked chicken and made a white sauce with sautéed vegetables served on bow tie noodles. Lacey said that when they'd had the meal as kids, her brothers would all get in trouble for fishing out the noodles with their fingers and holding them up to their throats like little sticky ties. Once she started telling stories, she kept them coming, and I happily listened, enjoying the way she painted a vivid picture of the chaos that had been her childhood.

I'd meant to ask her how she'd decided to be an auto technician, but when she leaned across the table and nestled her lips to mine, I forgot everything else. I meant to ask if the vegetables in her greenhouse were her idea or her gran's. I meant to ask how many girls she'd kissed, but all that slipped away as I learned how much my lips could say without uttering a single word.

CHAPTER TWENTY-TWO

Madison

People had tried to tell me about the wonders of dating, but I never got it, not until Lacey kissed me and turned my whole day into wondering when I'd get to see her again. My productivity suffered as I got caught in daydreams about her mouth on mine and how much I wanted her lips elsewhere, feelings so new they literally stopped me in my tracks.

Midway through the week the buzz of my cell snapped me out of one such pause.

"Hi Ruth," I answered, clicking the phone to speaker, so I could continue with the trim I was painting.

"I finished up the last set of curtains. They're ready when you are."

"I can't wait to get them up. I've got the living room painted and am almost finished with the first room." With the progress I was making, I would have no problem opening by spring, just a few weeks away.

"What did you decide for the living room?"

I'd texted her photos of the paint chips for the other rooms, remembering how good she'd been at talking me out of Pepto

Bismol pink when I was a child. "I went with that peachy color, Sippin' Cider, for the living room."

She clapped her hands. "I was crossing my fingers for that one. The name alone makes you want to sit and relax, which is exactly what you want in that space. It has a nice view?"

"A gorgeous panorama of the sunrise. You're going to love it. Once I finish up a bedroom, you and Bo have to come up."

"We'll be your first paying guests."

"You know I wouldn't let you pay. I already owe you and Bo so much." My words were met by a pause I didn't expect. I stopped painting, going over what I'd said again, wondering why it had caused Ruth's quiet.

When she spoke again, there was a sharper edge to her words. "Should I expect you for lunch Saturday?"

"My plans have changed a bit." I set down the brush and picked up the phone clicking it off speaker.

"Oh?"

"Turns out a friend of mine is looking for a car door at the junkyard in Chico. I'm going to drive down with her Friday morning. I really have no idea how long we'll be there, but we'll be in Paradise by evening." I rubbed at paint on my hands, not knowing how to tell Ruth that I'd invited Lacey to stay overnight. I'd danced around the invite, knowing that her sister and parents lived twenty minutes away in Chico. She had already told me she was overdue to see her parents, that she often spent weekends there, so I knew she could stay with them, and I could pick her up when I headed back on Sunday. I worried about it being too early to ask her to come home with me. When we were together, I still found myself bewildered by her attention, sure she must have something better to do. But I really wanted to spend the weekend with her and was thrilled she'd agreed to stick with me the whole trip.

"You won't be staying, then?" Ruth's voice remained formal as if we were conducting business. I wanted her softer voice back.

"I was actually wondering if it would be okay if she stayed too?" My thoughts raced. I was still working on how I was going to introduce Lacey. If I had her with me, maybe they would see how over-the-moon happy I was, and that would be enough for them to understand that we were dating.

"Of course, of course," Ruth gushed. "I was afraid you were going to say she needed to get right back up to Quincy. I'll make up another guest bed."

She'd returned to herself with the last statement, revealing how much Ruth had invested in my spending the weekend in Paradise. I was glad that having a friend along wasn't a problem. It had been a long while since I'd asked for a sleepover. While I was happy to end the call on a more normal tone, I kept thinking about the conversations I'd had with Ruth in planning the curtains and my trip to retrieve them. She had said that she was happy to have me close to home, but home was a tangled notion. I'd always assumed that Bo and Ruth would reclaim my room when I left for college. Now I realized they were counting on my using it more.

I lay down on my side, anxious to finish the trim on the bedroom closest to the kitchen. I'd chosen the smallest of the four rooms for myself and decided on a soft lavender. Lacey didn't see the logic in starting with my bedroom, but I argued that I needed my space to look nice too, and if I left it for last, I risked it getting pushed so far to the back burner that it would fall off forever.

"Madison?"

Her voice at my front door brought a smile to my face.

"In here. I'm almost finished for the day, I promise!"

She followed the sound of my voice and paused by the door. "Is it still wet?" she asked.

"That's where I started, so it should be dry now." I stood, paintbrush still in hand, to deliver the kiss I'd been dreaming about before Ruth had called. Her lips still impossibly soft on mine, she ran her hands along my tired shoulders and down my back. I groaned.

"Tired?"

"Exhausted. The walls took two coats, and the trim always takes so much longer than I think it should."

"It looks amazing. This is such a good color."

"I'm glad you like it." I turned to survey it with her, happy when she kept one arm wrapped around my waist.

"If I didn't, would you have changed it?"

"Seeing as I hope you'll stay with me sometime down the road, I weigh what you think pretty heavily."

"Sometime down the road?" She pressed.

"I..." I didn't really know how to respond. That our relationship was heading toward an intimate one was a given, but it seemed to be moving so fast.

"I wasn't putting you on a deadline," she laughed, squeezing me.

Relieved, I stepped away. "I have fifteen, twenty minutes to get these baseboards done, and then I can clean my brushes. Do you mind if I press on?"

"Not at all."

I returned to my spot on the floor and told her about my phone call with Ruth. "I hope you don't mind that she's making up a separate room for you."

"No, not at all. We haven't..." Her words trailed off to where I'm sure my mind had been wandering.

Quiet lingered between us and fueled my desire like someone winding an old music box.

"This is a nice door," Lacey said, snapping me back to my day's work. She tested the paint and then traced the beveled edges of one of the four raised panels.

"Someone must have locked a dog in here, and it tore up the bottom panel. It took me all morning to putty in where it scratched and gnawed on the wood." It had been a bigger chore than I had anticipated, but buying a new door as solidly built as the original one would have cost a bundle.

"I can't even tell now. It looks awesome. You want me to put the hardware on?"

I rocked back on my heels. "I didn't want to put it on until I fix the locking mechanism. Bo said he didn't have the first clue, and I didn't have a chance to ask Charlie."

"I'm guessing one of them is your dad?"

I went back to my trim, feeling the same unease I'd felt talking about Bo and Ruth with my friends. If anyone asked about my mom and dad, I answered from my experience with Bo and Ruth, but I'd always introduced them as Mr. and Mrs. Betters. I'd never called them Mom and Dad. I'd never called either Bo or Charlie Dad. I bit my lip trying to figure out how to explain. "Charlie was married to Shawneen."

"So Bo is married to Ruth, and they are the ones who raised you?"

"Yeah." For some reason laying it all out embarrassed me, like she'd see me as someone who didn't have real parents.

"Cool. Mind if I take a look at the doorknob?"

"No. It's in my glove box in the truck." Having sorted the names to the people in my life, Lacey left the room apparently satisfied. I wondered how to introduce Lacey in Paradise. What would happen if I claimed Bo and Ruth with the words Mom and Dad? Charlie had never argued when I used his given name, but Bo and Ruth had never suggested that I call them anything other than that. Ruth's voice came back to me, the way it had shifted during our conversation. For the first time in my life, I wondered if she had ever wanted me to call her more than Ruth.

CHAPTER TWENTY-THREE

Lacey

I sat on Bo and Ruth's wraparound porch with Madison's mortise lock case in pieces. I'd brought it along as a puzzle to tackle during any downtime. On holidays with my family, there were times I needed to step away from the group, and I guessed the same would be true meeting a girlfriend's parents. I was guessing because it was a first for me. I'd known from the start with Della that we weren't suited well enough to take that step. She'd made me feel giddy for a few weeks, but too soon, her negative outlook drowned out the sparks.

After that, I met a woman when I was visiting my family in Chico. I thought we had potential, but after a few months, she declined invitations to meet my family and never suggested I meet hers. We never saw any of her friends. She didn't need me to be part of her life. I felt like her dirty secret, best left untold. When it became clear to me that she was happy having an occasional lay without a relationship, I walked away. Now I know exactly what I want and don't see the point in investing time in something not likely to work out.

And then came Madison. My first impression had made me wary, but there was something about her that kept pulling me back. Despite our rocky start and the fact that we'd only just begun to date, here I was sitting on Ruth and Bo's front porch. They were lovely, making me feel immediately welcome. I woke to laughter floating up the stairs and had crept down to find Ruth and Madison making buttermilk pancakes.

The day before, Madison had driven me around the property. After lunch, I'd left Ruth and Madison to discuss curtain rods, and settled on the front porch with the knob and lock cartridge. Though I'd been careful when I removed the screw and separated the plates, the pieces of the internal mechanism spilled out randomly, and I'd been tinkering with them trying to figure out what went where.

Thus far, I'd made more progress on rubbing off the rust than figuring out where any of the pieces went, but it interested me and kept my fingers and brain engaged. A flash of orange caught my eye, and I recognized the Power Wagon Madison had driven up to Quincy the second time I saw her. A weathered cowboy tumbled out of the driver's side and ambled toward the trailer Madison had identified as Charlie's. He saw me watching and pushed his gray hat back on his forehead, squinting at me.

I smiled and waved. He looked at Madison's truck and then back to me and changed his trajectory. I started to stand, but he waved off my gesture.

"Madison here?" he asked, his tongue tracing the inside of his bottom lip.

"Inside with Ruth. I'm Lacey. I came down with Madison for the weekend." I wiped my hand on my jeans and extended it toward him.

He accepted with a gnarled hand, squeezing firmly. "You're the mechanic she met?" His cheeks were pocked and red, but his eyes friendly.

Knowing that Madison had told Charlie about me erased the annoyance I usually felt when people used the term mechanic. "I am."

His eyes roamed the pieces spread out before me. "You've got yourself a nice little project here."

"It would have gone faster if I'd seen where each of the pieces went, but they all tumbled out when I opened it up."

He nodded and sat on the edge of the porch taking the housing and the bolt first. He slid the bolt in and worked the other bits in without error. The muscles around his neck twitched involuntarily, and seemed to force him to blink, but he still managed to fluidly piece everything in perfectly in less than a minute. He handed it back to me, the only work left to put the top plate on and replace the screw. "Where'd you get this?"

"It's Madison's."

"I know. I took them pieces apart when she was just a little thing."

"You broke it?"

He nodded so slightly I almost missed it. "Had to." The muscles along the side of his jaw twitched.

Something had happened, surely with Madison, and I would have liked to ask about it. He rubbed his hand over his pained face, wiping his expression clean.

"You know I grew up in that house?" I said for something to say.

"Madison might've mentioned it."

"This was on my bedroom door. I always hated that it didn't work, but when I asked my dad about fixing it, he said I didn't need a bedroom door that locked. When I tore out the bedroom walls to add another bay to my garage, I gave all the old hardware to the woman who owns the antique shop next door. Madison must've bought it from her."

His lip twitched upward under his thick grayed mustache. He looked away from me, so I couldn't read what he was thinking. I replaced the screw and fit the beautiful red and black swirled handle through the plate.

"She's using it at the ranch?" Charlie asked.

"Yes, she's finished painting her room and is planning to use it there."

He stood, but his haunted eyes stayed on me. "I guess it's all right for a grown girl to have a locking door."

I sat flummoxed as he started to walk away. "She's right inside, sir."

"Maybe I'll see her a bit later. Pleasure." He tipped his hat to me before settling it firmly down on his head for the short walk to his trailer.

* * *

As the evening wore on I waited for Madison to suggest that we drop in on Charlie. She didn't mention it before dinner, and after Bo slipped off to his office and Ruth dismissed my offer to do the dishes, I couldn't hold back my thoughts any longer.

"I saw Charlie's Dodge earlier."

Madison nodded, refolding her cloth napkin.

"Did you want to say hi?"

"I don't need to. Did I tell you that Ruth is letting me have her mother's headboard and dresser for my room? I was telling her how I haven't found anything I like as much, and she said it never gets used here, and I'm welcome to it. Isn't that amazing?"

I wondered if she realized the significance of Ruth's gift, that it was one a mother made to her daughter to make sure that heirlooms stayed in the family, but I didn't want to lose track of the conversation I'd started. Ignoring that I'd spoken with Charlie earlier, I said, "I'd like to meet him."

Madison glanced at the clock although she had mentioned that Charlie hardly ever slept. "Okay." She stood and took my hand and paused at the kitchen doorway to let Ruth know we'd be back shortly.

Ruth's eyes bounced down to our joined hands and back up again. She dried her hands on her apron. "Hold on a minute. I'll make a plate for you to take over. That man doesn't feed himself properly."

Since she hadn't introduced me as her girlfriend, I was surprised by how much Madison touched me. Waiting for Ruth, she wrapped her arm around my waist, pulling me flush against her body. If that didn't announce *couple* in neon lights, I didn't know what did. I was already buzzing with pleasure at the contact with Madison and flushed all over again when Ruth smiled warmly at me when she returned.

With a foil-covered plate we walked in silence across the drive toward the trailer. She pulled back the screen and held it in place with her body and rapped on the door. She waited for Charlie to answer it, and the two didn't hug when she stepped inside.

"Ruth sent this," was the first thing Madison said as she handed the plate to Charlie.

He nodded and walked to the kitchen to set it down on the counter. They seemed more comfortable with the counter between them.

"This is Charlie," she said, standing a few feet from me. She introduced me and reminded Charlie that she'd stopped at my shop the first trip up to Quincy, and we all three stood there staring at the plate of food.

I didn't know what to say or do and felt the awkwardness press in on the small space. Dark curtains hung on dark paneled walls. He had a low bookshelf stuffed with books and a tiny TV in the corner. A tattered couch big enough for two took up one wall, and two old stuffed chairs faced the bookshelf with a table and lamp between. A book sat open on the table, and I wondered what we had interrupted.

"You're the reason there's a car door in the bed of Madison's truck."

"Yes, sir. I picked it up for a client." It occurred to me that Shawneen might have owned the Nova back when they'd been together. I glanced at Madison, still focused on the food. Was she thinking about Shawneen as well?

"I thought you worked on motors," Charlie said.

"I usually do. I got suckered into helping out." I had to be careful with what I said. In any other situation, I'd have been explaining Shawneen's ability to coerce me into doing what she wanted, but I wasn't about to talk to her ex-husband in that way.

"Careful what you say yes to. You lie down, a person'll walk all over you."

"I couldn't let her boyfriend weld the driver's side door shut. It didn't seem right."

He tipped at the waist, his shoulders jumping a bit, and I realized he was laughing. Madison looked at me in wonder.

When he stood again, the skin at the edge of his eyes was puckered in amusement. "As long as you're doing it for the car, I suppose you're fine. You girls get enough to eat up there? I hate to eat in front of you if you're hungry, but this sure looks good."

"We ate already."

The way she was turning to me, I could tell she was ready to go, but his last string of words gave me the impression he enjoyed our company. "But I'd sure like a cup of tea or coffee if you have it."

He put one hand on his hip and the other behind his head, and I was struck by the resemblance to Madison. "I've got it. Have a seat. Have a seat." He ushered us to the table in the kitchen, pushing papers into a hasty pile. "It's been a long time since I had company," he said, "but coffee I can do. Madison. You want a cup too?"

She looked from him to me like she was unsure of the right answer. "Sure," she finally said.

I butted her knee with mine under the table, happy she'd brought me home.

CHAPTER TWENTY-FOUR

Madison

"Are you okay?" I asked. Lacey hadn't seemed like herself since we'd left Paradise. She was unusually quiet, staring out the window as I drove. I thought the visit had gone really well, especially considering the warm hugs Bo and Ruth had given Lacey, but beyond asking after Charlie, who was out in the pastures at sunrise, she hadn't said a word.

"When are you going to tell Shawneen who you are?"

Her words threw me completely. "What in the world brought her up?"

Lacey scooted sideways to look directly at me. "Do you know how hard it was talking about why we were at the junkyard getting that door knowing it's Shawneen's car and who Shawneen was to Charlie? Things like that just spill out of my mouth, and I don't want to be the person who drops that bombshell. It's exhausting to dance around to keep it secret." Her eyes returned to the road, but I could tell she had more to say. After a few minutes, she added, "That's how it was when we saw Shawneen before we left."

"That was days ago."

"And it's still eating me up. Even if she's blind to you being her daughter, at the very least, she should remember she met you at my shop. How can you let that go?"

I kept my eyes on the road, not wanting to answer her question. "I don't know. Maybe it bothers you because you have all the pieces, and she doesn't, so I don't expect anything from her. She's caught up in what's going on in her life today, not what happened nearly twenty years ago."

"Still, she didn't even acknowledge that you were there at the grocery store the other day. It's like she's purposely ignoring you. It was all I could do to not say 'How can you not recognize your daughter standing right in front of you?'"

"I'm glad you didn't." I could only imagine the scene it would have caused in the checkout line. To be fair to Shawneen, I had been grateful that I was putting the snacks we'd picked up for our trip on the conveyor belt when Shawneen walked up behind us. I happily kept Lacey in between us because I didn't know how to act around her. "However little you think of her, she doesn't deserve to have her longlost kid drop a bomb in a supermarket."

"You have more restraint than I do," Lacey grumbled. "You have to tell her soon, or I will blurt it out. I swear. She already pushes my patience to its limit. Seeing the way she continues to ignore you just about makes me explode."

I laughed at that. "I'd hate to be responsible for that. Did your parents have short tempers?"

"My mom had a pillow that said *I can't cope.*"

"What would she do, scream into it?"

"Mostly it sat on the couch as a reminder for us to not push her buttons. She would pick it up and shake it at us when we were at our worst. Probably kept her from shaking us. If that didn't work, there were a few times she threw it. We knew to back off if it got that bad."

We sat in silence for a few minutes. Just because she was on the verge of exploding didn't mean that I had any better idea about announcing my presence to Shawneen.

"Nice try at distracting me, but it doesn't make me any less annoyed with your mother."

"Shawneen," I said before I even registered that I was talking.

"But she is your mother."

"I know, but the way you said it...It's like you hold me responsible for her, and I don't want any part of that. She is who she is, and she chose not to be my mother."

"Why come back to Quincy? Are you wanting her to be your mother now? You do plan on telling her eventually, don't you?"

I took a deep breath, calming the nerves that made me feel sick to my stomach. I couldn't really say what it was that I wanted from her now after all these years.

"Soon?" she pressed.

"I know that's what you want." I downshifted for a particularly steep, tight turn in the canyon. When the road straightened out, I continued. "I don't see how it's going to happen. I can't sit down at her station and say 'Hey, what are the specials, Mom?' or stop by her house. I've thought about calling her, but she's going to ask what I want or what I expect, and I don't have an answer for that beyond feeling like something was calling me to Quincy."

Lacey was still looking out the window when I glanced to check out how my destiny-coated answer had gone over. "I could introduce you," she suggested after a long silence.

"You don't think that would be weird?"

"I don't think there's any way around weird." She reached over and tickled the hair at my neckline. It felt so good, that simple touch, and I wanted to keep my attention there. The last week, all I'd wanted to do was forget about my mother and believe that Charlie's property was calling me back so I could meet Lacey. That was enough, wasn't it?

My mind drifted back to Steve's phone call and the sting that had pushed me to pursue buying the place my dad had worked. "People don't pick me," I said softly. Lacey's hand stilled.

"I pick you."

I chanced a quick glance at her and read concern in her eyes. I didn't want her pity, but I did feel like I needed to explain. For myself as well as her, I needed to try to put into words what I was doing. "Whatever happened with Shawneen and Charlie, neither one of them picked me. All through school, I sat at the edges, never getting picked. I invited friends for sleepovers, but they never reciprocated. When I was worried about dating in high school, Ruth told me that it would be better in college, so I was patient. I figured I would meet someone, but I didn't. I want to know why Shawneen let me go. That's not exactly an easy question to ask."

"Did you ever ask Charlie?"

"We don't really talk. Not like the two of you did last night. I've never heard the stuff he told you. That Rocky Mountain oyster story? I'd forgotten he had teeth until he told you that."

We hooted again, though my laughter was tinged with hurt that Charlie chose to share his past so easily with Lacey. He'd told us how a girlfriend had pulled him along to a branding party, and he had felt like he'd contributed to the day's efforts until the crew dumped the calf testicles right on the coals. He thought it was how they disposed of the bits, not how they cooked their dinner. It had been great fun listening to him tell how hard it was for him to finally put one in his mouth and chew. And chew. And chew some more as he tried to convince his belly that he was about to swallow it down.

"It's a good thing he ended up spraying it all over her brother's boots."

"Because it makes for a good story?" I asked.

"No, because it meant he didn't marry that girl. Where would you be if he had?"

"He probably would have told that kid the story about the first day he spent with his future in-laws."

"I'm glad he got the kid he did."

"Thanks," I croaked through a throat that had closed down on me.

"He seems to like sharing his stories…if you ask."

She said it like it was so easy, but what did she have to lose in striking up a conversation with him? "If he wanted to talk to me, don't you think he would have kept me? He was so relieved for Ruth and Bo to take me in. What if I say the wrong thing, and he disappears forever?"

Lacey's hand returned to her side, and I regretted saying as much as I had. I tried to push back tears pressing on my sinuses. Her reaction was exactly why I avoided talking to Charlie and procrastinated approaching Shawneen.

"Pull over." Her words surprised me. It seemed reckless on the narrow winding road. "Slow down. At the next lookout, pull over."

When I made no movement, she touched my knee. My leg responded, easing off the gas. I spotted the turnout ahead and pulled over onto a gravel shoulder high above the river. Lacey cut the ignition and unlatched my seat belt before doing the same to her own. She scooted closer to me and took my hands in hers. "We might have talked about other stuff as well."

"What? When?"

She leaned forward and pulled the knob from the antique store out of her backpack. "I fixed this. Actually Charlie fixed it yesterday."

I took it from her, turning it in my hands. "It's fixed? How do you know without the key?"

"I...Oh. Charlie put all the pieces back together. When he said *he* broke it, I assumed he knew how to fix it."

"He broke it? I'm confused. You said he fixed it."

"When you were a kid, he broke it."

"Why?"

"I don't know. He didn't say. Maybe you should ask him about it. Maybe he's got the key."

"Maybe." My whole life, I'd felt the distance he put between us, a door I'd never known how to open. I dug my fingernails into my palms willing myself not to cry, but tears were already welling. The moment Lacey pulled me into her arms, they spilled over. She wrapped her arms around me and pulled me as close as she could, one of her hands cradling the back of my head. I dropped the door handle onto the floorboards, so I could hang onto Lacey.

I am not one to cry. Before I'd moved to Quincy, I couldn't even tell you when the last time had been, but my tank was full, and I emptied it on Lacey's shoulder.

When I was spent, I pulled back from her but kept my face down. I didn't want her to see my red eyes or drippy nose. She interrupted my search for a tissue and brought my eyes back to hers.

"I don't know what you want from Shawneen, but you deserve to be seen. It's not right the way she overlooks you. Let me ask her to come by the house, so she knows."

I met her eyes, and she nodded. My breath caught and rattled out.

"You're making your home in Quincy. Eventually she's going to know who you are. Why not be in control of that? The longer you wait, the harder it will be."

I knew that. I'd waited almost twenty years. Telling her who I was scared me, but Lacey was right. She was going to find out, and it would be easier with Lacey there. I couldn't avoid her forever, and Lacey helped me feel strong enough to face her. I didn't argue when Lacey said she'd drive the rest of the way. As a passenger, I could watch the trees click by and run through what I might say to Shawneen. I pictured her at Lacey's house, the two of us under the same roof after twenty years. What do you say after all that time?

CHAPTER TWENTY-FIVE

Madison

"You are shitting me."

Shawneen had come straight from work, her perfume wafting into the living room before her. Lacey had asked her to come after her shift to pick up the Nova with its new tan door. Unluckily for me, she was already worked up about how it didn't match the maroon paint.

She slammed her fists to her hipbones and jutted her chin at Lacey doing her best to intimidate her into taking back what she'd said.

Shawneen, I really asked you here because I wanted to introduce you to your daughter. This is Madison.

Lacey held her ground, but under Shawneen's intense stare, I sat down.

"Is this your idea of a joke?"

I couldn't tell which one of us she was asking, but I answered. "It's not. I used to live here with you and Charlie."

"Charlie," she whispered. As if in a daze, she lowered herself to the couch next to my chair. We were all silent. I didn't know what to do or say. I watched her face, trying to know her heart. She covered her mouth then, her eyes wide on me.

"Maddie honey? You came to find me after all these years?"

My eyes flicked to Lacey who immediately inclined her head toward Shawneen. This was our moment, her gesture said. I looked back to Shawneen and saw a tear slip down her cheek. She held out her arms to me, so I nodded, finally, and said yes.

"Oh baby doll." She dropped to her knees in front of my chair and threw her arms around me. "Sweet, sweet baby. You don't know how many years I prayed you'd come back home to me."

She was right about that. I had no idea.

"Does Charlie know you're here? What did he tell you? What kind of poisonous things did he say for you to stay away so long?"

"I..." Again I looked to Lacey for help. I wished I'd sat on the couch where she could sit next to me. I needed to feel her arms around me. That would have grounded me. Having Shawneen so close made me feel like I was floating outside of myself.

Lacey came around to my chair and guided Shawneen away from me. She settled her back down on the couch and sat down next to her. The space allowed me to think more clearly.

"I didn't think you wanted me."

"Of course I wanted you, baby. A mama needs her baby girl. What did that man tell you? Because he stole you from me. He did. In the dark of night, he took you from me and left me here. I got one call. One call to tell me you were safe and better off without me, and if I ever came looking, he'd kill me." Her words were steeped in bitterness.

I cast back for any evidence of such violence in Charlie. I'd seen him wrangle some crazy bulls which could push the most placid person to lash out but had never seen anything but calm in him.

"Does he know you're here? What did you tell him?"

"He knows I'm here. I bought a place a few months ago, the place he used to run cattle on."

"Did you?" Her tone changed from the rapid-fire barrage. I didn't know her well enough to know what it meant that she slowed down. She pushed back on the sofa but sat upright. "Tell me about it."

"I'm fixing up the main house to rent rooms. Lacey's been helping me find an angle to pull people in. I'm almost ready to start working on a garden."

"You like to garden? This is so hard. I don't…I don't know nothing about you."

"I haven't really gardened all that much, but we…" Lacey smiled when I said we and held eye contact. My smile widened. I wouldn't have been able to do this without her. "Lacey and I were thinking that people might find it relaxing to get their hands in the dirt and know what they're eating came from the land they're staying on."

"I wouldn't." Shawneen laughed raucously. "If I could afford a vacation, the last thing I'd want to do is get my hands dirty." She held her freshly manicured hands out for us to examine. "Give me a spa treatment. Maybe a medicinal mud bath. You think about that?"

"I hadn't," I admitted.

She reached for my hand, petting it between hers. "You came home. Let me look at you."

I fidgeted under her attention feeling like she must be sizing up what she'd change about me. She pulled the hair I brushed to the side down on my forehead, arranging it like bangs. "I never thought your hair would be this dark. You were blond as a child. I always pictured you with long blond hair." Her hand stopped and cupped my cheek. "You have beautiful skin. Just like me. It's too bad you didn't get my blue eyes. You got Charlie's eyes for sure."

She said she'd pictured me. All these years she had carried a picture of me in her head. She was quiet again, and I thought about how I always found Charlie's eyes unreadable. Shawneen apparently hadn't been able to read them either if he'd slipped away without warning. I didn't know whether to believe anything she was saying, but her attributing my features made me lean into her hand. No one had ever played the game of matching my features or behaviors to the family tree, and I wanted more. I yearned to be claimed.

"So many years."

I nodded, and a tear slipped out. I quickly wiped it away. This was good, actually better than Lacey and I had predicted, so why was I crying? She stood, and Lacey and I followed suit.

"Dennis will be expecting dinner, so I've got to go. Did you want—?"

I cut her off. "No, thank you. I'm okay for tonight. Maybe we could have lunch tomorrow?"

"I work afternoons the rest of the week. How about breakfast? I could come out and see the old place."

Having her out at the house didn't feel right, so I suggested Lacey's friend's place in town. She hesitated a second before she agreed. After she'd wrapped her arms around me, she left me smelling of her perfume. Exhausted by all the emotion, I sat back down while Lacey walked Shawneen to the door.

When she came back, Lacey sat on the arm of the chair and took my hand. "I'm proud of you."

"Proud? What for?"

"You set a boundary on where to do breakfast. I speak with experience when I say boundaries are important with that woman." She ran her hands through my fine hair, and I sighed deeply. "Wrung out?"

"That's exactly how I feel." I closed my eyes and simply gave myself over to how good Lacey's fingers felt on my scalp.

"You stay here and let me put something together for dinner."

"Okay," I whispered, feeling the tears come again. I was glad Lacey left the room before they slipped down my cheeks. In the kitchen, she moved from fridge to cupboard, knocking pots to stove, lighting the flame, all the little motions required to take care of yourself or your loved one. I tried to imagine my four-year-old self playing in the living room while Shawneen cooked supper, but came up empty.

CHAPTER TWENTY-SIX

Lacey

The next day, I drove out to Madison's anxious to hear how things had gone with Shawneen at breakfast that morning. I'd called when I took a break for lunch, but it went to her voice mail.

I parked at the top of the drive next to her truck. I saw Madison wave to me through the picture window in the living room, but the horse resting by the porch would have indicated her whereabouts anyway. Content to stop and run my hand along his soft coat, I stayed outside and enjoyed the show Madison provided.

She stood on a stepladder, her head and shoulders out of sight. The picture window framed her torso and legs and the drill she had pinched between them. Though I knew it would embarrass her, I took out my phone and snapped a picture. After savoring the image for a moment, I couldn't justify standing by and letting her work alone. I climbed the stairs and let myself in.

"Hey," she said around the screws in her mouth. Having finished predrilling the holes, she was outfitting the drill with a screwdriver bit. With practiced efficiency, she tightened the bit and turned to mount the wall bracket. "I'm almost finished here. Really. This is the last one."

"Am I far off the mark in thinking that if I didn't come over, you would find something else to do after the curtains were up and work right through dinner?"

"I can stop."

"But you're not a clock watcher. You have no idea that I'm late and it's past dinnertime."

"You're late?" She glanced out the window instead of at a watch or clock.

"Days are getting longer," I reminded her. The sun isn't setting until almost eight tonight."

"Sorry I lost track of time." She glanced at the curtains she had picked up from Ruth that were draped across the back of the couch.

"Don't be sorry. I'm happy to watch."

"Why does that sound dirty?" she asked, setting down her tools and picking up a rod.

"I'll show you later." I met her with a curtain and held the sheer fabric while she scooted it onto the rod. With all the fabric in place, I grabbed a chair from the kitchen and helped her get them on to the newly mounted brackets. "These are awesome, Madison."

"Thanks! After dinner, I'll have to send a picture to Ruth. I'm so glad she convinced me to let her make them."

"They're perfect. I love the leaf pattern."

"Me too. Ruth said it would give more texture to the space when they're closed, and then once I mount hooks on the side, I can easily pull them back during the day."

The room was dimming in the twilight. Without curtains, the windows had been black holes. Madison turned on a lamp, and the curtains reflected the light back making the room bright and inviting.

"But first dinner. Don't worry. It's quick. I have some zucchini soup, and the corn bread won't take long at all, promise." Madison bustled into the kitchen.

"How did it go with Shawneen this morning?"

She pulled a box mix out of one cupboard and a bowl from another. She was quiet for a moment. With her back to me she said, "It was fine."

I waited for her to say more. I wanted to know if it had been easier to talk to her mother without me there. If it had been awkward or if they'd gotten past that. "What did you talk about?"

"Presidents," she said, turning away from the cupboard but still not looking at me.

"That doesn't seem very...personal."

"I didn't know if she'd be prompt, so I had the Taft/Roosevelt book with me. She asked why I was reading it."

"Why *are* you reading it?"

"It's really not obvious?"

When she put it that way, I stopped to think. "It wasn't obvious to Shawneen?"

"No."

"But you think it's obvious. Something obvious about Taft and Roosevelt."

"Not necessarily..."

"No hints!" I said, wanting to do better than Shawneen. We're talking Shawneen, here. It shouldn't be that hard.

"My name..."

"Wait! Let me think!" I insisted. But I played with what she gave me. "Madison."

"Carter..." she added, her dark eyebrows arched high in encouragement.

"Madison Carter," I repeated. "Taft and Roosevelt." She leaned forward, to encourage my train of thought. "They're all presidents!" I shouted. Her arms shot up as if I'd scored a goal. I furrowed my brow. "Shawneen named you after President Madison?"

"Don't be ridiculous. She named me after Madison Square Garden. When I told her that I *thought* I was named after the presidents and was reading the biographies from Madison to Carter, she said she should have named me Reagan and saved me the trouble of so much reading."

"I still don't get why you thought you were named after the presidents."

My question propelled her deep into her childhood, and the smile that followed was one of the most genuinely happy I'd ever seen. "Fourth grade, I sulked into Ruth's kitchen, and she asked me what on earth had put such an expression on my face. We'd gone over the list of presidents, and the teacher pointed out that I shared the names of both our fourth and thirty-ninth presidents. All the kids heard was that I had two last names, and they'd teased me about it the rest of the day."

"You like being teased?" I said perplexed.

"No, I do not. Not in school or in more intimate situations." She leveled her gaze at me, and I flushed realizing what I'd said. "Ruth said to ignore them and think about the honor of being named after two such important men. She sat me down with the encyclopedia and sparked my first interest in the presidents, and I still don't know how she managed it, but that night she convinced Charlie to have dinner at the house and tell me about how he'd picked which president to use for my first name."

"But it wasn't true."

"I didn't know that. It gave me something to give the kids at school. He told me to fire back that Madison was the father of our constitution, that he was the very voice of our republic, and I owed it to him to use my voice to defend myself."

"Wow."

"I know. It's one of the few times I remember Charlie talking."

"Did you tell Shawneen all that?"

Madison grew quiet again. "No. After the name fail, she said she's not a big reader and then talked a bunch about what TV shows she and Dennis watch."

"I haven't even seen a TV in your house."

"No, but that's okay. She likes crime shows. I didn't mind hearing about her favorites."

"Charlie seems like a big reader," I inserted.

"She mentioned that, too, but not in that tone."

"How did she say it?"

"I don't know, like if she had raised me, I'd be more like her, shopping on Madison Avenue maybe. She said it was wrong of him to try to raise a daughter on his own. She said there are things a girl needs to learn from her mother."

"You didn't tell her about Ruth?"

"No. I didn't really talk that much." She stirred the soup on the stove and peeked at the corn bread in the oven.

I'd spent enough time with Shawneen that this didn't surprise me. And I was gathering that Madison had a lot more patience than I did. "Aren't there things you wanted to talk about?"

"I don't know."

"Is she why you wanted to buy this place?"

She looked around with the expression she'd worn when she was first in my shop, as if the walls had answers. "I bought it because I felt like I belong. I never have before. Ruth and Bo raised me, but I didn't belong to them. I worked for a resort for three years, but when the owner's brother-in-law needed a job, they let me go. I've never had any real ties, and I thought maybe this would be where I tie myself. This town. This place."

"But not because Shawneen is here."

She took a thoughtful breath. "The way she reacted at your house when you told her? It's what I always dreamed about, that she wanted me. But she never contacted us. I wrote her letters, but she never wrote back. Why wouldn't she have answered them? And then at breakfast..."

"What?"

"I thought I was going to...feel something."

She sounded apologetic, and I remembered our argument about Fate. "It can't be easy seeing each other after all these years and know how to act. It's not like you were close and then got separated." I could see her processing that. "Are you going to see her again?"

"She asked to. I said I'd like to meet at Cup of Joy again, and she reluctantly agreed."

"You know why she's reluctant."

"No."

"Because Hope's a lesbian."

"But you're a lesbian."

"I didn't say she made sense. I'm just warning you that she was one of the more critical locals when Dani and Hope came out." When Madison seemed to retreat again, I was sorry to have made a point of it.

"You said that she's a piece of work. I was hoping you were wrong about that. I'm a part of her, you know?"

"You have her chin. Maybe her nose." I traced from bridge to tip of her cute button nose. "But you're your own person." I kissed her gently.

The timer binged, taking her away from me. She pulled the corn bread from the oven and dished up bowls of soup, grating cheese on top. "Let's eat in the living room. I want to enjoy the curtains," she said, moving us away from our conversation about Shawneen.

The room had no furniture, but the floor glowed from the new varnish. The meal was delicious and accentuated the hominess she'd created out of the dust. As she talked about all she wanted her resort to be, I could see it all happening. Once her guests arrived, they weren't going to want to leave. I knew *I* didn't want to leave. When I set aside my empty bowl, I said, "You've done an amazing job in the last two months." The silence that met my compliment puzzled me.

She tipped her face away from me. I put my hand on her shoulder, still not understanding what had changed. I thought our lighthearted dinner conversation had salvaged our day. "Did I upset you?"

"No. It's not you. It's… " She lifted a shoulder. "What if it's the same with Shawneen? What if she can't accept me because I'm gay? What if that's more important to her than having me back in her life again? I don't know why I said I'd meet her again. If she never wrote back, maybe I should have stopped wondering about her."

I leaned against her unsure of what I could say. I couldn't help but question Shawneen's motives. If she wasn't interested in learning who Madison was, why spend more time with her? Shawneen always had an ulterior motive, and what it was with

Madison worried me. "Maybe you said you'd see her again because you need to ask about the letters."

I traced a pattern up and down her strong forearm, admiring her lean musculature.

She set her bowl aside as well. "Maybe."

Before I could figure out something more to say, her lips were on mine. She offered a dessert of kisses, so many I thought we might forget to stop. I knew though, that she would. Where she lost herself in her work and in fantasies of reconnecting with her mother, she never completely lost herself in me. I craved the intimacy she kept guarded from me but knowing all she was struggling to sort out, I was not about to ask for more.

CHAPTER TWENTY-SEVEN

Madison

I let the door to Martha's antique store settle behind me and walked next door to Lacey's shop. She'd recently found new taillight covers for her VW and finally had the time to put them on. "That does make a difference."

The smile she flashed made my belly bottom out. I still couldn't wrap my head around the idea that she liked me, that I had something to do with her smile. She was the princess, the prize that everyone wanted, not me. I wanted to kiss her, but I still didn't quite trust that I could lay claim to her perfect lips.

"These are the little joys of car restoration—making her look as beautiful as the day she hit the lot. How'd it go with Martha? Did she have anything good for you?"

Since I'd set up my bedroom with the furniture from Ruth, I'd been talking about finding antique sets for the other rooms to keep with the rustic feel of the place. Lacey had suggested that I talk to Martha. "She found two bedroom sets that are perfect. I can't wait to get them out to the house." I took a deep breath in, remembering the sweet smell that escaped when I pulled out the drawers of Ruth's dresser. I'd been trying to think of what it reminded me of.

"This means you're almost ready to open, doesn't it?"

"Really close. I need to run to Chico or Reno for mattresses and bedding. Towels and all that stuff I can pick up when I get the dining room and living room furniture."

"That's a lot to haul in one run."

"Bo and Ruth are lending me a trailer."

"You must be so excited. I remember when all of my remodeling was finally finished, and I was about to open!" Lacey's eyes sparkled, and she gave me a quick hug.

The oil and metallic smell of her shop hung about her, resonating with me on some level. I closed my eyes and searched deeply. Charlie. I mostly saw Charlie when he was tinkering with something in the shop. If I stopped in to chat, he'd sometimes rest his calloused hand on my shoulder. I always preferred Bo's hugs and how he seemed to carry the outdoors in with him. I suddenly remembered why the dresser drawers smelled familiar. They smelled like Bo. Even washed, his clothes held that mixture of sunshine and sweat. I remembered sleeping in his old undershirts and how it felt like being held by Bo. I squeezed Lacey tighter remembering how safe I'd always felt in his arms.

"What was that for?"

"I found another piece of my childhood. It seems to happen a lot when I'm around you."

"I like that." Lacey squeezed my hand before turning back to her work.

"You almost done?"

"Almost finished," she corrected.

"Auto technicians aren't done?" I asked, remembering how she'd corrected me before.

"Turkeys are done. People, whether they are mechanics or auto techs, are finished."

"Not that anyone is a mechanic." I couldn't take my eyes off her mouth.

"If you keep staring, I'm not going to be able to help myself." Her voice dropped to a sultry whisper.

"Who said I was asking you to?" I had been ready for more but was waiting for Lacey to take us further. The way we'd been kissing, I thought she wanted more too, but she'd been pulling back from me. I was scared that I liked her more than she liked me. I couldn't risk pushing her away by letting her know how much I wanted.

Lacey busied herself installing the second taillight. "I figured going further than kissing was your call since…"

"My call? You're the one with experience dating. I was waiting for you to make a move."

"Oh, no. You make the call on your first time."

My laugh came out a surprised bark. "Wait. You think I'm a virgin?"

"Um, yeah. If I recall correctly, you said you'd never been on a first date before."

"No, but just because you've never bought a car doesn't mean you've never been on a test drive." She kept her face turned toward her work, but I could see the tension in her body. "That bothers you," I observed.

"You don't seem like the kind of person to have one-night stands." Her tone was serious.

"Wait, wait, wait," I stammered. I didn't want her to get the wrong impression. "I never said I had one-night stands. I said I'd tested out the equipment. There's a difference."

"I guess I'm not clear on how that happens without dating."

"I had a friend in high school. We fooled around together. First kissing and then…more. We never dated—we hung out like friends do, but it never went past that emotionally." I tried to say it as straightforwardly as Susan had, but the air I breathed felt tight in my lungs.

"Until it did for you."

I nodded, unable to find my voice. I didn't want it to matter after all these years. It was foolish for me to have thought for an instant that she would pick me. I knew better than to think she'd pick me for a school dance or anything so public, but I told myself that in private she picked me, and that was enough. When I discovered that she preferred the boy she went to the dance with more in private too…

Lacey set down her tools and pulled her shop doors down, leading me in to the house through her back door. Immediately inside, she stopped at a small washroom and scrubbed her hands and forearms with Borax soap. She turned to me and took my hands in hers. They were chilled from the mountain-cold water. I told myself that's why a shiver zipped up my spine.

"Do you remember the first time we touched?" Her bedroom was right next to the washroom, and she took a few steps inside. She kicked some stray shoes and clothes toward the closet as she led me toward her bed, a simple mattress on a box spring, no headboard, blankets thrown back.

Our destination obvious, I was grateful for the task she had assigned me. I ran our intimate moments through my memory working backward from when we first kissed. Pausing briefly at obvious things like being at Bo and Ruth's and running into her at the restaurant, I settled on her shop. "When you gave me the box. We were sitting in Shawneen's Nova, and your fingers brushed mine when you handed me my box of treasures."

A sly smile crept across her face. "Correct on the fingers barely brushing, but it was the day you came in with your flat tire. I was so frustrated with you, keeping me in the cold garage. I didn't know then what had you frozen."

"We touched?"

"You were so lost that day. But I noticed your fingers, how long and slender they are with those big half moons like smiles at the base of each fingernail. I've been thinking about what your hands would feel like on me ever since then."

My heart felt tight in my chest. How could she feel that way about me? Nobody had ever wanted me like that. "Since I drove into your shop, really?" I took a step closer. I'd expected her to have the sharp oily tang of her shop, but her room smelled of lavender, and so did she.

"You handed me that valve cap."

"You make that sound so sexy."

"I'd love to check your tire pressure." My brain started to default to how she could possibly be flirting with me, but then she slid her cool hands around my hips and pulled me flush to her. Her hands on my body overrode my fears. I surrendered myself to her kiss and welcomed the cool palms that crept up under my shirt. She had made me so hot so fast that I hissed with pleasure. She immediately pulled away with an apology.

"No. I like it. I want them everywhere." My fingers flew to the buttons on my shirt, making quick work from bottom to top. I remembered my first impression of Lacey when I'd believed she was the customer, not the shop owner, when I assumed that she would never take note of someone like me. She did now. I saw her chest rise and fall with her rapid breaths. She stepped forward and pushed the shirt from my shoulders while I released the clasp on the front of my bra, which she peeled away as well. Instead of shrinking from her cool fingertips, my skin seemed to be drawn toward them as if they were magnetic. My nipples begged her to touch them. Her hands hovered for a moment but did not settle or linger. Instead, she took a step back, watching me as she undid one of the buttons of her blue work shirt. For each step back, she released another until she stood by the side of her bed. A step ahead of her, I had my hands on the button fly of my jeans, matching her button by button.

My heart pounded in my ears, in my fingertips that ached to touch her, and at my center. I fought against following the tempo my heartbeat set and slowly propped one of my booted feet up on the bedframe, pushing the lace from the eyehooks without having to untie it. When I bent to take off my boot, Lacey shimmied back on her bed to remove her work boots. I took each from her to set down before I propped my other foot up between her legs, disengaged the laces and slid my foot out.

She shed her shirt as I inched my jeans past my hips. With my head start, I stood in front of her fully naked. She moved to stand, but I stepped forward between her legs to keep her where she was. She lay back to let me pull off her functional work pants, and I found that the green lace of her panties matched that of her bra. The contrast made me smile.

"Glad you like what you see."

"Oh, I do," I said, tracing the delicate material. "You weren't wearing your mechanic's duds that first day, and I thought you were a girly girl dropping off her car."

"And when it turned out I was the technician?" she said, correcting me yet again.

"Blew me away. Almost as much as finding these…" She shivered as I traced the garments I'd left on her.

"I hope what happens from here doesn't disappoint," she said, pulling me down to her.

She got the motor I'd let sit idle for far too long purring under her expert hands. She wasn't just passing the time or lost in what made her feel good. Her lips, tongue and fingers asked questions and listened to what my body had to say and asked me to keep talking. I never knew I had so much to say, but her hands were like pressure on the accelerator, building the horsepower of the engine, our parts revving at the precise calibration.

She liked me as much as I liked her. She wanted me as much as I wanted her. That alone would have been enough, but she asked for more, holding me, stroking me, letting me feel her everywhere, places I'd never even knew existed. My orgasm shot through me like gears finally engaged, and I rode it full throttle never wanting to slow down.

And when we switched drivers, I touched without the fear that there might never be another time. The smile on her face, the catch of her breath, the way her body pressed into mine: it all said more. I always worried that I wanted too much, but that anxiety fell by the side of the road as we accelerated once again. I didn't give it another thought as I took in the scenery and sped toward my destination.

"Just so we're clear," she panted as we lay spent in each other's arms, "I pick you."

"Hmmm. What if I need occasional reminders?" I asked, thinking that my time with her felt like a tune-up for my confidence.

Her reply made me feel like she was reading my mind. "I take scheduled maintenance very seriously."

CHAPTER TWENTY-EIGHT

Lacey

I let myself into Madison's place amazed at the transformation furniture made. The living room now had a dark leather couch that I would have loved to sink into had I not promised to return to the field to help Madison figure out what was wrong with the irrigation. Coffee table, area rug, and prints on the walls gave the room a definite finished and homey look.

On closer inspection, I confirmed that the prints were of Dani's prize barrel racing mare, Daisy, some of her in action and others of her nuzzling a mule colt. I recognized Kristine Owens's signature on all of the shots I found around the house, all local scenery that I hoped would encourage Madison's guests to get out and explore the area on their own. I was admiring a huge print of a bald eagle, wings spread wide above the branch its great talons gripped.

"Isn't it beautiful? I might have to buy that one to keep permanently."

I turned and smiled at Madison leaning against the doorframe, a glass of water in hand.

"It's perfect. When do Bo and Ruth arrive?"

She checked her watch. "'Bout an hour."

"They are going to be so impressed. I know I am." I swept my arms around her and planted a kiss on her. "There are other ways to spend that hour."

"You're a bad influence." She swatted me with little conviction. "What if they get here early?"

I kissed her again but not as deeply to let her know I'd heard her. "What do you mean you might buy this one?" I motioned to the eagle.

"Don't you know how I got all of these?"

"Why would I?"

"I was sure you'd put Hope up to it. The last time Shawneen and I were there, she pulled me aside and asked if I liked the art hanging in her diner. I told her I loved it but was sure I couldn't afford it. Turns out the artist is local and is happy to have businesses hang her work on commission."

"If guests like what they see, they can buy it? That's a fantastic idea!"

"I'm so glad you agree." A shadow passed over her face before she zeroed in on her glass. She drained it and then asked if I was ready to take a look at the pipes.

"What's up?"

"I told you I can't get the water pressure I want down there. I got a couple of the fixtures turning, but I think there's a blockage somewhere because I'm getting a tiny bit at the closest faucet and absolutely nothing further out."

"There's something else. I know about the pipes. And everything you've done up here looks incredible. Once you have your website up, you're going to be booked solid. I don't see why you'd think I'd question a thing you've done, not that it matters what I think. This is your place."

"I know." She headed toward the kitchen to deposit her glass. She was distracted by something, and it drove me nuts that she thought she could walk away and pretend like she wasn't.

"Spill."

She looked at the floor as if she expected to find that she'd unknowingly made a mess of water in the kitchen.

"Madison. I can tell something's wrong."

She pressed three fingers to the center of her forehead and fanned them toward her hairline.

"Sit down and tell me why you're upset," I said, guiding her to the red chair that she kept in her kitchen.

"Shawneen says I should give up on the gardening idea. Yesterday, I told her about the issues I was having with the water lines, and she said it was a sign. Instead of doing a big garden out there, I should offer a day spa."

Madison picked up a large stack of papers on the counter and let them fall again. I shuffled through them, some ads for local massage therapists, others for mud baths and saunas in town. "If you're interested in this, you should talk to Cal."

"You think I should?" she asked, crestfallen.

"No. Remember I voted garden."

"She said that I should let Dennis come out and walk the property to see if I have a hot spring somewhere that I could use."

"Whatever you do, don't call Dennis. That woman believes that he can do anything just because he has a penis. How is he more qualified than you are to find a hot running spring on your property?"

She shrugged. "Keep looking through the stack. It gets better."

"Palm readings?" I blurted before I considered that maybe Madison would actually be on board with palm readings since she believed in Fate.

"I know, but she's serious."

I was so relieved that we were on the same page about palm readers. "So what. This isn't her place."

"I feel bad that she spent so much time gathering all of this information. What am I supposed to say?"

"You say no." I gathered up the papers and tossed them into her recycling. "Don't let the time she decided to invest surfing the Internet and dreaming up what she would do in your position make you feel obligated in any way. She's a big girl."

She stood there brooding.

"What?"

"I didn't think it was going to be so difficult to irrigate that field, and…"

"And the garden was my idea," I said, easily hearing Shawneen's argument that the garden hadn't been Madison's original plan either.

"Don't be mad."

"I'm not mad. It's fine with me if you don't want to put a garden in down there. Wait until Bo gets here and ask him what he thinks about whether it would be worth it to run a small herd of cattle up here. Cattle can at least walk themselves down to the river for a drink. Squash don't." The joke finally relaxed her. I crossed the kitchen and put my arms around her. "You're really nervous about Bo and Ruth seeing the place?

"Yeah," she said into my neck.

"They're going to be so proud of you. Really. So proud. Whatever you choose to do from here, make it be what makes *you* happy."

"I can visualize people getting their hands in the soil here. That feels right."

"Then let's see what we can do about the irrigation. Where's your sexy tool belt?"

She pulled her eyebrows together. "My toolbox is down by the field. I don't see why we'd need the tool belt."

"You're right." I pulled out my phone and grinned at the picture I'd taken. "It really was more the drill…"

She peeked at the screen. "Oh, jeez. Delete that, would you?"

"Never! I love that picture! I clicked it to camera and squeezed her close to me clicking a photo of the two of us before we got back to work.

CHAPTER TWENTY-NINE

Madison

"Well these are awful, don't you think?" Shawneen asked, fingering Ruth's curtains.

Of course I didn't, but it was my fault that Shawneen didn't know that Ruth had made them. We'd been having breakfasts together for a month now, and while I wanted to talk more about the part of my life she'd missed out on, Shawneen generally kept bringing up what I was doing in Quincy, specifically what I'd done with the old ranch house and how she'd really like to see it. I'd held her off when I was still getting the last of the furniture in, but having had Bo and Ruth up for the weekend, I didn't have that excuse to use any longer.

Luckily, she didn't count on an answer and continued without any participation from me. "They're not as bad when you pull them open. You could leave them tied like this until you get some new ones."

"I just put these up."

"The rods are nice, honey, and these'll do for now, but they're clearly not right. You need something with more color to liven up this room. Some throw pillows for the couch would be good too. You can work with minor colors in the curtains, accent them with the pillows. Definitely get ones that you can take off and wash. That's important. These bitty little clocks aren't going to work either. You've got to get something big. Take down one of these prints, and a big wall clock would look super on this wall."

Forehead resting on my fingers, I just stared at my palm instead of following her as she criticized my decorating and talked about what she would do. Without looking up, I explained how my old employer placed the clocks unobtrusively on purpose, encouraging guests to forget about their everyday schedules. "Only bathrooms and closet doors got mirrors because it doesn't matter how you look on vacation."

"Oh, a big mirror! I take it back. A big mirror would be even better than a clock."

I immediately regretted bringing up the subject. Had I mentioned it when I gave Ruth and Bo the tour, they would have congratulated me on applying something I picked up from working at Steve's place. They didn't barrel in with their unsolicited opinions. I had happily led them from room to room, excited to talk about what the challenge had been or what I was particularly proud of. Shawneen didn't ask about the work I'd done, so I followed mutely, trying to grasp something positive.

She was the first stranger looking at the place, so at least I was getting an objective view. I glanced out the window of the front-facing bedroom while Shawneen argued the benefits of supplying wooden hangers in the closets instead of the plastic ones I'd bought. Houdini was nosing around the Nova with its incongruous tan door. Shawneen complained about it, but she wouldn't spend the money to have it painted.

After viewing all of the rooms, she asked about how I decided to book and price each and started making calculations about what she anticipated the place could make each month. I felt as uncomfortable as I had the first time we'd had breakfast together. I'd waited to order, and neither of us specified separate checks, so the waitress had delivered one check. I assumed that she would sweep it up and pay. The whole assume and "ass out of you and me" saying was exactly how I felt sitting there agonizing about whether to pick it up myself. The longer it sat there, the more I stewed, feeling like she *ought* to pick it up. After all these years, couldn't she spring for my pancakes?

Lead. My stomach had felt full of it then and did again now. At least at breakfast, once I'd paid for the both of us, I could jump in my truck and get along with my day. Standing back at the living room, I had no idea how to signal that I really wanted to get back to figuring out my irrigation down in the field.

"I should get the measurements for these windows. In case I see something I think would work." She smiled brightly at me and then turned back to the window. Something out front caught her eye. "What the hell…"

She leaned forward as she drew out the words, and I came up beside her. By the time I'd reached her, she'd spun and stomped toward the front door.

"Get!" she screamed at Houdini. "Get out of here you god-damned disgusting thing! Look at this!" She waved her arms at the hood of her car.

I was looking. And inside where I knew she couldn't see me, I had a good laugh. In the kitchen, I grabbed a handful of paper towels and a bottle of cleaner. I composed myself as best I could and jogged out front to meet her. "I am so sorry, Shawneen."

Hands on hips, she glared at the steaming pile of horse manure on the hood of her car. "He did that on purpose!" she raged, veins in her neck standing out.

"He's kind of a wild card." I grabbed a shovel from the garage and moved to scoop it off the hood.

"Are you kidding me? That'll scratch my paint," she whined.

I stared at her quizzically. With all the dings and scratches elsewhere on the car, I didn't see what harm the shovel would cause. Nevertheless, I returned with a broom and swept the manure onto the ground before spraying and wiping down the hood, all this with my tongue bitten tightly between my teeth to keep myself from laughing again.

While I worked, Shawneen returned to the house and grabbed her big metallic-silver purse and slung it over her elbow. "You had better corral that thing before you open. Can you imagine if he did this to a guest's car? Can you imagine?" She shook her keys for emphasis before getting in the car and slamming its tan door shut.

"See you next week," I called as she gassed the car in reverse.

She paused before she turned in the drive and rolled down the window. "At the diner," she spat.

That suited me just fine.

I swept the pile of manure out toward the trees before focusing on my irrigation problem. I'd hoped that Lacey and I could figure it out, that I wouldn't have to embarrass myself by asking Bo for help. I didn't want Lacey to think that I was asking him because he's a man. I was hoping he could teach me from his experience, but he'd insisted that Charlie was my guy.

It shouldn't be so hard to dial a number I chided myself, pulling my cell from my pocket. Getting him to talk in person was tough enough for me. The way he and Lacey got on, I almost wanted to have her call him. The awkward silences that were our norm were even more pronounced on the phone. Resigned, I pressed the call button. "Hey Charlie," I said, glad he answered. I could picture him rubbing the back of his neck thinking about what to say, so I saved him the trouble and launched into why I was calling. "I've been trying to fix the irrigation down to the field by the road. Bo said you might have done some work on it back when."

"Sure I did. Not a lot I can do on the phone though. That Lacey seems pretty handy. Did ya ask her to have a look at it?"

"We had a go at it. She got all the spigots cranked open, but we're still not getting anything." I was tempted to explain how impressed I'd been when she added a section of pipe to gain the torque needed to get the old cranks moving again.

"You sure it's running from up top? They should've shut it down at the house to keep the pipes from freezing."

"I opened that up first. I know there's water up here because it's dripping."

"Well, if it's not flowing down below, shut that sucker off. You've got some kind of trouble in the line. Don't need to be adding stress to those old pipes if they're not working."

"Short of digging up the entire line, is there anything else I can do?" In the silence, I could picture his tongue checking where he used to stow his chew.

"Guess I could come up and have a look. There are a couple of places you can check first, but I know 'em by feel not by any measurement."

I hesitated to ask. "Would you? I'd really appreciate it."

"Sure. Let me talk to Bo about when he can spare me. You need it soon? He was saying how you're wanting to get some plants in the ground." I couldn't imagine him and Bo having a conversation about me. Even more shocking was that in my stunned silence, Charlie continued talking. "He says you've really done something with the place, that it's really something to see."

"Thanks." Bo's praise made me stand tall. "I look forward to showing you around."

"I'll be up this week then."

"Okay." I said, clicking off. And it really did feel okay.

CHAPTER THIRTY

Madison

I was out at the corral pushing over rotted-out fence posts with my borrowed tractor, my eye on the road. Charlie said to expect him before lunch. He would take off after his morning chores. For him, that might mean daybreak. He wasn't one to wait on the sun to get his work started, so I'd begun early too. As I maneuvered the tractor, I brainstormed things to talk about and worried over whether he'd approve of what I'd done. I'd asked Lacey if she could stay, so it wouldn't just be Charlie and me, but she insisted that maintaining her regular hours was important. Though I argued that everyone has to stop for lunch, frustratingly, she had not made any commitment to join us.

My stomach flip-flopped when I finally saw Charlie's truck pull up the drive to the house. I watched him creep up the road, the wheels of the old "Love Machine" kicking up almost no dust. The way he paused before parking in front of the house, he perhaps considered going to the barn as he must have back when he managed the cattle. Stepping out of his truck, he didn't put his hat on immediately but stood with it in his hands instead as he took the place in. Was he thinking, as I had, whether the place would have made it if he'd stayed on? His eyes landed on me, and he quickly settled the straw hat on his head and strode over to the corrals.

"What do you think of our place?" I asked.

"Our?" He looked confused.

"With how much you invested…"

He waved off my words. "It's your place. You got a name for it?"

I hadn't assumed a check that significant would be a gift and sat stumped at how to reply. "Nothing yet. Can't exactly call it Hot Rocks Cattle Co. if I'm not running cattle."

"Still got them hot rocks, though, don'tcha?"

It was my turn to look confused.

"You haven't been out to the hot spring?"

I thought about Shawneen suggesting there might be one but felt uncomfortable saying her name. "The realtor didn't mention it."

"It'd take too long to walk out there today, but I could draw you a map. Where'd you think they got the hot rocks for the name from?"

"The piles of manure?" I suggested.

He shook his head as he turned from me. "I'll grab my tools and get to the irrigation. Manure…" As he turned, I thought I caught a glimpse of a smile, but I wasn't certain, and he wasn't sticking around to talk. Without Lacey, he didn't seem as comfortable.

My chest felt tight as he ambled away. I sat on the tractor and watched him reach into the bed of the truck for a shovel and his toolbox and head down to the lower pasture. Movement by the barn caught my eye, Houdini propelling himself up from where he'd been resting. He shook himself soundly and turned his big head in my direction, waiting. He reminded me of how Lacey had engaged Charlie by asking for a cup of coffee. Houdini bobbed his head as if he was impatient with me, so I finally swung down from the tractor and headed for the lower field. Charlie looked surprised when I caught up to him.

I told myself it was the horse, but he said, "You don't have to stop what you're doing."

"Lacey will want to know what you did to fix it," I said. "Like the lock."

He hmphed at me and ran his hand along Houdini's thick neck. "Nice-looking animal. Had myself a big white gelding like him once," he said, before grabbing the shovel and sinking it into the dirt.

My heart pushed at my chest, and normally I would have accepted that he didn't want to talk and walk away, but I remembered how good it felt when Lacey told Shawneen who I was. Borrowing courage from how that had gone, I said, "Why'd you take it apart?"

"What's that?"

I didn't want to ask again, but I did. "The lock. Lacey said you broke it on purpose."

Air puffed out between his lips like I'd stuck a balloon. "Didn't want you getting stuck in your room."

"I got stuck in my room a lot?" I tried to picture how a kid as small as I must've been could have gotten locked in. Maybe if I locked it and took out the key but couldn't get it back in again? I knew skeleton keys could be tricky, but if I didn't have the key, I wouldn't have been able to lock or unlock it at all. "Why didn't you keep the key out of my reach?"

"You weren't the problem."

"I wasn't?" I felt like he'd given me a riddle, but no solution.

"Shawneen." He scratched his sideburn and settled his hat back into place. He wouldn't look at me. "Sometimes I'd come home and she'd have locked you in there." He slammed the shovel down into the earth with much more force.

I felt unstable and sat on the pine needles he'd pushed away to begin his digging. They pricked at my thighs even through my work pants. "Was I bad?"

A sound escaped him, an angry guffaw. "You bad? You didn't have it in you. She said…she needed personal time. I said to find another way and broke the lock so I knew she'd listen. She put you in gymnastics class. I thought it was all settled."

Charlie strode toward the lower field, poked at the soil a bit as if to test his memory, and started digging a new hole. I followed him knowing the story wasn't over but uncertain of how to ask for more. Lacey would have known what to say next, but she said that she couldn't get away from the shop. Houdini butted his muzzle against my hand, and I reached up to stroke his broad face. "It wasn't?"

"What?"

"Settled," I prompted, testing whether he'd say more.

"You asked her?"

"No."

"But you've seen her." He stopped digging and leaned on the shovel. He looked like he'd chewed something hard on a bum tooth.

"I'm sorry."

"What are you sorry for?"

What did I say? I didn't like to see him agitated and thought that if I told him I'd seen Shawneen a bunch of times since we'd picked up the door for the Nova, he'd be hurt.

"I didn't tell you that the door Lacey and I picked up was for her."

I could see his jaw working as he tried to control anger I didn't understand. "She tell you whose car it is?" He punctuated the question with the shovel biting hard into the earth.

I'd never seen him so angry. "No."

"I'd wager it's not hers, that it belongs to whoever she's got in her bed. Never meant to get her pregnant, you know, but I did the honorable thing. I married her. Found a house that we could fill up with kids. A house she ended up bringing other fellas to. One afternoon, I was at work and I got a call from the police station saying that they had you and couldn't find Shawneen."

"Why was I at the police station?"

Loosening big bites of earth Charlie widened the hole, his heavy boot sinking the spade. "You were at your gymnastics class. Patrol officer found you hours later huddled in the doorframe, nobody around, no coat on. They'd picked you up asking you about your mama. You were wide-eyed and shivering. Shawneen was supposed to pick you up at five. They asked if you knew where your mom or dad was. You told 'em your dad worked at Hot Rocks."

I felt hot, like I was somehow to blame for it all. "You never told me."

"Never wanted you to know. A girl doesn't need to know that about the woman who birthed her. You were in the truck with me when I saw the car outside our house. His goddamned car in *my* drive. I told you to wait in the truck. And it's a good thing I had you with me. I might've killed him otherwise."

"And we left that night?"

"We stayed here for a few nights while I tried to sort it all out. I couldn't divorce her. The judge would have given you to her. I couldn't leave you with her. She was never fit to be anyone's mother."

"Wait. You never divorced her?"

"Nope. If I went all legal like that, no judge would've given you to me. I was pretty sure she wouldn't come lookin' for us—hell, I think she was glad to see us go—but I couldn't take the chance. Best to let sleepin' dogs lie. She was a nasty, vindictive bitch then, and no doubt, still is."

All those years of Charlie's living in Bo and Ruth's trailer started to make more sense. I'd always thought that we couldn't afford a house. Charlie said he'd taken the job Bo offered because it paid as well as the one at Hot Rocks, but with a place to live thrown in. Now I realized that if he had owned any property, Shawneen would've had a claim to it. And then he'd given me that huge check. He'd had the money but chose to save it. For me, it seemed. Would he have put it toward his own ranch if I hadn't moved up to Bo and Ruth's place?

Charlie hit the pipe and started following it, exposing a longer section as I sat processing it all. Had I really ever called him Dad? I had no memory of ever using the name Dad for anyone, certainly not him. The realization felt like a piercing hole. I hugged my knees to my chest feeling like I could squeeze it away.

"Yup. Here it is. Here's your split. This joint was always vulnerable. You've got to flush the line or leave a drip going in that lower field before winter sets in, or it'll bust it right here. I got some pipe in the back of the truck and some elbows in the cab. You want to grab 'em?"

I nodded and pushed to my feet. In the truck, there was a battered cardboard box with pipe joints and cement. Next to that was a plastic-wrapped plate of peanut butter cookies, my favorite. I remembered Ruth teaching me how to roll the dough between my hands to form a perfect ball before pressing the crisscross pattern into it with a fork. Bo had loved the way the house smelled when Ruth and I made them. He always took his with a big glass of milk. I grabbed two from the plate.

I set down the box and handed one of the cookies to Charlie. "Still your favorite?" he asked, taking his carefully between his dirt-covered fingers. He bit nearly the whole cookie, leaving just a small crescent he fed to Houdini.

I nodded, taking a bite of cookie and tasting home.

"Ruth sent them. Said I'd be saving her the trip to the post office."

"She sends peanut butter cookies in the summer. When it's colder, she sends peanut butter balls."

"Those the ones dipped in chocolate?"

"Yep. The first time she sent them to me at university, I made myself sick on them. I couldn't stop."

"You always did love peanut butter. You'd eat anything if it had a little bit of peanut butter on it. Even broccoli."

"That's disgusting."

He chuckled. "You didn't think so when you were a little thing. Still need that length of pipe."

We never did go back to talking about the day he left Quincy for good. Once he'd repaired the pipe, he looked anxious to get back on the road and back to Paradise. Later, long after he'd gone, on my kitchen counter I found the map he'd drawn directing me to the hot spring. With it was a skeleton key. I held it in my hand feeling the metal grow warm in my palm.

In the quiet of my house, I walked to my bedroom and retrieved the doorknob Charlie had fixed. I slipped the key into the lock. When I turned it, the bolt poked out. I swallowed. Charlie had kept the key? Still disbelieving, I turned it again, housing the bolt. The hardware felt heavy in my hands. He'd left Shawneen. My room. My things. He'd left it all in the house he had fled. A little girl waiting in a truck. An angry father leaving without looking back, pocketing a key he'd never be able to use again. Yet he'd kept it all these years.

Lacey noticed it straightaway when she arrived for dinner. "He had the key after all?"

"He did." All the things he'd told me about Shawneen tumbled out at once.

Lacey took me in her arms. "Knowing all that, you still put it on your bedroom door? It doesn't creep you out?"

I'd thought about that. I considered installing it on the pantry or out in the barn, but it had called to me, so loudly Martha had heard it too. I couldn't ignore that, and as I told Lacey, now I was the one with the key.

CHAPTER THIRTY-ONE

Lacey

"What's that smile for?" I asked Madison on the drive over to Chester Friday night. She sat next to me with her feet up on the dash of the Bug and her arms resting on her knees.

"I love this old car. Reminds me of Charlie's 'Love Machine.'"

"Do I want to know?"

She raised her hands as if to present herself as evidence.

"Is that why..." I stopped myself, but she knew my train of thought.

"I never straight out asked Charlie, but..."

The road's curves had my full attention. When I risked glancing over at her, she was looking out the window.

"You okay over there?"

"Thinking about how he said he never meant to get Shawneen pregnant."

I'd made the right call staying away from the ranch when Charlie was there fixing the irrigation. If I'd been there, she would have counted on me to do the talking. When she'd shown me the key, I could see that they had done some repairs on what was broken between them. Not everything, but a start. "There are plenty of unexpected pregnancies."

She nodded. "And I suppose there are plenty of parents who give up their kids."

"Heck yeah," I said. "Be careful, Trevor will be trying to foist his two on you tonight for sure."

"They can't be as bad as you've described."

"Don't let your guard down," I warned.

"I held my own with your game night group."

"My friends play nice. My family are all trained pranksters, even the youngsters."

"Still better than being a piece of work."

There was quiet between us for a few minutes. "I'm sorry I said that about Shawneen."

"Apparently you were right about her."

"It doesn't mean I'm not sorry. If I could take it back and change things, I would."

"You like to fix things."

"That I do. Too bad people aren't as easy to figure out as cars."

"No, they're not," she said, barely loud enough for me to hear. When I looked over, she was looking out the window.

* * *

My brother and his family must've lined up when they saw us pull up to their curb because when the door swung inward, they stood posed like a family portrait: Trevor with an arm wrapped around his wife, Iris, and a boy in front of each. The younger one had lost a few teeth since I'd last seen him and the older looked more grown up with his enormous adult teeth in his small head. Both sported shaggy hair that came with the end of a school year.

"Trevor, Iris, Bruno and Eric," I said, ending on the six-year-old, "this is Madison."

"She's your girlfriend?" Bruno, eight, asked up front.

"Yes."

"Are you going to marry her?" Eric followed up.

"Well, maybe you should invite us in first," I suggested. I bent down to give the boys hugs. "And treat her nice. This is kind of like an interview to find out if she likes my family." I stood to hug Trevor as well. "That goes for you too, mister."

"Best behavior," he said, ushering both of us into the house. He shook Madison's hand. "Very nice to meet you. Lacey exaggerates about the family, by the way. Most of the stories she's told were probably tricks that she pulled and is now blaming on us."

"Lacey, come see my new remote control car!" Eric pleaded pulling her arm.

Iris shook Madison's hand and asked what she'd like to drink.

"Should I stay?" I asked, one arm extended toward Eric's door like a stretchy superhero. I was surprised to find how hard it was to hold my ground against someone half my size.

"I'm good," Madison said as Iris directed her to the kitchen.

"Come oooooon, Aunt Lacey." I followed him to the end of the hall where he had the car and controls. "My turn first!"

"Of course." I sat cross-legged next to him on the floor and watched him maneuver the toy car. "You looking forward to summer?"

"Yeah!" He launched into all of the activities he and his brother had planned. Knowing Iris, they had them written down, so she could remind them the second *I'm bored* passed their lips.

"Hey sport," I said the moment he stopped for air. "I'm going to go get a drink too."

"Okay," he replied, still distracted by the car.

When I got to the kitchen, I found only Iris working on dinner. "Where's Madison?"

"Bruno abducted her. They're in the den with his new Lego set. She seems like a sweetheart." She pulled ingredients from the fridge and checked whatever was boiling on the stove. "Trevor said you were down in the valley a few weeks ago. Did you take her to meet your parents?"

"Not yet. We stayed with hers."

"That's a first for you, isn't it? Do you like them?"

Three of the four of them, I mused, but I didn't want to get into all that. Sitting on the porch with Charlie and having coffee had been a highlight. I felt like I got him. "A lot," I said simply.

"Are you ready for summer?"

"Not even close. I sure hope you're up for some activities. I am not taking those boys to the lake by myself."

I laughed knowing that she included my brother in that list of boys.

Iris never complained the way some women do about having just boys, but I sometimes sensed she missed having another girl around. She wore her almost-black hair long and always up in a new twist or complicated braid. The way she liked to show me styles I could try made me wonder if she would have liked a little girl to go shopping and talk fashion with.

Madison and Bruno were around the corner in the TV room. I could hear her asking Bruno about the Lego, but I didn't hear my brother's voice. The amount of time he'd been unaccounted for raised a red flag. "You need my help with anything?" I asked, even though I knew she would decline.

"I've got it. You can go rescue Madison."

As I anticipated, Madison looked completely at home with Bruno in the center of a Lego island. "You seen your dad?"

"Out front."

Closer to the garage than the front door, I poked my head in to see the garage door open. I slipped out and met Trevor crossing the lawn, a big smile on his face.

"You got the baby blue exactly right," he said.

He crossed his arms over his chest, the spring evening turning cool, and turned back to look at the car. It was the same as I'd left it, and I knew I locked my doors. I patted my pocket to make sure I still had my keys. You don't leave your doors unlocked or your keys accessible around my brothers. Chrystal learned that the hard way when she got blasted by baby powder someone had put in her vents. I always check to make sure my vents are off before I crank my engine.

"It looks good." He smiled. I didn't trust that smile. "You send a picture to Dad yet?"

"I texted him one right when she came back from the body shop."

"What did he say?"

"'Looks like the one I sold.'"

"Good thing you already knew how he's not sentimental?"

"Yeah." I already knew that I was alone in getting attached to cars and had spent some time swearing about the work I put into Shawneen's Nova because I'd become emotionally involved with it. But then Charlie's "Love Machine" came to mind, and I remembered how I'd connected Madison to the treasure box picture with that same truck. It had a history, and even if it was a complicated one, it was something that Charlie had hung onto. While I was proud of how far I'd brought my own Bug, it would never be the one my dad sold.

"You're still looking for that old horn, aren't you?"

"It's the last thing."

He chuckled at me. "C'mon. I was bringing the boys' bikes in," he said, turning back to the garage.

Had the bikes been out? I glanced again at my car before following him back into the house. Trevor had already joined Madison and Bruno on the floor, so I picked my way over to the couch, enjoying my family. Bruno dominated the conversation, explaining what Madison needed to do to build a plane that could land in the water and become a submarine.

Iris noticed how Madison pointedly said she'd wash her hands in the kids' bathroom, so I confessed that I'd let her in on the water trick Trevor had perfected.

"We don't want to scare you off," Trevor said loudly enough for Madison to hear.

When she came back, Iris added, "Once they figure out you're serious, watch out. I almost peed my pants when I found a mummified lizard in my crisper."

"Just preparing you for parenthood," Trevor said.

The evening hummed along, and I was glad to have brought Madison. We left the house hand in hand having given and received hugs all around before the boys bounded down the hall to get ready for bed.

Madison squeezed my hand before letting it go for me to walk around to the driver's side. "I like your brother and his family."

"Asshole!" I shouted before I could help myself.

"Excuse me?" Madison looked ashen.

I gestured her over to see the car from my side, the Bug up on the jack and front tire nowhere in sight.

"Where's your tire?" Madison asked, astonished.

I narrowed my gaze toward the house where I knew Trevor was watching. I heard laughter and then a window slam. "If he was feeling nice, he stowed it in the car." I lifted the Bug's hood and sighed with relief to find the tire and tools waiting for me.

"Aunt Lacey, Aunt Lacey, what are you doing?" The boys burst through the door, the big one wearing jammy bottoms, the little one in nothing but his tightie whities. "Dad says you need a lantern."

I intercepted Eric as he chased his brother with a lantern which was more likely to clock his brother than help me see what I was doing.

"Boys, back inside," Iris called. "We still need to brush teeth."

"We're helping Aunt Lacey," Bruno said, climbing into my car. His brother followed.

"Out of the car."

"But it's cool," Eric whined.

"Aunt Lacey will drive you around next time but only if you get out. Right. Now."

"Do you get stories before bed?" Madison asked.

"I can read now," Eric shared.

"How about you read me a story while Lacey gets the car fixed," Madison suggested. Both boys tore up to the house to find books. A very thankful looking Iris linked arms with Madison. It only took a matter of minutes to get the lug nuts secured and tools stowed away. I washed up as Madison finished the stories and collected another set of hugs from the boys.

"This was really fun for me," Madison ventured as we pulled away.

"We'll see what you think when they pull something like this on you."

"I think I'll say the same thing," she whispered.

I reached over and found her hand. Her answer surprised me until I considered it from her perspective. For the outsider, it would be an initiation. In that way, I could see how tonight's display was already a welcome to the family.

CHAPTER THIRTY-TWO

Madison

Ruth's curtains lay in a puddle by the front door as if Shawneen had a plan to haul them to the trash on her way out. As she bustled about getting her "perfect" curtains, I retrieved Ruth's wondering why I had opened the door. I wasn't ready to see Shawneen after what Charlie had told me and had canceled breakfast with her. She was the last person I'd expected to see when the doorbell sounded. Without invitation, she'd crossed the threshold, ushering in a man I didn't know, his arms laden with bags.

"Now I have the receipts for these if you need them. If you love them, and, oh, aren't they just the thing? Well then, you know how much to reimburse me."

They were dark. The bold multicolored geometric patterns were far better suited for a motel in Phoenix where the goal is to block out the sun. I couldn't form the words to say how absolutely they did not speak to me. And would she expect me to pad the amount for her time? When Ruth had volunteered to sew curtains, I assured her that I would pay for the material.

She was very clear about the materials and time being her contribution to my business venture. I hadn't told Shawneen that I wanted her to be on the lookout for anything. But then, I hadn't shared how much I loved Ruth's curtains when she had criticized them. I draped them carefully over the back of the couch aware of the hours Ruth had spent ironing them for me.

How had I allowed this to happen? Shawneen's curtains were out of the package before my brain even comprehended what they were. And now they were about to be hung. Shawneen and a straw-hat-holding boy I prayed wasn't Dennis held them up for me to see. The thought that she could be dating someone my age made me feel sick, but the story Charlie had told me about her leaving me at gymnastics to carry on with a guy made me think it was entirely possible.

"Oh, where are my manners? I was so excited about these curtains I didn't introduce you. Hagen Weaver, this is my daughter, Madison."

Flustered by her introduction, I shook hands with the immaculately pressed cowboy as she prattled on about the multiple properties Hagen's parents owned. I'd waited a long time to hear someone claim me with the words "this is my daughter," and yet they felt so wrong. She wasn't matching up to the woman I'd dreamed about. Part of me wanted to turn the two of them around and march them out of my house, but the four-year-old me wanted to know if Shawneen had any remorse. The way she'd reacted when Lacey told her who I was made me think that she regretted losing Charlie and me.

"I never knew Shawneen had a kid, and I'd never have taken you for her daughter." He paused and combed his manicured beard with his fingertips before he continued. "You look more like sisters, honestly."

Flattered, Shawneen smacked him lightly on the shoulder. "Oh, you're too kind. My years of youthful beauty are spent. What I wouldn't give to be in my twenties again, and courting one of the Weaver boys."

She said it as if men were steps on a social ladder she hoped to climb. Hagen's face flushed pink when he glanced at me.

Had he not seen the rainbow sticker on my truck, or was he unclear on what it meant? If Shawneen had seen it, she didn't understand its significance if she thought I would take her place in courting this boy she held in such high esteem.

"Hagen, get on over here and help me with these curtains. I'm sure you don't even need a ladder to reach the other side there."

In case I ever forgot, Hagen was stamped into the leather along the back of his finely tooled belt. His ridiculously pointed boots were obviously custom-made as well. I didn't think much of the outfit that had never seen work, and worried about the weight of Shawneen's introduction and what they both expected from me.

"All I'm asking is that you give these a chance. I can take 'em back if you don't like 'em."

The curtains or the guy? Hagen stood with one thumb hooked on a belt loop, and I did my best not to stare at the large bronc on his gold belt buckle. I shifted my focus to the pencil-perfect part of his hair, dark waves that he'd tamed with gel. Still worried about Shawneen's intentions in bringing Hagen along, I threw out a line to see if it might be because he could be an asset to my resort. "Are you a masseuse?" I asked, using the title on purpose, my thoughts on Lacey.

His laugh revealed straight white teeth. "Not for hire," he said in his rich voice.

"Hagen grew up here and knows more about ranching than anyone I know," Shawneen said. "We talk about it whenever he comes to the restaurant."

"Which is kind of a lot," he admitted. "It's too tempting right across the road from my parents' feed store."

"Oh, I've been there. It's a few shops down from Lacey's," I said.

"Of course he's familiar with Lacey," Shawneen said dismissively. "Before you go any further with that garden idea of hers, you should talk to a rancher about how to use the property. Hagen agreed to take a look around and see how well suited it would be to run livestock."

I sighed with relief. "It wasn't enough to keep Hot Rocks going."

"But Charlie's boss didn't think about guests like you do. Maybe the two of you could team up. Hagen saw the field you were thinking of planting down by the road. Couldn't hurt to show him the rest of the place. You two go on. I'll get these curtains all set."

Watching her mess with the curtains was making me feel sick, so I thumbed in the direction of the back door. Hagen followed with an eager look that unnerved me almost as much as Shawneen's showing up.

"Hey Houdini," I said absentmindedly as I patted his head and walked down the steps.

"There's...a horse on your porch." He held both hands up to protect his shirt as he scooted around Houdini's big noggin.

"He might follow, might not. He does his own thing." I kept walking. "I've got this corral here. The holding pen and barn."

"You don't have a stall for the horse?"

"I tried to keep him in the barn, but he escapes. He has a fondness for visiting Lacey at work."

"She's over in East Quincy."

"Weird. I know." I couldn't suppress the smile that accompanied the shared puzzlement Lacey and I had over Houdini's visits. He hadn't been back to her garage since we'd started dating despite the invitations she extended to him when she was at my place.

"Couldn't you make the barn more secure?"

"I kind of enjoy his company around the house."

"Shawneen said that he took a dump on her car. If you're running this as a guest ranch, you don't want him damaging property."

"So I've heard." Houdini had ambled over to the barn and stood in front of the latch.

"You don't have any livestock in the barn?" he asked following my line of sight.

"No. I've got a loaner tractor holed up in there, but mostly empty space." I didn't feel like moving Houdini to give Hagen the full tour. Had it been Lacey, I might have pulled her inside and had her show me what our first kiss could have been like the evening she came out to talk about my field. Or maybe we could have a literal roll in the hay.

"You have a pretty smile," Hagen said.

I quickly turned away from him, trying to shoo away the image of Lacey stretched out on a bed of straw and get my face in order. I didn't want him to get the wrong impression and think that I was reacting to him. I had to redirect my thoughts, but the more I tried to push Lacey out of my mind, the more ideas I got. My skin tingled as my imagination fed it memories of how good Lacey's hands felt on me, and I was shocked to feel moisture pooling between my legs. I gulped, genuinely flustered, grasping for anything to save me.

"Hey you two," Shawneen called from the porch. "How's it look?"

"Real good!" Hagen said. I couldn't see his face, but I still felt his eyes on me.

"Aren't you two a picture. Wouldn't it be exciting if the two of your dreams matched up?"

So she *was* matchmaking. I didn't like her smile, and suddenly I felt pressure on the small of my back. I whipped around to find Hagen attempting to guide me back up to the house. Could he feel the heat my daydream of Lacey had generated? I stepped away quickly and returned to the house, nodding and agreeing with Shawneen as she pointed out what she liked about her curtains, anything, anything to get the two of them to leave.

I didn't even wait until their car was out of sight before I dialed Lacey.

"I need you," I said without preamble.

"Madison, what's wrong?" She sounded alarmed.

"I've got a problem."

"What kind of problem?"

"One only you can help me with."

"Is that so?" I could hear the relief in her voice. She dropped it a notch as she engaged in the flirting I'd started. "Can you describe this problem?"

"I seem to have developed a drip."

"Oh, that does sound bad."

"When do you think you can trace the source?"

She sucked in a breath. "I'll be there in fifteen."

I flopped down on the couch holding the phone to my chest. My eyes flicked to the curtains. "Damn," I whispered, wishing that problem were as easy to solve.

CHAPTER THIRTY-THREE

Lacey

I'm embarrassed to admit how quickly I became accustomed to eating dinner with Madison. When she called to say that she was running late and had not even started cooking, I said it was fine, we could fend for ourselves, but had proceeded to stand in front of my refrigerator with no motivation to cook for myself. Two weeks into dating Della, and I was finding excuses to keep my evenings to myself. Two weeks with Madison, and home alone, I felt like a single horse hitched to a double yoke.

"Hey Lacey," Hope greeted me ten minutes later when I pushed through the door of Cup of Joy. "It's been a while." She smiled at the reason behind my having been away from her diner so long.

"I forgot how important it is to support local business," I shot back. Whenever I berated myself for not cooking, Hope would argue the positive side of my decision to eat out.

"Uh-huh. Do you know what you want?"

To be at home chatting about my day with Madison, I almost said. It was more than the pleasure of cooking for two. I missed her company. I missed feeling her next to me even when she was fully clothed. "How about a chicken pesto sandwich, fries and a soda?"

I realized that if Madison had come alone, she would have brought the biography of Woodrow Wilson she was now reading. Not in the habit of carrying a book, I spent the time running through a shop problem. The Ford sedan Gabe's mom drove had developed a vibration that I couldn't pinpoint. I'd already checked the obvious—tires and wheels were balanced and all of the suspension pieces were tight and functioning properly. I hated to give it back to Gabe with the issue unresolved, but I was stumped.

Hope returned with my soda, forcing Mrs. Owens's car to my mental back burner.

"What are you doing working, anyway?" I asked, knowing Hope had cut down the hours she spent at the diner to spend more time with her family.

"Our waitress went home for the summer. Dani didn't take any summer classes, so she's home with Joy until the fall semester. By then Jalisa will be back to take my hours, and I'll be MOD again."

"MOD?"

"Mom on Duty. That's what Dani calls it. Every once in a while, she's Administrator on Duty at the college."

"It sounds like a nice trade-off for both of you."

"It is, so why do you sound like I ran over your cat?" She rested her elbows on the counter, propping her chin.

"I couldn't track down what's wrong with Mrs. Owens's car."

"Hmmm. So it has nothing to do with you being here alone?"

The bells chimed before I could answer, and the one problem I had with Madison walked through the door.

"Evening Shawneen," Hope said, sweet as syrup. "Did you want to add anything for yourself to Dennis's to-go order?"

"I already ate," came Shawneen's curt reply.

While Hope retrieved Dennis's dinner, Shawneen sidled in next to me at the bar, muttering about how miserable Dennis could make her life.

I called Madison. I frowned when her voice mail picked up. "Hey, I didn't end up cooking. I'm at Cup of Joy if you haven't eaten yet."

I couldn't help but notice a sly smile creep across Shawneen's face. "She might be busy for a while if that was Madison you were calling. She was talking about some electrical work the other day, and I suggested Hagen go out and give her a hand. You should have seen the way she blushed over him when they first met. I don't get why he didn't ask her out right then, but that'll change."

Hope paused ever so slightly before taking the credit card Shawneen slid across the counter. "Hagen Weaver?"

"There aren't two Hagens in town as far as I know." Shawneen barely glanced in Hope's direction, even when she returned with the receipt. Shawneen signed her copy with a flourish and left it on the counter. "Take care Lacey," she said over her shoulder as she left.

"I don't see how you put up with how rude she is to you," I said incredulously.

"It got better after I had the baby. Now she can go back to pretending I don't exist. She couldn't ignore the baby or how it got there. What's your excuse?"

"My excuse?"

"For putting up with her?"

"If I don't, I give her more ammunition to hate lesbians. If I'm nice to her, she'll eventually see how wrong she is."

"What's this about Hagen?"

"Let's find out." I already had my phone out and had typed in *Is Hagen really at your place?* I hit send.

"You know that you fix cars, right, not people?" Hope asked.

"I know that," I said, distracted by Madison's reply: *Y.* I flushed hot, not liking her evasive question, or the fact that she hadn't told me that he was there when she called off dinner. How could she not guess why I would want to know if he was with her? I typed back, *Because I thought we were having dinner together.* To Hope, I said, "But clearly you think that being nice to Shawneen could help bring her around. Otherwise, you'd refuse to serve Shawneen and make Dennis come in for his own food."

"Fair enough."

My phone rang. I apologized to Hope and answered it. She waved off my apology and disappeared into the kitchen.

"Sorry. Got lost in one last project. You seemed off in your last text."

"*I* seemed off," I snapped. "You're the one asking why I want to know if he's there in the first place."

"I told you he was here."

"No, you said 'why?'"

There was a long pause. "Doesn't the letter Y mean yes?"

I rested my head in the palm of my hand. "I thought you didn't want me to know he was there."

"You were jealous?" She sounded relieved, and there was something else in her voice, a squeal of disbelief. "You're still at Cup of Joy?"

"Yes." I overenunciated the word.

"Get me whatever you got. I'm starving, and I'll be there in five."

"Madison wants one too," I said to Hope when she came back with my sandwich.

"Everything's okay?"

"I really thought there was a chance what Shawneen said was true, and she was out there having fun with that brat." I'd never been a fan of Hagen's. Nobody wanted to be friends with the snob his parents had raised him to be, and he did nasty things to try to fit in. My brothers were always part of the in-crowd, and he tried to ingratiate himself by impressing them with pranks that always went a little too far.

"Madison doesn't seem like the kind of person who would mess around on her girlfriend."

"I know," I said, realizing how quickly I'd let Shawneen's insinuation get to me. Hope had been right. "Seems Shawneen knows how to push *all* my buttons."

"That she does."

I sat with that new knowledge until Madison arrived and slipped her arms around my middle. My body said yes to every spot she touched. I noticed the twinkle in Hope's eyes when she saw me resting against Madison. It meant a lot to be confident about affection in public. I had Hope and Dani to thank for the trailblazing example they set in town, and the look she gave us made me think she was happy to see another couple being affectionate.

Hope delivered Madison's sandwich. Madison squeezed me before sitting to eat. "You didn't seriously think that I was choosing Hagen over you."

"I thought you were blowing me off."

"You know how I lose track of the time. I was trying to do better in wrapping up, but Hagen stopped by, and I saw my opportunity to get that bum outlet squared away."

"I'm sorry. I let Shawneen get me worked up about why he was out there."

"I don't see why you're worried about it. It's like Gabe bringing the tractor by, and I like that I'm making my own friends and not relying on yours."

"It's not like Gabe. Gabe doesn't expect any favors in return."

"Neither does Hagen." Though her reasoning didn't match mine, she'd already moved on to another topic with Hope. "The whole reason I needed to get to it today is that I have my first real guests coming in tomorrow."

"That's wonderful!" Hope said.

"I wanted to thank you for your help. I've booked several weekends since you suggested where to start my advertising."

"I'm so glad."

"The one coming in tomorrow requested the room with the private bath. I thought I had all day to get everything ready, but I kept getting interrupted by the phone."

"Reservations?" Hope asked.

"A few." They high-fived. "Some queries too, and then Shawneen who was especially chatty."

"Probably keeping you on the phone, so she'd know you were there when she sent Hagen over."

"He's not her puppet."

"I don't trust him. That's all. You didn't grow up with him."

"No. I didn't."

The way she said it, it hit me that she would have if Charlie had stayed in Quincy. What would we have been to each other if we'd all grown up together? I softened when she draped her arm around my shoulder.

"Nobody's ever been jealous of who I spend my time with before." Madison beamed.

That smile mixed everything up. All I wanted to do was keep that very smile on her face. That felt more important than insisting that she set up some better boundaries with Shawneen and Hagen.

CHAPTER THIRTY-FOUR

Lacey

I was under Mrs. Owens's car tightening a hose-clamp around the driveshaft when the Nova pulled up. After a week of mulling it over, it hit me that the vibration could be a problem in the link between the transmission and the rear end. I'd gone over the driveshaft carefully and thought I'd found a spot where a balance weight was missing. When I drove it with the hose clamp, I'd be able to tell if I was right.

"Be with you in a minute," I said.

"Take your time." Despite my signs warning customers to stay out of the shop, she'd drifted toward my bench while I had snugged the hose clamp in place. Gritting my teeth, I rolled out to deal with her latest problem.

"How can I help you, Shawneen?"

"The car's fine. It's Madison I wanted to talk about."

That stopped me short. My belly clenched in anticipation.

"I'm so grateful to you for bringing Madison back into my life. It was real sweet of you to arrange for us to meet each other here after so many years apart. A nice gesture, if you will, seeing as we spent the first four years of her life together here."

I felt a *but* coming.

"But I was thinking you could give her a little space. Seems like the two of you spend an awful lot of time together."

"I didn't realize anyone was keeping track."

"Well, I'm sure she appreciated all the help you gave her settling in, getting to know the area, but don't you think now it would be best to…step back…give her some breathing room?"

"We happen to enjoy each other's company," I said, wishing I could be blunt and claim Madison as my girlfriend.

As if reading my mind, she sighed dramatically and said, "Well the amount of time you spend together could start to give folks the wrong impression."

I stopped wiping my hands and crossed my arms across my chest. "The wrong impression…"

"That she's…well, that she's like you."

"You say that like there's something wrong with my being a lesbian."

She thrust her hands to her hips. "Well, it's not my place to say, but look at you. You could have any man you wanted."

"You're right. It's none of your business."

"But what man is going to want a woman who does a man's job?"

If she didn't shut her trap, I was going to do something I'd regret. I held up my hand. "Shawneen, stop. This has nothing to do with me."

"But it does. I see the way you look at her, and it's not right."

The last thing I needed was a woman I'd barely tolerated for years standing in my shop telling me how to live my life. I'd put up with her crap long enough. "You can leave now."

"I am just asking you to think about Madison's future. What is Hagen supposed to think if she's too busy with you to see him? I'm sure you don't want to ruin her chance of a future with him."

"Madison's future is her own choice," I said between clenched teeth.

"I'm her mother. Why do you think she came back after all these years? I can help her."

My mind flashed back to the phone call Madison made to say she had a problem only I could help her with, and I couldn't help but laugh.

"You think that's funny?" Shawneen spat.

"If you need help with your Nova, I'm your gal. I'm sorry, when it comes to Madison, I don't see a problem, so you're wasting your breath. Leave my shop."

"You think it's wise to talk to a customer that way?" she challenged.

"I think if you want me putting any more of my time into a car I care about a whole lot more than you do, you'll turn around and leave."

"Don't forget what I said," she threatened before she slammed the car door Madison and I had tracked down for her, hours I had not billed her for since it was a chance for me to spend time with Madison.

I grabbed the keys to Mrs. Owens's Ford, trying to stop my brain spinning. Before Shawneen interrupted, I'd been so excited to solve the vibration problem, but now my blood was boiling. I gripped the keys hard trying to distract myself with the bite of the metal. It didn't help. I'd reached my limit and threw the keys across the shop. I swung my leg back to kick something, anything, but realized how with my doors open I was very much on display. Raging through my back entrance, I slammed the door. It felt so good, I opened it and slammed it again, growling on the other side of the closed door.

If Hagen had been there, I would have very much liked to bash his head in with a very large wrench. I sat down in the hallway, chest heaving, hands clenched. I pulled out my phone. Madison had to tell Shawneen that we were a couple. I wasn't going to do it and out Madison, but I wasn't going to put up with Shawneen threatening me either. Shaking, my thumb hovered over the call button. I was too angry.

Midnight lazed down the hall mewing. I raised my hand, and she walked under it, arching her back as she snaked back and forth. Her purring recalibrated my heart rate. I finally calmed down to realize that this was yet another example of Shawneen manipulating me. Now close enough to five to justify closing up, I pulled the doors and shut off the lights with a promise to return tomorrow in a more productive frame of mind.

I showered as my mind drifted to Hope and Dani's monthly games night in a few hours, seeing Madison there and then spending the evening doing far more than what friends do. Feeling foolish for letting Shawneen get to me, I hummed along the familiar route out to Madison's place in a much-improved mood. I would have buzzed up the hill after turning left into the drive as I usually did if Houdini hadn't been standing on the little bridge, one leg cocked and fast asleep.

That's when I saw them walking across the field. My gaze dropped to their hands. Not linked. Had I really thought she'd be holding his hand? I hated myself for even looking. I knew she didn't like him, but I couldn't understand what she was doing walking the pasture with him. We'd walked that same pasture, and I'd been thinking about kissing her the whole time, my body alive next to her. I had hoped she'd asked me to take a look at the place because she was interested in me, so why was she now walking it again with Hagen?

It did not sit well with me to be the tucked-away lesbian lover. I'd done that for too long with the woman in Chico. A long-distance girlfriend had been easy for her to hide away. Was Madison parading around with Hagen to hide what was building between us? Was she trying to build a public façade to hide her private life?

She waved to me. Of course she saw me in the Bug, and she would have heard its distinctive engine a mile away. I sat as they approached. Did she have any idea that the two of them looked like a couple? Call me paranoid, but it didn't seem right. I pulled to the shoulder, cut the ignition and stepped out not wanting to leave them at this charade any longer than I had to.

Hagen held his chin up the way he always did around my brothers. It seemed like he was trying to measure up to them, and I was glad to read that I intimidated him.

"Hi Lacey," Madison said, all smiles. Her face was pink from the cool evening air and the walk through rows of starts she had planted over the weekend. I loved the way she glowed when she walked her property and remembered that excited smile the afternoon we'd borrowed Gran's tractor and taken turns tilling the soil. "I was telling Hagen about what else we've got planned for the garden."

"And I pointed out she could easily hold twenty bulls down here."

I caught Madison's eye roll and wondered what it was about.

"I got the irrigating done, so I'm ready to roll. Once I lock up, we can go."

"You want a ride up to the house?" I asked them.

"Sure!" Madison said, heading to my car.

"I won't fit in that thing," sneered Hagen.

"You could ride Houdini," I suggested jokingly.

As he had on the road, Houdini came to attention at the mention of his name. He took a deep breath and sneezed all over Hagen.

"Damn horse!" he bellowed. Hagen always worried about whether he was pressed or not.

His work done, Houdini turned and headed up the road. Madison looked at me, and I shrugged. I couldn't care less about Hagen. I wanted only to get Madison alone to talk about how she had to shut down his advances.

"I'll climb in the back. You ride shotgun," Madison said.

I clenched my teeth but angled my head to let him know it was okay with me. Once he'd folded in his long frame, I gunned the motor and zipped up the drive ready for Madison's gentleman caller to hit the road. In the rearview mirror, I locked eyes with Madison, trying to convey how very important it was for her to give him the boot. In case she'd missed my meaning, I highlighted it by taking a few steps toward the house after I parked. I was not going to stand around and make small talk with Hagen and pretend that his presence didn't make me furious.

Hagen did not move toward his truck. His glance alternated between me and Madison, who said nothing. I pocketed my keys. Signal three. He goes. I stay. Madison reached up to rub her forehead the way she did when she was stymied but caught herself and lowered her hand back to her side. Did he know her habit of fanning her fingers on her forehead as if she could massage her thoughts into place? I doubted it. Why did I feel so threatened?

I broke the stalemate by leaving them. Let her explain, I reasoned, letting myself into her house. In the kitchen, I opened the fridge for something to do more than because I was thirsty or had any intentions of finding something for dinner. If I didn't do something, I would hover by the window, and hovering made me even angrier. A minute went by. Two. What the fuck were they talking about anyway?

Don't get jealous. Don't get jealous. Don't get jealous, I chanted to myself. *It's not jealousy!* I answered back, allowing myself to fan my feelings instead of stuff them away. *You will not date someone who doesn't acknowledge you as her girlfriend!*

Five long minutes later, Madison came in. "I'm sorry," she had the grace to offer.

Don't say it's okay. I bit my tongue. "Do you know why I drove over?"

Her eyes flicked to mine but didn't stay. She easily read my mood.

"Shawneen came by my shop, that's why. Because she doesn't want me standing in the way of what you could have with Hagen. You have to know that walking the fields with him is leading him on. Surely you can see that."

"I was showing him all the work I've already put in."

"That's not how he interpreted it."

"How do you know?"

"Because the guy likes you, and until you tell him that you're gay or even better that we're dating, he's thinking that he has a chance. Out there, the way you stood closer to him than me, that tells him that he's in the game."

"Lacey, you know I'm not interested in him. I know you don't like him, but he's harmless and not that bad to be around. He can be useful, even if he doesn't know the difference between a bull and a steer."

Her comment froze my brain, and I stared at her in confusion.

"Twenty bulls in one pasture! Absurd! They'd kill each other. Clearly he doesn't know his ass from his elbow."

I closed my eyes briefly to find my focus again. "I don't care if you spend time with him as long as he knows the terms, that you and I are the ones who are together."

"I spend all my time with you. I have the rainbow on my truck. He can't be that dim."

"Yes he can! You just said he doesn't know the difference between a bull and a steer."

"What would you like me to do? Hold your hand?"

"That might be a start, but a guy like Hagen…If you don't lay it out in words, you're leading him on. Not everyone is as perceptive as Ruth. Some people have to be told."

"If I tell him, he'll tell Shawneen."

"Shawneen is exactly why I'm here! She obviously thinks that Hagen has a chance with you, and I'm sure Hagen's buying that hook, line and sinker." Through the doorway, I could see Shawneen's curtains still hanging where she'd placed them. "That woman is toxic."

"I just met her. I came up here to…" Her eyes pleaded with me to drop it, to give her time to negotiate things with the mother she'd never known. "How am I supposed to tell Shawneen when I barely know her?"

"Do you really want to know her?"

"She's my mother."

"If she wanted to be your mother, wouldn't she have tracked you down after Charlie left? You said she had letters from you."

Madison recoiled as if I'd slapped her. "She's making an effort now," she said quietly.

Shawneen's motives had crept into the tail end of our last conversation, and now that she'd had her little chat with me, I thought I had a pretty good read on what her motives were. "With your resort," I pointed out, "she sees an opportunity. That's who she is. Do you really see her as making an effort with you?" She turned from me, making me regret my words. "Madison…"

"Charlie didn't exactly make an effort either, but you encouraged me to spend time with him and try. Maybe the same thing is true for Shawneen. Do you know what it's like to live a stone's throw from a parent who totally ignores you? I moved here, you know. I want to settle here, and it would be really nice to have a mother. If I tell her I'm gay…What if she hates me? I'm stuck here with that."

"Then it's her loss," I said honestly. Madison sucked in a breath. "I know it's a loss for you too. I know how badly you want to find something with her, but at what cost? You *have* to tell her who you are."

Her shoulders drawn forward, she looked as lost as she had the first day I'd seen her in my shop. I could see how she'd been searching for something, trying to fill a hole she'd felt her entire life and how maybe Shawneen could fill it. But that wasn't the Madison I loved. The thought gave me pause.

I was in love.

My anger told my heart to shut up.

Everything aside from my heart said to push by Madison and leave, let her see what she was losing. I wanted what I felt to matter more than Shawneen, for Madison to put us before anything else. I wanted her to hurt as much as I did…which was absurd. I didn't like what I was feeling, but in punishing her for my feeling frustrated, I was punishing us both. No words would fix this. Despite my rational reservations, my heart persevered and prompted me to step forward and wrap my arms around her.

"I can't…" whispered Madison.

"We'll figure it out," I whispered, hoping there could be truth in my words. She held on to me like a lifeline, so hard I almost suggested we cancel going over to Hope and Dani's.

She sucked in a long breath through her nose, held it and whooshed it out. "Ready to go?"

"Are you sure? I could text them that we can't make it."

"If we don't go, they'll all think that I'm stealing their friend away from them. I don't want to be that girlfriend."

"They'd understand." I didn't want her to feel pressured.

"Give me a minute, and I'll be ready."

I waited on the front porch hoping to talk to Houdini about Hagen. He lived up to the elusiveness of his name, so when Madison joined me, I shelved the issue.

* * *

Gabe and Brenna had beaten us there and were sifting through the boxes of games. There was no sign of Della.

"Hide that one," I heard Gabe say as Dani hugged us hello.

"What are you hiding?" I asked.

"Nothing!" He shoved a box under a couch cushion.

"You're not hiding Taboo, are you? It's my favorite," I said.

"We don't stand a chance with you if we play Taboo. You killed us last time."

"You can be on my team."

"I want to play Apples to Apples," he said.

"That game requires no skill at all," I complained.

"Which is why it's fun. Am I right?" He looked for support in Brenna.

"Apples to Apples works," Brenna said.

When he looked to Madison, she threw her hands up and said, "I'm too new to vote."

Hope joined us with a bowl of chips in one hand and tray of assorted chocolates in the other. "What about cards tonight?"

"Don't say Hearts. We are *not* playing Hearts," Dani said.

"Too many players for Hearts," Hope said. "I thought we should play…"

Dani shook her head. "No cards. Let's try that new Smart Ass one."

"I'm surprised that's not the one you said to hide," Madison quipped. "I'm sure Lacey kicks ass at it."

Dani high-fived her, and Gabe threw his arm around her shoulder and squeezed. "I like this one. She can stay."

"Glad she got your vote," I said, beaming at Madison's grin.

"How did your first guests work out?" Hope asked Madison.

"They really enjoyed their stay. They said it was the perfect spot to honeymoon. The time they weren't in their room, they were out at the hot springs. I think that's going to be a great selling point!"

"Hot springs? I love a hot spring," Dani said. "Do you have to be a guest to take a dip?" She sidled up to Hope.

"Between guests, I'd be happy to point you in the right direction. I've got the path there all evened out and marked. Now I'd like to make the actual spring less rustic."

"What do you want to change?" Dani asked.

"Right now it's about as big as an old claw-foot tub. I'd like to push out the sides a little bit, pull in some of the large, flat stones from nearby and make a more comfortable place to sit."

"But it's private?"

"Absolutely. Can't see a soul. And sitting there listening to the wind in the trees…" Madison and I had spent many evenings there listening to the forest orchestra in the treetops.

"It sounds great," Gabe said. "What do you think about Quincy as a honeymoon destination?" he asked Brenna.

"Good for commerce. Want a drink?"

"You sure you know what you're doing?" I asked him when Brenna disappeared.

He rocked back on his heels. "Oh, yeah."

"I'm so excited that it went well. Pretty soon, you're going to have more business than you can handle, and you'll be pining for the quiet days," Hope said.

She left with our drink orders, and we settled in the living room. Madison scooted close to me and rested her hand on my leg. Hope set up the game and ran through the instructions. All of the afternoon's anxiety washed away to be replaced by ribbing and laughter. I saw that the people who mattered most accepted Madison and me together, and that was all I needed. At least for the night.

CHAPTER THIRTY-FIVE

Madison

As much as I'd enjoyed game night with all of Lacey's friends, her words about Shawneen ate at me. Over and over, I heard *That woman is toxic* and *Shawneen's a piece of work*. If we were talking about a potential guest, I would have accepted her assessment and avoided the person. There was certainly enough about Shawneen that grated on me, but I just couldn't seem to walk away from her. She was my mother, and part of me was still waiting to hear that she was sorry for abandoning me.

Lacey was right about Hagen though, and it wasn't fair to her for me to let him hang around just because I didn't want to risk pushing Shawneen away. I was going to have to be honest with them, and though more daunting, it was better to start with Shawneen. My stomach in knots, I slid her curtains off the rods and folded them carefully before slipping them back into their bags.

As I waited for Shawneen to arrive I rehung Ruth's. I'd asked her to meet me at my place and heard her voice shift when she accepted. It was too bad I'd raised her hopes only to dash them, but I couldn't say what I needed to in a restaurant or on the phone. I rehearsed various versions, anticipating her response along a spectrum of anger to hurt to nastiness.

She was late, and I was antsy with guests set to arrive in a few hours, so after I'd swapped out the curtains, I moved the bag to the porch and picked up a mallet and punch I was using to craft a sign for my place. After Charlie had told me about the spring and the origin of the ranch's original name, I decided I liked the ring of Hot Rocks Resort. Lacey had helped me split a log, and I was pounding small dents in the wood around my lettering to make it raised. It was tedious, but I enjoyed the simplicity of the task and the rustic product taking shape under my mallet.

The Nova finally pulled into view. I didn't get up to greet Shawneen, dressed in her black slacks and red work blouse. She hated the soft-soled black sneakers she wore to save her back. I considered the waitress who had once charmed Charlie and had kept on charming her customers when she tucked her wedding ring out of sight. Even now, I saw that her hands were bare. Was Dennis happy to live together without being married, or did she continue to find that she got better tips without a ring on?

I swallowed my anger and pointed to the bag. "I didn't want the receipt to expire on the curtains."

She walked to the bag and peeked inside, then glanced at the original curtains. "I thought you liked them."

I almost softened my reason, saying that I was hoping they would grow on me, but I heard Lacey saying subtlety would be lost on her and leave me open for another pitch. "The truth is someone made those curtains for me, and I like them. They're what I wanted."

"Well why didn't you say so before I spent all that time hanging these?" She rested a fist at her waist.

I rested the mallet against my thigh. "Maybe because I didn't want to be rude in front of the guest you'd brought. You kind of threw me for a loop, and I..." If she'd known me at all, I wouldn't have had to explain how long it takes me to process how to react and what to say. But she had already decided that she knew what her daughter would like. It didn't matter to her that it didn't fit me at all. With a deep breath, I continued... "I didn't know how to say that Lacey and I are seeing each other."

"I know you two are friends."

"She told me that you stopped by to say you were concerned that if she was here too much Hagen would start to think I'm gay. I thought the rainbow sticker on my truck made it pretty clear that I am."

"Well you've hardly given Hagen a chance."

"I don't need to. I'm with Lacey."

"My daughter isn't a queer."

I didn't know how to respond to that. Was I supposed to correct her? Comment on who my mother was? Lacey would have fired back something like *my mom isn't a whore*, but like I said, it takes me a long time to figure out the right way to respond, especially when my feelings are in turmoil.

"Is this because I let Charlie raise you on his own? He raised you like a boy and got you all confused, didn't he? I told him a girl needs a woman to raise her."

"I am not confused." I stood up and faced her squarely. "I know I'm a woman, and I love women. And for your information, I grew up in a pink room with a loving couple who modeled what a family is way better than you ever did. Ruth never forgot to pick me up from girl scouts or soccer."

"What do you know about being a parent? What do you know about a child ruining your life, your dreams?"

"How did I ruin your dreams? You're still doing the exact same thing you were when Charlie left you. If you felt so saddled by us, you could've done anything you wanted when he left. You didn't have to take care of me anymore. You could have done anything. Why didn't you?"

"He didn't divorce me, did he? How was I supposed to know if he was gone for good or if he'd come back for me? I was never free. He made sure I wouldn't forget, sending me those letters you wrote."

I gasped with surprise. "You got my letters?"

"A few scribblings. I couldn't make out what they said. Didn't have a return address, did they? And sent from Montana. Wyoming."

Those first years we were with Bo, he often sent Charlie on trips to pick up new breeding stock. It stunned me to realize the lengths Charlie had gone to mislead Shawneen. Where his concern was to protect me, I didn't get the impression that she would have checked those details because she missed her little girl enough to track her down. More likely, she felt like Charlie owed her something.

"Left me with a rent I couldn't afford," she said, confirming what I'd suspected. "When I got evicted, I had to find somewhere to live, but anyplace I checked out around here meant I had to answer a lot of questions. Where you two went. Why you left. How exactly was I supposed to get over that? How was I supposed to make anything of my life with the whole town talking about me like that?"

Tense silence strung between us. She still felt like Charlie owed her. She wasn't interested in who I was. She was interested in how she could recoup her losses. She wanted my property, not me. It had never been about me. It was and would always be about her.

"No," she continued. "I didn't expect you thought about any of that, about how what he done affected me. And you can forget about seeing that McAlpine girl. No child of mine is going to parade around this town like those freaks with their child."

Even though Lacey had told me exactly what Shawneen thought of Hope and Dani, her words stung. I heard her ice-cold heart in them and knew no words of mine could ever warm it. There was no point in arguing with her, and I wanted nothing more than for her to leave. She had let me down despite how low I'd set my expectations. "I am not your child, Shawneen."

"You are sorely mistaken if that's what you think. You don't think people got to talking after we started eating at that filthy place? I should have spoke my mind from the beginning. No way in hell people didn't put two and two together. You don't know how small this town is. You can't think that it's okay to set up some gay getaway here in the mountains. We won't stand for it."

As mad as I was, I couldn't help smiling at her use of that phrase.

"How is that funny?" she sneered. "We won't stand for it."

A professor I'd had in college had explained that the common phrase so many used originated from farm culture. He explained that "I can't stand it" is tied to horse breeding. Most of the time when a mare in heat is introduced to a stallion, nature takes its course. But sometimes, the mare won't let the stallion mount her, won't stand still, hence the phrase *she can't stand him*. After that visual, I never used the phrase again. Given the choice, people will say the stallion is more powerful than a mare, but listening to Shawneen made me see that the mare has power too. She can say no. "It's not funny," I agreed. Without waiting for a reply, I turned and strode across my porch.

"You overestimate how fond this town is about people like you," she called after me as I entered my house and gently closed the door. I didn't respond. I had nothing more to say to her. I'd overestimated how much I needed to make peace with the woman who had birthed me instead of focusing on what really mattered—the people in my life who were fond of me.

Inside, I pulled my cell phone from my back pocket and was about to select Ruth's number when her ringtone came through. I punched receive. "Ruth?"

"Madison. I hate to ask this of you when I know you're just getting your feet under you, but..." her voice cracked, and she sobbed.

"What is it? What's wrong?"

"Bo's had a heart attack. He's...he's at the hospital now. Can you...?"

Dust from the Nova rose up into the trees as Shawneen sped toward the road.

"I'll be there as soon as I can. How is he now?" I ran to my room to throw my nightshirt and a change of clothes in a bag. I did my best to tick through my nighttime routine, adding my toothbrush and phone charger as I strode from room to room.

All I heard was Ruth crying. I'd never heard her cry before, and I felt helpless, like she was locked on the other side of a door to which I had no key.

"Ruth…" I got no response which worried me. How was a child supposed to help her… "Mom…It'll be okay. I'll be there as soon as I can."

Her sobs continued, and I felt my heart breaking. Not waiting for her reply, I told her I loved her and disconnected.

I had to leave but I couldn't without taking care of Hot Rocks. My guests would be arriving in an hour, which was what I was trying to explain to Lacey. I needed someone to stand in for me. How had I not seen how alone I was? Even without a full house, I was completely stuck without staff. Until I had a steady income, I had thought that I could swing everything on my own, but I hadn't considered what to do in an emergency. All I knew was that I had to get to Ruth and Bo.

"Slow down, slow down," Lacey said, interrupting my rapid-fire words. "Where are you going?"

"Home. Ruth needs me. Bo's had a heart attack."

"You're not driving like this." I heard her tools hitting her bench as she tossed them down.

"I'm already packed but I'm stuck until I know Hot Rocks is okay," I insisted. I bent over at the waist, trying to ease the spinning sensation.

"You sound like you're a mess. I'm not letting you drive down to Paradise alone. Let me drive you."

"I just need you to be here as soon as you can in case they want to check in early, okay? That's all I need from you right now." Too late I heard how my words sounded and knew how she had taken them when she answered.

"All you need…"

If I'd remembered what I'd said to Shawneen, I might have been able to salve the wound, but there was only one word in my mind, Bo, and the easiest way to get to him was to have Lacey step in for me. "I don't want to fight. I just want to be on the road."

"Give me five minutes to see if Hope or…"

"I don't know if Bo has five more minutes. I'm leaving a key under the mat. Can you help me or not?"

"Call me when you get there, okay?"

I finally sighed with relief. "Okay. Thank you." I clicked off before she could even reply. I jotted a quick note for Lacey, letting her know how to check in the guests. I knew she wanted to be with me, but she had to see how much it meant to me to be able to walk away and trust that she could manage my little resort.

Tossing my stuff into the passenger seat, I swung around in the drive and sped down to the road as fast as Shawneen had, to hell with the dust I usually tried to minimize. I needed to call Lacey and tell her that I'd told Shawneen. Feeling my hands shaking on the wheel, I knew it was better to focus on driving. We could catch up once I was down there and knew that Bo was going to be okay.

CHAPTER THIRTY-SIX

Madison

I wished I'd asked Ruth what was happening, but she was crying so hard, I don't know if I could have gotten any more information out of her. Questions for my mom about my dad. I smiled as the truth of the words hit me. I'd told Shawneen they were my family, and they were. How had I ever doubted that? They had raised me as their daughter, but I had kept them at a careful distance, always worried about hurting Charlie's feelings and wondering about my "real" mom.

Now Mom needed me. After all the years I'd invested thinking of a figment called Shawneen as my mom, I was finally pointed in the right direction and heading to the woman who had been my mom for twenty years. I catalogued my memories with Bo and Ruth in the hour and a half it took to get to the hospital, ending with their meeting Lacey. I wished I could go back and introduce her to my parents more officially, acknowledging not only how important Lacey was but how important Bo and Ruth were to me. I vowed to fix that as I found parking and jogged to the building.

Ruth was right inside the door. And Charlie.

Why wouldn't she be by Bo's bedside?

In his room?

Why didn't he have a room?

My heart felt like lead as my footsteps slowed, realization settling on me like a heavy blanket. If I stopped my feet it wouldn't be true. But Ruth stood and held her arms out to me, pulling me forward into a truth I didn't want to hear.

"When?" I sobbed as we fell into each other.

"He died in the ambulance," Charlie supplied quietly. He lay his warm palm on my shoulder.

"You...you didn't tell me." My brain was swimming. She'd known when she called, and she hadn't said anything? She'd let me hold on to the hope that he was alive?

"I couldn't. I couldn't," Ruth said.

"But..." I gasped.

"I'm sorry. I'm so sorry. I needed you here. It was so fast," she sobbed.

"Where is he?"

Ruth pulled away from me and looked to Charlie. His face was drawn. "Are you sure you want to see him? You might want to wait for the viewing. Right now..."

"No. I have to see him," I insisted. "I didn't get to tell him...I never said..." I gulped for air. Did I dare say what I'd felt about Bo to Charlie?

"He knew." Charlie's Adam's apple wobbled stoically.

My anger flared. "How could he have known?" Inexplicably, my fingers closed to a fist that landed on Charlie's chest. He jumped but didn't move away from the blows. After I'd landed a good six or seven punches, he got his arms around me. I struggled to free myself from him but couldn't. It should have been Bo holding me. I tried to imagine what he would have said to my calling him Dad. His blue eyes had told me everything he ever felt, but they'd never mirror my claiming him. "I never told him," I said over and over as my tears fell. "I never told him."

"He was a better father than I ever was. We all knew that, even you. Even if you didn't have the words for it. It was in your eyes."

"Mom?" I tested Charlie's claim on Ruth.

"He knew." She pursed her lips trying hard not to cry. Her shoulders came back a speck, as if my label gave her back a little of her strength. "I knew you'd want to see him. I wanted us to say goodbye together. Can you?"

My eyes welled, and I nodded, unable to speak. We linked arms, and she led me to the emergency room where a nurse walked with us to a curtained-off bed. She paused before drawing it, waiting for my signal. I nodded again, completely unprepared to say goodbye to the man who had contributed so much to who I was.

Tears slipped freely down my face as I stepped forward. Bo's eyes were his best feature, and I'd rarely seen him asleep, so to see his face without that sparkle hardly felt like looking at Bo at all. Ruth wrapped her hand around his, and I lay my hand on his lifeless arm. "Thank you," I whispered. "I wish it hadn't taken me so long to figure out how much you gave me."

"You stole his heart from the beginning. Both of ours. You don't know how much it meant when you moved to the house and shared yourself with us. You have been our gift." We held each other and cried. I was aware of Charlie by the door, but he kept his distance until we'd dried our faces.

I left the room in a trance, let Charlie take my car and rode home with Ruth. After we got to the ranch, he handed me the keys and hugged the two of us tightly. Though Ruth invited him to join us, he silently retreated to his trailer. Only when Ruth turned the key in the lock did I picture Lacey finding the key I'd left her. "I have to call Lacey," I apologized, not wanting to leave Ruth alone.

"I don't know about you, but I haven't eaten all day. I'm going to put some things out. We'll feel better for having something."

"Maybe huevos rancheros?"

She smiled like she was watching Bo pour on Tabasco sauce complaining that she never made anything spicy enough. "That sounds good. Make your call."

It was hard. I didn't want to cry again. I didn't want to admit that I'd been wrong about needing her with me. I wished she could somehow hold me before I fell apart. Start there, I told myself. "I wish I could have your arms around me right now," I said when she answered. My voice caught, and the tears came.

"Madison. Oh, Madison. Is he gone?"

"Yes."

She growled her frustration. "I need to be there. With you."

"But I needed your help there. I still do. I...Can you stay the weekend, so I can be here with Ruth?"

"I can get someone else to run things here."

"I don't have anyone else to ask, Lacey."

"Yes, you do. You have friends here who will help you."

"I couldn't possibly ask your friends..." I stopped unable to imagine calling any of Lacey's friends to ask them for such a favor.

"Please trust me?" Lacey asked gently.

Though still uncomfortable with the idea of burdening people I barely knew, I remembered how much I wanted her to hold me. I rested my head on my fingertips appreciating how cool they felt against the pulse at my temples.

"Madison?" Lacey prompted me. "Can you let me take care of things here my way?"

I took a shaky breath. "Okay. But I've got to go now. Ruth wants to feed me."

"Madison?"

I'd been about to hang up and was standing at the doorway of the kitchen watching Ruth slide fried eggs onto tortillas. "Yeah?"

"Madison, I love you."

Ruth looked up at my stunned face. I didn't know how to respond. The words echoed around in my head looking for a place to settle. "My eggs are done."

"What?" She sounded confused, and rightly so.

I shut my eyes as her words found their way into my heart. My chest had felt so tight from the moment I saw Ruth at the hospital. That now eased, ever so slightly, and I felt my chest expand enough to take a deeper breath. "I love you too," I whispered.

"Good."

We said our goodbyes, and I stood there holding the phone as Ruth added avocado and homemade salsa to our dinners. She passed a plate to me.

"How's Lacey?"

"Frustrated with me for not waiting for her to make the drive down with me."

Ruth's expression told me she agreed with Lacey. "I expected to see her with you when you came to the hospital."

"I was worried. I asked her to stay at the resort. I don't know what I was thinking."

"You were thinking that you could protect yourself. You've always thought that if you kept to yourself, you could creep through life without touching people or being touched. You think that by keeping to your space, you won't get hurt." There was a sternness behind her usual caring tone.

She was right.

Ruth set down her own plate and came around the table to wrap her arms around me. "Let her be close to you. She lights you up from the inside. Bo saw it too. I know you never asked our opinion, but Bo and I talked about what it meant for you to bring her here, and I want you to know he liked Lacey a lot."

"I should have told you."

Ruth laughed, startling me. She sat down across from me and said, "Thank Charlie for that. One of those trips you made home from college, he shuffled up after you left asking what we thought of that rainbow flag sticker. The three of us sat here at this table for an hour wondering whether you had a girlfriend you were too scared to tell us about. I remember Bo said it probably came through his side—his favorite aunt had herself a lady friend. I had to remind him that he hadn't actually contributed any genetics. We both looked at Charlie who waved us off. 'Don't look at me!' he hollered." Ruth smiled. "There. That's a fine memory."

I shut my eyes to imagine the three of them sitting at this table talking about me while I was away at school, all of them trying to figure out who I was. I took her hand across the table.

Ruth swallowed hard. "No more should-haves. Only what was. Agreed?"

"Agreed." Though she sat back, she used only her right hand. The two of us ate our dinner that way, our left hands joined in the middle of the table. At the same time that I felt Bo slip away, I felt closer to Ruth than I ever had. I wanted to say how I wish I'd been able to call him my dad but stopped myself hearing the *should have* I said I'd avoid.

CHAPTER THIRTY-SEVEN

Lacey

"Are you out of your mind? Do you even hear what you're asking? Do you?" Della blew up in my ear.

"I know." I put my thumb between my eyebrows and shut my eyes. "Madison would never ask..."

"But you would. You know what it feels like to have your ex-girlfriend call to ask if you will do her girlfriend's work? No! Because I. Would. Never. Do. That. To. You."

"Understood." I should have skipped asking Della, but I thought that she might be swayed to help out the newcomer to the neighborhood. The fact that I was dating and she wasn't clearly overshadowed that.

"But tell her I'm really sorry her dad died." The concern seemed genuine.

"I'll be sure to pass that along. Bye Della."

Next, I called Hope who was characteristically empathetic as I explained what was going on. Sadly, she could only offer to help feed the weekend guests with food from Cup of Joy. She pointed out that sleeping in a house with a child who called during the night was nowhere in Madison's brochures, and Joy didn't sleep well when her moms messed with her routine in any way at all. "How are you doing in all of this?" she asked before I could slip under the radar of her concern.

I glanced at the clock. I hadn't made any promises to Madison about when I'd be there, and her asking made me realize how much I wanted to get off my chest. "I don't really know. The last time we really talked, I told her that I was frustrated with her for not telling Hagen that he doesn't have a chance."

"How can he not know?"

"People know what they want to know. The real issue is that Madison won't just tell him."

"She's not you," Hope said gently.

I opened my mouth to say I knew that, but shut it again realizing that I did, in fact, want her to deal with Hagen the way I would. "That's fair. But if I lost my dad suddenly, I'd want her there with me. I wouldn't be asking her to sit tight and hold down the fort." I waited for Hope to say something and then heard what I'd said. "Oh. Shit. Is driving down there the worst idea ever?"

"No. I think that once you're there, she'll realize how wonderful it is to have someone to lean on. It sounds like she doesn't have a whole lot of experience with that. So you teach her."

"Thanks Hope."

"Anytime. And you know Gabe would be a great stand-in host. His dad can manage without him for a bit, and he makes a good show looking all Western the way he does."

"Yeah. He was next on my list."

* * *

Many hours later, after I'd made more phone calls, settled the second set of guests in and handed off all other Hot Rocks duties to Gabe, I finally held Madison. The way she stepped into my arms and the look I caught on Ruth's face before she disappeared into the kitchen to give us privacy confirmed that

I'd made the right decision. I didn't think about anything else, just wrapped my arms around Madison as protectively and reassuringly as I could. She wept, and I rocked her, and we stayed like that for as long as she needed, until she stepped back and mopped her face.

"I'm sorry. Do you need…" She looked around as if trying to place what she was supposed to offer.

I waved off her concern. "Don't worry about me."

"I can't believe you're here."

"I can," Ruth hollered from the kitchen. "Now that you've said your hellos, come have something cool to drink. I'm sure you need it driving down into this heat."

"It is cooler up in the mountains," I said, following Ruth's voice to the kitchen. She set down the pitcher of lemonade and hugged me. "I'm so sorry about Bo."

Ruth squeezed me again before she released me. "Doesn't quite seem real. I keep thinking I dreamed the whole thing, and he'll be coming in and moving that damn hand towel from the bathroom. Forty-two years he carried the hand towel with him as he dried his hands…more than that. He did it when we were dating. The years we were together…I barely remember the girl I was before I met him. We spent most of our lives together."

Madison moved to her side and guided her to the table. I tried not to react when Madison chose the chair next to Ruth's. She pulled it close, the whole length of her body in contact with Ruth who had closed her tired eyes and rested her head against Madison, whose eyes held the same weight of sadness. The gravitational pull had shifted between them. I was sitting with Madison and her mother.

"But now you've got me," Madison said.

"Yes. Not a day goes by that I'm not thankful for that. And you have Lacey."

I smiled weakly, uncertain of their new dynamic.

"Hope and Dani didn't mind being asked?" Madison asked, reminding me of how self-conscious she'd been about asking for help.

"No, but they couldn't stay out there, not with Joy."

"Who was there last night?" Madison's posture shifted to worry.

"Gabe was happy to."

"Gabe!" Madison exclaimed.

"Gabe's the one that thinks he's a cowboy?" Ruth asked.

"No, that's Hagen. Gabe's Lacey's friend. He *is* a cowboy. He lent me the tractor, but I barely know him."

"That's not true," I argued. "He was as happy to do this as he was to haul Gran's tractor over for us. It's the weekend. He doesn't really have to do anything. Hope's on dinner, so he'll occupy the place while they're there and lock up when they're gone. I'll get my keys from him whenever I'm back."

"Still. I wish…" Madison looked at Ruth as if to gauge what she should say. "I hate having to owe someone. I have no idea how to repay him."

"That's not how he thinks. It's not how any of them think." I lied a little remembering Della's answer when I asked her to stay.

"Well, at least it's only this weekend."

"What does that mean?"

"I'm canceling the reservations I have for next weekend and closing the online booking calendar."

"Madison!" Ruth exclaimed.

"I need to be here with you."

"But you only just opened," Ruth argued.

"I know, but I can't be up there right now. I can't leave you down here alone."

"Charlie and I can manage. Honestly, Charlie could manage on his own. You're starting your life up there. After the funeral, I thought you'd head back."

Madison threw her arms around Ruth. "I need to be here with you," she whispered.

I stared at my hands in my lap thinking about how I'd driven down to offer my support only now realizing that didn't mean she would accept it, or that it was needed. Over Madison's shoulder Ruth caught my eye, urging me to say something. But what was there to say? If she wouldn't listen to her mother, I couldn't imagine her listening to me, but Ruth's look was insistent. I had to say something.

"Don't do anything yet, Madison. You don't want to ruin anyone's vacation, especially not when you're building your reputation. I could always run the place next weekend if you need to be here. Don't cancel anything. Block off a few days on the online calendar if you need to. You've put so much work into your place."

Ruth nodded, satisfied. I felt like I'd passed an important exam. More importantly, Madison sat up and met my eyes. She nodded mutely, but at least she nodded.

CHAPTER THIRTY-EIGHT

Madison

I woke up too warm, the sun already high in the sky and the body next to me radiating heat. I opened my eyes but resisted stretching, not wanting to wake Ruth. Sleep made the sadness that tightened her features when she was awake disappear. I lay quietly in Bo's spot wondering why I'd never crawled in with them. Why had I stayed a guest in their home for so many years when they had so obviously welcomed me into their hearts, not just their home?

What I would have given to have been there in bed with my parents. In that space between sleep and wakefulness, I allowed myself the fantasy of rewriting my youth. I imagined snuggling next to Ruth and having her put her arms around me. Or would I have put my head on Bo's strong chest? Surely, he would have carried me back to my own bed when I had fallen back asleep feeling safe and comforted. I'd thought about it before. I remembered hovering at their doorway, afraid of waking them, to say that a storm or a shadow had startled me from my sleep.

The sound of the back door brought me more fully awake. Lacey had woken by herself again. I willed myself to fall back asleep where I could avoid the hurt in her eyes. We went to bed together in the queen-sized guest bed across the hall from my childhood room, and it felt wonderful to relax into her arms and let her comfort me. She did her best to settle me into sleep by running her fingers through my hair, but she was always first to fade, her hands slowing and then stopping, resting on my shoulder until I shifted away into a position from which I could watch her sleep. She slept deeply, uncomplicated by the worries that floated around in my head.

What was it like to have parents who were still together, who enjoyed each other's company and who had always wanted her? It was simply the life Lacey had always known. These thoughts spinning, I couldn't stop listening to Ruth as she wandered around the house, lost without Bo.

Unable to resist, I would slip out and join Ruth downstairs. We sat up late looking at photo albums, Ruth avoiding the bed Bo would not be sleeping in ever again. She only agreed to go up to bed when she was past exhaustion, falling almost immediately into sleep and leaving me to think about how Bo had been a father figure to me and worry about what my role would be at the funeral. Did his friends and family already see me as his child, or would they find it strange to see me standing by Ruth?

Lacey climbed the stairs, hesitating at the top step. She would be worrying about Ruth and me getting up and getting ready for the service. My feet found the floor, and I slipped out as Ruth reached for the clock.

"I'll put on the tea. You can shower first."

Ruth blinked her approval of the plan, and I stepped out into the hall.

"I didn't know if I should wake you."

"I know," I said, realizing that she'd been restless for a long while wandering around the unfamiliar house by herself. "What have you been doing?"

"Helping Charlie with the stock. He's getting cleaned up now."

For the service. I needed to start breakfast.

"How's your mom?" she asked.

My eyes met hers, and I was so grateful to see genuine concern instead of the veiled hurt of the previous day. I loved that she had begun calling Ruth my mom without my having said anything. Tears of gratitude sprang to my eyes. I didn't quite understand what I had done to deserve Lacey. She got me, sometimes before I even got myself. I stepped into the arms that were always waiting for me and tried not to think about Ruth missing Bo.

"Come on." Her voice was gentle. "Let's get some food into you."

She guided me to breakfast and then prodded me to the shower. I resisted each step of getting ready as if avoiding the service would change the fact that Bo was dead, and she directed me as patiently as Charlie did the cattle. That's what I felt like as Lacey and Charlie shut the doors on Ruth's sedan. Lacey rode in the front and Charlie drove, and I sat in the back with Ruth, watching the scenery and wondering what the cattle must be thinking as they zoom down the highway to the slaughterhouse.

Arms linked, Ruth and I made our way into the sanctuary of the Methodist church we attended sporadically. I recognized the minister but not the hymns. I only knew the joyous Christmas and Easter music, not these slow, somber songs. Ruth sang. I held the hymnal without singing, staring at the closed casket, my shoulder pressed to Lacey's.

When the minister finished his eulogy, I was surprised to see Charlie approach the pulpit, looking foreign to me in a suit two sizes too big, pressed but hanging loosely from his body. I'd seen Bo in a suit before, but I'd never seen Charlie in anything but his dusty, rugged work attire.

He swallowed, and his Adam's apple bobbled. He fidgeted and tried to look at the small congregation. His eyes flitted over to Ruth and me ever so briefly before he took out a piece of paper that trembled in his hand.

"I don't see how it's fair for me to be standing here talking to you about this man who succeeded at everything I failed. Bo married his high school sweetheart, and he and Ruth cherished each other the way the Lord intended. He was a proud father and a good one, raising Madison with strong morals and a stronger work ethic." He swallowed hard, and tears stung the back of my eyes. His voice cracked as he continued. "I don't know a finer businessman. Honest. Always more concerned about the animals than profit. He was the very definition of generous, sharing himself like he did. It isn't right that I'm the one standing here talking. If God had any sense, he'd have taken me, but I guess lookin' at it that way, he'll make better company. He'll be sorely missed."

He folded his paper and held it for a moment. His hands didn't know what to do without his hat to spin or settle back on his head. He finally shoved them in the deep pockets and sat back down next to Ruth. I watched as he crumpled. Holding his face in his hands, his body shook with sobbing. Those around us stood for the final hymn, but I was immobilized by Charlie's grief. I'd never seen a single tear slip down his face let alone witness such a flood of emotion. I had to go to him. Already at the center of attention sitting in the front row, I didn't want to invite more, but I simply had to comfort him.

Bending as if I could slip across the row undetected, I inched over and crouched by his side, awkwardly slipping my arm over his shoulder. He started at my touch and turned tear-filled eyes to me. I suddenly felt guilty for abandoning him in his lonely trailer. I'd voted Bo the better man too and was only now seeing how much Charlie had sacrificed. I pushed into his arms and felt his hesitation as I hugged him hard, my own tears falling on his shirt. As his arms tightened, I burrowed my head on his chest. I felt his breath as he pressed his face into my hair.

Only when he pulled away did I realize that the song was over and Charlie was expected to join the pallbearers. I stood and was grateful for Ruth's arm. We followed the coffin and stood at the door for people to press their hands to ours, grip our shoulders, say the words they needed to say.

As the crowd thinned, I looked for Lacey. She was on her phone and caught my eye. Holding up a finger, she smiled apologetically. Still, it was the happiest smile I'd seen in days, and I figured she'd been on the line with someone in Quincy about how she was through with all of the grief in the valley and ready to return home.

I stopped short on that. I'd gone to Quincy looking for home and remembered how certainly I had felt the call of Hot Rocks from the minute I had arrived. But I also felt at home right where I was, Ruth's arm tight around me. How was I supposed to resolve those two things?

CHAPTER THIRTY-NINE

Lacey

I was itching to be home. I'd said as much to my gran when I had called her the day before to say I'd be back in the morning to take over the care of Midnight. It would be good to be in my shop which had been shut four work days. I was happy to have been able to close up as long as I needed to be with Madison, but I couldn't help looking forward to getting back to our life, the rhythm we had when it was just the two of us. Us. The pronoun slammed up against my chest as I remembered that Madison was staying in Paradise with Ruth. I remembered how hard it had been to have one meal without Madison, and now the only solace I had returning to Quincy was that she still hadn't closed the online booking system.

I should have been thrilled for her to finally find the family she had been searching for, but I couldn't help but wonder if she was going to sell Hot Rocks and disappear back to Paradise. What did that make me? I didn't want to be the shit who said *What about me?* to the woman who had lost her dad, but I felt cut loose by her need to stay. I wanted her to come home. I wanted to be the one holding her.

My phone buzzed in my pocket. "Hey Gabe," I answered, unable to feign a good mood.

"You already heard?"

"Heard what?"

"About Madison's place. Did Brenna finally get through to Madison?"

"Why is Brenna trying to get Madison?"

"To talk about Hot Rocks."

"What's going on, Gabe?"

"A neighbor called in a disturbance out there. Brenna responded, and they have someone in custody. She's trying to track down Madison." I was in motion now, running down the stairs. Madison and Ruth were sorting through papers in Bo's desk. I thrust the phone in her face. "Gabe says that the police department's been trying to get you on the line."

Madison reached for my phone while she pulled hers from her pocket. "Gabe? This is Madison. I've had my ringer off all day." Her eyes flicked from me to Ruth. Her face reddened, and she nodded even though Gabe couldn't see her. "I understand… Okay…Yes. Sure." She called up contacts on her phone and punched in a number. "I'll call her now. Thank you, by the way, for helping out last weekend. You didn't have to and…it really helped." It took another minute for them to wrap up the call. When she was finished, Madison calmly handed my phone back to me.

"What the hell's going on?" I blurted.

"My garden's torn up," she said. I didn't think it was possible for her to drift any further away than she already had, but she managed with the short phone call and that phrase.

Ruth took Madison's hand.

"Did he have any other details?" I pressed.

"Not really. All he said was Brenna needs to speak with me. I'd better call her."

She hit send on the number she'd entered into her phone. It must have been Brenna's direct line because once Madison identified herself, she mostly listened. Ruth and I sat by, shut out of the conversation. Ruth still held Madison's hand, and it didn't feel right to step closer. I stood there wanting Madison to acknowledge my presence. She knew I was upset about her staying in Paradise, and now she sat there communicating nothing. I had almost reached my blowing point when she finally spoke.

"No. I appreciate your getting in touch with me, but go ahead and file the report. I'm not interested in taking it to court."

Ruth and I looked at each other. She looked as concerned as I felt. Shouldn't Madison be running any of this by us before she answered Brenna?

"I'm sorry you got roped into any of this. I'm sorry for the misunderstanding." She righted the edges of a stack of papers she'd been sorting. "I really don't think the extra patrol is necessary. I'm sorry for the bother."

She bit her lip as she ended the call. The hesitation in her eyes made me sit down. Whatever it was she had to say, she really didn't want to. "What is it?" I asked.

"I forgot to tell you I came out to Shawneen."

"What! When? When was this?"

"The day that Bo died. I…I told her to come out to the ranch, and I gave her the curtains back, and I told her everything. She didn't take it well. It's all muddy in my head, but she said that I absolutely could not be gay. I'm sure she told Hagen. Brenna has him at the station because he was doing doughnuts in the lower field. A neighbor drove by and reported it."

"What was the stuff about her report and court?"

"She told me she had the official report for me and could send it to the prosecutor if I was interested."

"But you told her to file it?"

"Yeah. It's just a field. He's angry. You were right. I should have said something instead of letting him keep coming around. I'm sure he feels like I led him on."

"You have to take him to court. That's a hate crime!"

"It's not a hate crime," she shot back. "It's a dumb guy being jealous. Why would I want to prosecute when I don't know…"

That's why she'd hesitated.

"You don't know what, Madison," Ruth prompted.

"She doesn't know if she's keeping Hot Rocks." I stood.

"That's why you won't go to court? You're thinking of selling?"

Her eyes went to Ruth, not me. I bit my tongue. I needed to feel something other than my surge of disappointment and anger. "Or have you already decided?"

"I haven't. I haven't decided anything. I can't think right now. All I know is I can't be up there. I need to be here. I need to be close to Bo's things, to Ruth. Everything up there—Shawneen…Hagen…I can't. You understand, don't you? That I can't go back up there?"

"What nonsense are you talking?" Ruth said. "This boy tore up your field, and you're going to walk away? That's *your* place. It's where you belong, and you have to protect that and yourself. You call back and tell her that you changed your mind. That boy has to repair what he's damaged. You can't afford losing all the work you put in."

"It's a field. I can put in more plants, and I could always just wait until next year."

"But he's trying to intimidate you," I argued.

"I'm not there right now to tend it anyway."

"Well you should be," Ruth said determinedly. "Get your things together. I'm calling Charlie to tell him to watch the place."

Madison remained rooted.

"I'm serious, Madison. You have to stand up for yourself." Ruth waited.

"I was wrong about needing to go up there. Wrong about needing my own place, about fulfilling some dream of Charlie's. Everything I always thought I wanted is right here, not up in Quincy."

Her words felt like a punch to the gut. Part of my brain tried to argue that she meant her parents, but that was a tiny sound compared to the reverberating hurt that shouted *she said everything. She never needed you.*

"You don't mean that," Ruth said softly but sternly.

Madison's head snapped up at that and her eyes moved from Ruth to me. *Hi there*, I wanted to wave. *Remember me, the solid girlfriend who came down to be your emotional support?* She might not have meant everything she'd said the way I'd heard it, but she was scared. Whatever Shawneen had said to her had rattled her. She was pulling into herself the way she'd been when I first met her.

I didn't know what my part was in all this. I was on Ruth's side, wanting Madison back in Quincy, but I certainly wasn't objective in my reasoning. I felt bad too, because I'd been pushing Madison to come out to Shawneen and Hagen. "I'm sorry," I said.

Madison looked confused, and I realized that she had no way of following my train of thought.

"About Shawneen. I'm sorry that she reacted the way she did. I wish you'd told me."

She nodded but didn't say anything.

"I'm glad she knows. I…" What I wanted to say was difficult with Ruth standing right there. "I want everyone to know about us, but I'm sorry she reacted like that."

Ruth punctuated my words with a nod and rubbed my shoulder as she left the room. I waited for Madison to speak, but she stood frozen as if her system was simply overloaded. When the shop computer did that, I rebooted it. Maybe that's what she needed. I stepped forward and put my hands on her hips. Her eyes were wide as I leaned in to kiss her. They fluttered closed as our mouths met, and I stepped closer, wrapped my arms around her and tried to convey with my kiss how very much I needed her to come back to Quincy. I felt her relax in my arms. When I pulled away, I said, "I love you, Madison."

Her eyes fluttered open and found mine. "I know. But I don't know why you do. You're so strong and certain about everything, and I'm…not."

"Maybe it's because I never had to search for my family. They were always there. Sometimes too much."

Finally, she smiled.

"So Shawneen was awful. I can't really say I'm surprised. This means I don't have to try to be nice to her, right?"

"Only if you want to keep her business."

"I want to keep you."

She rested her head on my shoulder. "It feels scary to be so far away from Ruth and Charlie."

"But you're not alone. You've got me. How many times do I have to tell you that?"

"Maybe it would be better if you showed me."

I kissed her again for all I was worth. I gave her the kiss that only a fool would walk away from, and for the time being it worked. She took my hand in hers, and we went upstairs to pack our things together.

CHAPTER FORTY

Madison

Lacey dropped me at Hot Rocks. We'd had a quiet ride up the canyon, holding hands whenever the windy road allowed. I was glad for the dark masking the damage Hagen had done to my field as we headed up to the house. Ruth was right behind us. Unlike Lacey, she paused at the gate. I couldn't tell whether she could see the damage to the property or if she was giving me and Lacey a few minutes to ourselves before she drove my truck up to the house.

"Should I stay?" Lacey asked after helping to carry in our things.

"I know you're anxious to get back to your place."

"But if you need me," she whispered.

"I do need you." I buried my face in her neck. "And I'm almost home."

She stepped away from me, and I worried that she'd ask me to explain what I didn't quite understand myself. Instead, she squeezed my hand and said, "I like the sound of that."

On the porch, Ruth hugged her goodnight. "I hope I'm not scaring you away."

"Not at all. I've got to get back to my shop. I have an early morning tomorrow, and it's a lot easier to get up and get going when I don't have any temptations."

It had been a while since I'd made it hard for her to get out of bed. I could see that in her eyes, the question of when I'd be back in that capacity. I winked at her to let her know it was inevitable. Emotionally, I was still sapped, but physically, I still very much wanted her. Being back on my turf made that even clearer. I walked her to her car. In the short time we'd been inside, Houdini had parked himself next to it. He rubbed his head up and down her body.

"Your horse is more feline than equine," she said, bracing against the force.

"He wants you to stay so he can curl up on your lap." I reached up and ran my fingers through her hair, settling back into place what Houdini had rumpled. Cupping her cheek, I kissed her, thanking her for being so supportive but also for giving me space.

"Thanks for that." She lingered a moment longer and then was beetling down the hill. Houdini and I watched until she disappeared around the bend.

"Hope you managed okay without me. It looks like you got yourself fed." I rubbed his ears for a moment until his lip stuck out like an old man with too much chew. Back in the house, I found Ruth standing in the doorway of the room she and Bo had shared when they'd visited together. She hadn't tucked her bags inside any of the rooms. "He was so proud of all you've done. You did so much more than we expected all on your own up here. I'm glad he saw it."

"Me too." I gathered her bags and set them in my room. "I figured you'd bunk with me tonight."

"I really don't want to scare Lacey away. She's lovely for you."

"I know. But she gets it. I promise."

I steered her to the kitchen and pulled out a package of cookies and put on some water for tea. Though I could have crawled right into bed, I sensed that she was still finding it difficult to stop.

"Bo'd be really disappointed if you sold. He knew, we both did, that cattle ranching isn't for you. I don't want you giving up your dream up here. This is where you belong."

"Were you mad at me when I came to Quincy? With Shawneen being here and everything? I wasn't thinking…"

She shushed the rest of my thought away. "I had the gift of your childhood. Even if she had been exactly who you need right now, she can't ever take that away."

"I spent twenty years being mad at Charlie for taking me away from her. He never made sense to me."

"He didn't feel like he knew what to do. He got it into his head that all he could be was a good rancher, so that's what he did. I had no idea he was saving all that money for you, but now it makes sense. That was what he felt he could give you."

I got up and made our tea, standing by the steeping pot. "I thought he didn't like me. I thought I messed up his life, that I'd roped him into a life he didn't want and then forced him to leave the one place he loved. I guess that's what brought me back here. I thought I could fix things, not that he'd get back together with Shawneen, but that…"

"You'd finally be able to understand?"

"Exactly."

"He only ever wanted the best for you," Ruth said gently. "He asked us over and over whether you had enough, if you were happy enough."

"I wish he'd asked me."

I poured our tea, and we stayed up talking until midnight. When she saw that I couldn't keep my eyes open, we tucked into bed, Ruth promising that in the morning she'd pick her own room. I accepted that, knowing we were both figuring out the baby steps back to ourselves.

We were drool-soaked pillows asleep when we heard a truck rumbling up the drive, not the rattling hum of Lacey's Beetle but the knocking of a large diesel. I sat up wiping my face. Ruth put her arm around me to keep me in bed, and we listened as the noisy engine passed the house.

"Hagen," I identified for Ruth. He knew the layout. He angled the truck to the back of the house so the headlights poured right through my bedroom window.

We both stood and instinctually moved out of the flood of light. "You need to call the police," Ruth said.

"He'll go away," I said with a prayer.

He slammed the truck door and both Ruth and I jumped when something hit the side of the house. He'd clambered out of the truck with something in his hand. He popped open a can of beer, and I realized it must have been an empty that he'd thrown. "Came to see the show!" He hollered. "I see you girls in there, just like Shawneen said." He leaned back against the grille of his truck as he chugged down the next beer.

I flattened myself against the wall.

"Madison." I heard the edge in Ruth's voice "You cannot ignore this."

The can he'd been working on hit the window.

"I'm not talking to a drunk guy."

"I wasn't saying you should. I'm saying it's the police department's job to deal with it."

"It's not natural," Hagen growled. "You think you can give her what she needs, Lacey? You don't have what it takes. You'll never have what it takes."

"He's…"

"I don't need to know what he's doing," I hissed. "Get away from the window, would you? If he knows we're listening to him, it'll only encourage him."

"This is ridiculous. You cannot let him camp out and insult you."

"…not safe for a woman to be all alone…Hey!"

"What happened? Did he fall off the truck?" I peeked out of the window. Houdini was butting at Hagen with his giant head.

"Get your damn horse off me, Madison!" he bellowed staggering to his feet.

"Get off my property!"

Hagen grabbed another empty can and crushed it on Houdini's forehead.

"Leave my horse alone!"

"Not until Lacey leaves. Someone's got to put a stop to what you two have been doing."

"Lacey's not even here."

"Don't lie to me," he said, grabbing a hefty rock. "I can see the pair of you." He switched his aim from Houdini and heaved it toward us instead. I jumped back as it shattered the double-paned window.

"That's my mom, asshole!" I stuffed my feet into a pair of work boots.

"Liar! Who do you think sent me out here?"

Cool mountain air poured in through my broken window. I stood in the glow of his headlights and shouted, "Shawneen is not my mother!"

"She said you need a man."

"Well I don't, so go on home."

"Come out and make me."

I crunched across the broken glass and dialed 911. Hagen continued his drunken monologue about our future as he looked for something else to heave. Bent over, Houdini butted him to his knees. "Get!" Hagen shouted, kicking out at Houdini. As the horse advanced, Hagen scrambled up the hood of his truck and up onto the windshield.

"This is Madison Carter," I said when dispatch asked me to state my emergency. "Hagen Weaver's back on my property and sent a rock through my bedroom window."

"I'm sending the officer on duty now, ma'am. Please remain in the house and on the line."

"I am."

"If possible, do not engage him."

"On their way," I whispered to Ruth when I went back to find her throwing on sweats and some shoes. I grabbed pants and a light sweatshirt. When he saw us dressing, Hagen moved to jump off the truck, but Houdini seemed to be having fun blocking him.

Ruth and I waited for the blue and red lights to make their way from town. Brenna parked and approached the house, her hand on her belt. The others swept out to either side of the house, and the drivers stayed by their vehicles.

I stepped out onto the porch. "Hagen's still spouting off back behind the house. Houdini has him pinned on his truck."

She hollered for them to take the patrol car around back and then turned back to us. "What time did all this start?"

Everything I'd been through, the flashing lights, and the late hour had frozen my brain. I just stared at Ruth.

"Twenty minutes?" she guessed.

Brenna's radio on her shoulder crackled to life. "We've got a runner!"

"Is he armed?" Brenna growled.

"Not that I saw," I said. "He was chucking beer cans and rocks, but I couldn't see in his cab to know if he had anything on the gun rack."

"Stay inside." She ran down the steps pulling her flashlight from her belt. We followed her instructions and made a beeline for the kitchen. Three powerful beams sweep over the forested area behind my house.

"I feel like I need a drink." I sank down into a chair searching inside of myself. "I wish Lacey had stayed."

"There's a quick way to fix that."

"I can't call her at three in the morning."

"Why not? She'd want to know. And she'd want to be here. Why is it so hard for you to wake her up?"

"I don't want to impose."

"It's not imposing. It's leaning on someone, letting someone be close enough to you to help you. Don't you see that she would rather be woken up than feel like she was kept at a distance?"

Ruth's words hit hard as I realized how many years I had kept her at a distance. For so long, I hadn't wanted to be a burden, and all that time, she had been waiting for me to call her.

I still cringed ringing Lacey at such an early hour.

"What's wrong?" Her voice was heavy with sleep.

"I'm sorry to wake you," I said.

"Madison?" She sounded confused.

"Brenna and her guys are chasing Hagen, and…" I closed my eyes, hating to ask for anything.

"I'm on my way."

Was it really that easy? For so many years I'd tried to do things on my own figuring that people would respect the one who could take care of herself. I hadn't realized how lonesome that imposed self-reliance felt until I accepted how much better everything was with Lacey by my side.

"I'm fine," I kept assuring her when she got there, her hair sleep rumpled. She'd thrown on the same jeans she'd been wearing when she left and a lightweight fleece. I sank into the softness of her as she ran her hands over my arms and back. "I'm not hurt."

"You could have been," she said, having seen the hole in my window. "You should have had Brenna file her report."

"I thought that would be the end of it."

"Well obviously it wasn't."

Someone knocked on the door, and Ruth jumped up to open it.

"How do you call off the horse?" Brenna said. "Hey Lacey," she said, not batting an eye. "You got him off the road. Care to get him away from the tree Hagen's roosted himself in?"

Lacey laughed. "Houdini's got him up a tree?"

"He had Hagen stuck on the hood of his truck for the longest time. I don't know how he managed to run in the first place," I said.

"All I know is Hagen won't come down with the horse camped out, and my guys can't get that beast to move. Seems to be his MO."

"I've got some grain in the barn," I offered. Lacey grabbed the Maglite I kept on top of the fridge and escorted me to the barn. I knew she was waiting for me to respond about the report, but she didn't press as I grabbed a bucket and a handful of the corn, oats and barley mix. "I'll ask her to file this report."

"That's a start. It's not enough, but Brenna's waiting to give this to Houdini."

"No, she's not." I heard Houdini's hoofbeats slow at the door. He nudged it open, and I met him with his prize.

"Glad you were here to protect her," Lacey said, stroking his neck. "How did he know?"

"You're ready to talk about Fate now?"

She reached out to me, and I set the bucket down, sliding into her arms.

"If I had known about Shawneen being your mom, I like to think that evening would have gone differently."

"Isn't that something to imagine. If I'd have known coming here was about finding you, I wouldn't have wasted any time at all on Shawneen. I'm the one who poked at that beehive. I'm the one who has to fix it."

"You don't have to fix it alone, okay?"

Tough as it was for me to accept, I knew she was right and followed her out past Houdini.

Brenna was waiting outside. "We've got Hagen in the cruiser. Madison, mind if we get your statement now while it's still fresh?"

"Sure. I'm too wired to sleep anyhow."

Lacey took my hand as we walked across the yard. From inside the cruiser, I could hear Hagen yelling his head off, but Brenna paid him no mind at all and followed us to the house.

CHAPTER FORTY-ONE

Madison

"You didn't have to do this," I told Gabe when he showed up the next morning with Mrs. Wheeler's tractor again. Lacey had already headed over to her shop, and Ruth was in town picking up groceries.

"Oh, I do."

"Seems like Lacey and I are the ones who owe you for looking after the place."

"Oh, that wasn't anything. And it wasn't Lacey who asked me to come out now."

"She didn't?" I was confused. Since it was her grandmother's tractor, I'd assumed that they had set it up on the sly.

"Brenna did."

"Brenna? What, she thinks that if you help fix my field, I'll file the official restraining order?" Once he'd busted my window, I conceded that I wasn't made of money and gave my statement to the officer. Brenna had insisted on a temporary restraining order and had sternly suggested that I file my own with the court.

He shrugged. "I don't really get how it all works."

"See, but this is the problem. You're out here doing something nice because…" Did I say your girlfriend? I still wasn't sure. "Because Brenna sent you. The only reason Hagen was out here is because Shawneen got him all worked up. She's the problem, but it's not like I can file an order telling her to stop filling Hagen's mind with crap. *I* have to do it. I know that. But I'm not up to it yet."

"If you're not going to talk to Shawneen, then you've got to do the restraining order. She didn't drive him out here that night, Madison. And he could've hurt you or lashed out at Lacey. A field, a window, you can repair. Your being stubborn makes you vulnerable, and people…They aren't as easy to fix."

Worried his concern might make me cry, I walked over to open the gate, giving me some time to swallow back my tears. He backed the antique tractor out of his stock trailer and putted into the field. After he cut the engine and jumped to the ground, he walked out to where I'd been working with a shovel. I'd spent the morning breaking my back trying to repair the rows by hand, righting the plants I could and pulling the ones I couldn't.

"What'd you lose?"

"Squash, mostly. Half my tomatoes."

"Okay." He already had his phone out of his pocket and up to his ear by the time I realized he wasn't just making conversation. I started waving trying to get him to hang up, but it was too late.

"Hey, Mrs. W. A lot of it is fixable, and the tractor will speed her up a bunch. Yeah. She was down here with the shovel when I got here." He turned away from me and listed out the plants I'd mentioned as well as others I hadn't. I didn't want the damage to seem as bad as it was, but poking through the discard pile with the toe of his boot, he easily read the field's casualties.

"She'll be over in a half hour," he said when he turned back to me.

"What do you mean she's coming in a half hour?"

"That's all we need to get the furrows repaired. Then she'll be here with the crew to get the new plants in. Good as new by the end of the day. Did you need any help with the window?"

"Lacey and I hung some plywood over it. It'll be a week before the glass comes in. Wait. Quit trying to distract me. I can't take more of Mrs. Wheeler's plants. I'll be fine with what's left for the season."

"You want to argue with Mrs. W? I'll get her back on the line for you." He pulled out his phone and angled his head waiting for me to gesture him to call. I couldn't find any words, which brought a satisfied smile to his face. "I figured you had the sense not to argue with her. And you'll save yourself an earful if you get on board about the restraining order before she gets here. You want to do the driving or directing?" He asked without missing a beat, shooting a thumb at the tractor.

"Direct. I don't trust myself not to rip up everything that's left."

"Fair 'nuff," he drawled, sounding a little like Dani.

Before he'd finished with the rows, two cars pulled up the drive—Hope, Dani and Joy with Lacey's gran in one and Della in the other. The first three women hugged me warmly and reiterated how glad they were that all the damage to my field was repairable. I shot a look at Gabe who shrugged as if it were coincidence that they were using words so similar to his. I didn't know whether to hug Della or not and wished Lacey was here to act as a buffer. I wasn't sure why she'd allowed herself to get roped into the act of kindness, but she answered the question about whether she expected a hug by stepping forward and pulling me into an only slightly awkward embrace.

"I was promised snacks," Della explained.

"Which we've got in the car," Hope quickly added before I could worry about what I was going to feed this impromptu crew.

Suddenly, I was thankful to have Della there. Had she not been, I could not have accepted the kindness from those whom I considered Lacey's family and friends without crying. Della made it all business, carrying the trays of plants from Hope's car to the field. Knees in the dirt, we made fast work as the sun crept high in the sky. Nobody talked about why they were there. Mrs. Wheeler discussed her hopes for the crops, Dani and Hope chatted about their plans for the summer, inviting me to join them all when they took a pontoon boat out on Lake Almanor. Gabe shared stories of leaping from a rock formation at Indian Falls into the icy Feather River.

"Joy won't be jumping off any rocks," Dani said.

Having both grown up in Quincy, Hope and Gabe shared a look, but it was Mrs. Wheeler who said, "If she grows up here, you won't be able to stop her. That place has a mighty pull."

Dani spoke again. "What about you and Lace? Are you two talking about babies?"

Her questions stopped me short, but I was the only one. Everyone else kept working as my mind spun. Hands on my thighs, I looked at Joy happily playing with clods of dirt in the shade of the tractor. Lacey and I hadn't talked about it. We hadn't even talked about living in the same house. She was over in East Quincy at work in her shop, the house where she'd spent her youth.

Yet here I was literally putting down my roots at Hot Rocks. I recalled how it had felt to stand on the property for the first time that snowy day, how I'd felt like I'd finally found my home. I could not have imagined this scene, that there were others who would be invested in my success.

"You don't have to answer that," Della said, making me realize how long I'd been silent. "She doesn't mean to get personal. She's got to know about everyone's breeding potential."

"That's not true," Dani insisted.

"You asked me if I wanted kids when we first met. I wasn't even dating anyone!"

"Yeah. And it's how you introduced yourself to me," Hope agreed.

Dani glanced at the others. When neither Gabe nor Mrs. W disagreed, she hung her head and laughed. "Hi, I'm new in town. Are you interested in having babies with me?"

"Pretty much." Hope laughed too, before leaning across the furrow to kiss her wife. "And that was it. How could I say no?"

"Your family is here in town, aren't they?" I asked Hope, remembering what Shawneen had said about how I overestimated what the town felt about having an out lesbian couple.

"My father is. Now that my sister is in school, it's just me and him."

"And he let you jump off rocks into the river?" I asked because I couldn't ask about how he and the town treated her and Dani like I really wanted to.

The way she smiled at me made me feel like she knew exactly what I was asking. "Indian Falls was a favorite spot of ours, and Dad already talks to Joy about how much she'll love it when she's old enough to join her cousins in the water."

"This town will surprise you," Dani said. Her words were for me, but her eyes were on Hope.

"It already has," I answered. I was so glad that Lacey and Ruth had insisted I come back. I knew it was time to talk to Lacey about how lucky I was that a blown tire had led me to her shop and how she'd repaired what I hadn't even known was broken.

CHAPTER FORTY-TWO

Lacey

The '66 Mustang was back in for an annoying leak in the rear transmission seal. I was going to have to remove the whole driveshaft and was settled in on the creeper when I heard a familiar clop. Though it had been a while since he'd visited, I was prepared for the nudge on my boot and Houdini's four hooves visible from where I lay.

I was totally unprepared though for the set of boots that dropped to the floor. I wheeled out and looked up at Madison. I blinked in confusion. "What on earth are you doing? How'd you get here? Are you trying to get Brenna to give you a ticket?"

"It's nice to see you too." She dropped one of the reins to the ground and fished through the saddlebags hanging from the horn of her saddle.

Straddling my creeper, I sat there trying to wrap my brain around her being in my shop with Houdini. When she turned around, she had her childhood cigar box in her hands. She knelt down next to me and pressed it into my hands without speaking. It was heavier than it had been when I'd found it tucked away in our bedroom wall. Did she realize we were sitting within throwing distance of where it had been? I pushed the lid up and gasped.

The last time I'd seen that golden Wulfsburg crest was when I was sixteen and learning to drive in my dad's Beetle. "Where? How?" I didn't have words. When I'd first begun the project, I thought it would be so easy to piece the old car back together, and as I checked items off the list and the horn continued to elude me, I'd begun to think the hole in the middle of the steering wheel would mock me forever. An alternative to the genuine '53 was simply unacceptable. This one was perfect.

"My pop found it."

I considered her impishness that had sometimes made her seem timid or vulnerable but now I knew was part of her quirkiness. "Your pop," I said because she'd said it so easily.

"Charlie. I asked him to be on the lookout for it."

The fact that she'd had the conversation with Charlie meant as much to me as the object in my hand did. "And you knew the right one."

"It is? You didn't say…I was worried…"

I set the box down next to me and threw my arms around her, even though I itched to install the horn that instant. "It's perfect. You're perfect." I felt my words work their way past the insecurities that had guarded her for so long. It was like she'd been wrapped in thorns that now bloomed instead.

"That first day I stood in your shop, I was so lost. I didn't think there was any place I really belonged."

"And then you left, and Della yelled at me for letting a hottie drive away."

"What exactly did you tell Della?"

I blushed. "It wasn't what I said. She read it in my face."

"Hmm. That sounds suspiciously like Fate." Her eyes locked onto mine.

"If that's what you want to call it." Everything around us felt still.

"I don't know how this works," she whispered.

"How what works?"

"I belong with you. I rode out here because I needed the time to think of what to say or how to solve this problem. I know I can't ask you to give up your childhood home, but this isn't my home. Hot Rocks is, and I have to be there for the business anyway and..."

I saw no logical end to the words tumbling out of her mouth, so I planted a kiss on her. "Is this your roundabout way of asking me to move in with you?"

"If you wanted to. But not just that. Would you...Do you think you could take a look at the horn?"

Puzzled, I picked up her treasure box again and lifted out the horn. Beneath it was a band. My blood whooshed faster as I lifted it out. "It's beautiful," I said, admiring the square setting that held four small diamonds around a slightly larger one in the middle.

"It was Bo's mother's. Ruth found it one of the nights we were sorting."

"And she gave it to you."

"She did."

"How do you know she didn't mean for you to be the one wearing it?"

Real confusion swept across her face. "Because then what would you wear?"

I jumped up and ran to the bench. I searched through the hollow locating dowels I kept for locating the cylinder head when I was positioning it on the block. Different sized engines required that I have a variety of sizes on hand. I selected from the shorter ones, slipping one after another onto my finger until I had one that fit in a makeshift way.

Madison had followed me to the bench to watch what I was doing, and when she saw me slide the thick band of metal over my knuckle, she met my eyes. I still had her grandmother's ring and held it up. Madison offered me her hand, and I slid the diamond into place. "It fits perfectly," I said.

She reached diagonally between us and took my left hand in hers. "We can shop for your ring."

"You don't approve? I think it's appropriate."

"I don't want your family and friends thinking that's all I can do."

"I don't need anything fancy."

"That's not what I thought when I first saw you standing in your shop."

"When you thought I was the customer?" I egged because I loved to hear her tell stories about us.

"I thought you were the homecoming queen. No homecoming queen would wear a…what is that, anyway?"

"A hollow locating dowel," I said like everyone knew.

"No homecoming queen would wear a hollow locating dowel as an engagement ring."

"Luckily, I was never homecoming queen."

Madison stepped forward and kissed me deeply. "I don't want to spend any of my nights without you. Ever."

"Good. But what are we going to do with Houdini?"

"Gabe said he'd pick him up with his trailer on the way out to Hot Rocks this evening."

"Wait, we're going back out to your place?"

"I wanted to have everyone out to say thank you for all their help."

"Tonight?" I couldn't hide the disappointment in my voice. I'd imagined the two of us celebrating the bands on our hands in private.

"I know it's not the best timing, but Charlie's here to pick up Ruth, so it has to be tonight."

"But no guests."

"No guests, and Charlie and Ruth will be heading off tonight. Early morning for Charlie and all."

"I didn't know Ruth was so anxious to go home."

"She was starting to think about it. When Charlie said he'd deliver the horn, it made sense for her to head back with him."

"When's Gabe going to be there?"

"Tonight around five. I thought I might be able to convince you to take a long lunch."

"You expect me to come back to the shop and get any sort of work done when you proposition me like that?"

She shrugged. "That's for you to decide. Aren't you glad you own the place?"

"And Houdini?"

"I'll put him in the backyard if you don't mind."

"I don't. And I'll close up shop while you get him settled." Without another thought to the driveshaft or the leak in the transmission, I pulled my shop door down and locked up, grateful there was no one around to see my goofy grin.

CHAPTER FORTY-THREE

Madison

I loved Gabe's bear hugs enough to not let myself think about whether Brenna had a problem with how long I held on. Even when I saw her out of uniform, she still carried an air of law enforcement, her black hair pulled back in a severe ponytail, and dark buttoned-down shirt as serious as any uniform. I squeezed Gabe tightly anyway, loving how in his hug I felt like I really belonged. Lacey had always belonged to a clan. Being surrounded by family was a completely new feeling for me, and I reveled in it.

"It's nice of you to have us all out," he said as Brenna shook my hand in a very official manner, looking around as if scoping out trouble. Gabe had already met Ruth, but I took the chance to introduce him to Charlie. Until then, Charlie had been talking stock with Dani. They were by the big picture window, and Charlie's gestures suggested Dani had him talking about what the place was like back when he managed the cattle ranch. I was a little jealous to see them talking so easily, but I knew that like Lacey, Dani had a knack for getting people to open up.

Hope and Mrs. Wheeler were already at the kitchen table feeding Joy. With Gabe and Brenna there, we all gathered around my family-style table with rough-hewn planks and benches along each side. My heart felt like it might explode—family and friends pulled together around a summer meal of corn, slaw, potato salad and barbeque chicken. I'd spent so much of my life feeling like I had no one, and here was this huge gathering pulled together at my request. Lacey must've read how I was feeling because she reached out and grasped my shoulder.

I looked over at Charlie who was lost in thought. I'd have given anything to know what he was thinking and his reminiscences. Feeling my eyes on him, he blinked over to me with a huge smile. He picked up his beer and held it aloft. Everyone went quiet, their attention on him.

"To bein' home."

Everyone echoed his toast. My throat was too constricted to give voice to what I felt in my heart. We clinked glasses to bottles, cheer all around.

"It's somethin', innit? When you find the spot that makes your heart sing?" Dani said.

"Or the person," Hope said.

Ruth bowed her head, and my heart ached for Bo's absence.

"So y'all made it official? You gonna share the story, or are you keeping it secret?" Dani gestured at Lacey's left hand.

Lacey and I both displayed our rings, and everyone raised their glasses again. Ruth beamed as I shared the history of my ring and puzzled over whatever it was Lacey had shoved on her finger arguing that I didn't have to go ring shopping anytime soon.

"Are you two ever going to talk about rings?" Dani ribbed Gabe.

"Believe me, I've tried," Gabe said. "She's still not sure."

"How long have the two of you been together?" Ruth asked.

"Two years…" Gabe said. "Maybe eight months," said Brenna at the same time.

"Two years? How in the world." We watched her search back. "That would take us back to…?"

"When you gave me that ticket when I was hauling ass outta town on my way to Reno."

"I'd hardly call that our first date." Brenna sounded exasperated.

"I knew. Why do you think I fought the ticket in court? Guaranteed second date," Gabe said with confidence.

"I don't know that arguing your guilt can be considered a date."

"That wasn't the point. The point was for you to get to see me all cleaned up in my tie."

She rolled her eyes, but the edge of her lip held a smile. Her voice had a gentler tone. "I can't think of a thing I've done to encourage this."

Dani said, "Gabe you remind me of a story I read way back about a boy who straight out had to have this wild horse and chased it day after day after day until that horse gave up and accepted him."

"I'm the horse in this story, I gather," Brenna said.

"Exactly," Gabe said. "And now that you've accepted that I'm not going anywhere, you agree to get hitched."

"So now we're both horses. Pulling a wagon," Brenna deadpanned.

"Believe me, being the horse is a huge compliment. I hear all day long about how horses aren't the problem," Hope said with a smile on her face.

"It's the humans," Dani inserted. "Every damn time."

Hope cleared her throat and pointedly looked at Joy who sat happily playing with the remains of her meal. "*Language.*"

"Every stinkin' time," Dani revised. "Horses listen to instinct. Humans fight it."

I thought about how Lacey fought Fate while I embraced it. It didn't feel like the time to nudge her about that, but I smiled and took her hand. The way she smiled back made me think she already knew.

I enjoyed my friends so much that night that it was tough to say goodbye. Of all the work I'd done and success with my guests, this gathering had been my best moment. I understood when Hope looked at her watch and then at Dani that they had to leave, and their gathering kid stuff was the domino that tripped the others to look for keys and also make their way to the door.

Hope and Dani were securing their passengers, young and old, in the back of Hope's car when another set of headlights swung into my drive. Lacey looked at me questioningly, but I was as puzzled as she. The maroon Nova provided the answer.

She took in the group as she stepped out of the car. Night had already chased the last light from the property, but the porch light spilled wide and invitingly in contrast to Shawneen's anger as she slammed the door and stalked to the porch. I watched her take in the crowd, especially when her eyes landed on Charlie. She stopped and inhaled so deeply I could see her chest expand.

Her emotions battled each other but she quickly shoved aside all but her rage. "How dare you file a restraining order against Hagen?"

"He damaged my property twice, Shawneen. I didn't want to wait around and see what would happen a third time."

"You know that's just heartbreak speaking. There's no need to put something on his record."

"They wouldn't let me file one against you, but now maybe the judge would reconsider." I glanced at Brenna and was relieved to see her nod in agreement. Her wide-set shoulders reminded me to stand tall when Shawneen spoke again.

"Me? Why the hell would you file a restraining order after you went to all the trouble to find me after all these years?"

"I was looking for home, Shawneen, not you. I found everything I need, and I think you should go."

"Me? You're the one who should go. You and your filthy friends who parade around like they're God's gift. I don't know what the college was thinking hiring the likes of you," she spat at Dani before shifting her attention to Hope. "And your mother'd turn in her grave if she knew that you carried that bastard child."

I stood horrified, trying to find a way to rewind and get Shawneen off my property before she could continue her insults. Chancing a look at Hope, I was surprised to see her face sympathetically neutral. "You obviously didn't know my mother. And it looks like you don't know Madison either, which makes me sad for you." Looking to me, she effectively dismissed Shawneen. "Do you need us to stay?"

They were going? For a moment I wanted to say yes, that I needed all of my friends to face this foe. But then I realized that in staying they only gave her more fuel. "No." I walked down the stairs of the porch to deliver an extra hug to Hope and Dani. After they left, Ruth came down behind me, Charlie following with her bag which he tied in the corner of his truck.

Ruth hugged me long and hard. "Thank you for sharing your home and your friends." She must have seen the tears I didn't want to spill in front of Shawneen, because she tenderly patted my cheek with her palm before hugging Lacey as well. At first it looked like she was going to walk around to the passenger side, but instead she turned to address Shawneen. "I'm sorry life hasn't handed you what you think you deserve, but you'll have more luck if you start with yourself."

"Who the hell are you to talk? You know that man is married to me?"

Charlie shot back, "Only because it was the only way to keep Madison away from you. You know the court would never've given her to me, and you would have only kept her to hurt me."

"I would've at least raised her right."

"She seems more'n all right to me," Charlie said.

"You know she's having sex with that woman." Shawneen pointed at Lacey.

Lacey put her arm around me, which made Shawneen twitch.

Charlie looked from me to Lacey, and for a moment, I could see that Shawneen thought she'd pierced him. That was before Charlie threw back his head and guffawed. I'd never heard such a loud sound exit his wiry frame. He placed his hand over his mouth as if he'd surprised himself. "I certainly hope so." He shook his head and put one hand on my shoulder and one on Lacey's. Lacey took her arm away, and Charlie awkwardly wrapped his arms around me flooding me with the memory of being carried by him. When would he have carried me? Had he carried me when we lived in the East Quincy place? He whispered, "proud of you" and released me to walk to the driver's side of his truck.

"You are not leaving. You don't get to leave again," Shawneen hissed.

"Long drive and an early morning," he replied, tipping his hat in her general direction.

Because he'd turned a bit to address her, when she rushed him, her hands hit his chest and he stumbled backward until his back hit the truck. I heard the oomph of air leaving his lungs. His arms shot up away from Shawneen as she continued to beat her arms against his chest. He did nothing to stop the blows. Brenna quickly intervened to restrain Shawneen.

"That's enough. Unless you want to take a ride with me and spend the night at the station. Time to go home."

"I'm not leaving. You leave." She lurched toward Charlie again. "You obviously know how. Leave and take her with you again without a thought about me."

Charlie swallowed a few times before replying. His voice came out as a growl. "I thought about you plenty. Thought no mother in her right mind hurts her child. Thought about how you threatened to tell the judge it was me even though I never raised a hand to my girl. Thought the only good thing that ever came outta you was Madison. Maybe that's why you hated her so much."

I felt sucker punched, and Charlie's eyes held apology when they met mine. He'd never told me. When I looked at Ruth, I knew his words were true and that she'd known. She took a few steps and took my hand. There would have been a time when knowing Shawneen had hit me would have set me into a spiral. I felt Ruth's hand warm in mine and saw how lucky I was to have been raised with her love and kindness. Whatever Shawneen's problems, they didn't concern me.

"You never loved me. The only reason you married me was because of her. I never asked to be a mother, and I got all the crap. All the dirty diapers, all the barf and screaming. Then you'd come home, and she was all sunshine and roses. She never wanted me. Should've never happened. Shouldn't have let you talk me into letting her take over my body."

"Thought she'd take over your heart." Charlie's voice was quiet.

What would it have been like to grow up with them? All those times I'd imagined us in Quincy together as a family. They would have fought like this. I'd have grown up with insults hurled at each other, with her hurling insults at me.

"She certainly took over mine. Mine and Bo's both." Ruth smiled with joy and sadness, and I suddenly missed Bo fiercely.

"I don't need you, Shawneen. I don't need a thing from you. You can't hurt me anymore," I said, my voice strong and sure.

Brenna released her arms, and Shawneen dramatically smoothed down her shirt, pumping up her pride. "You'll regret this…"

Brenna stepped closer again capturing her attention. Like I said, she didn't need her uniform to be intimidating. "I'd be real careful about what words left my mouth," she said.

Without another word, she returned to her Nova, slamming its tan door. I expected her to tear out of the yard and down the hill, but she didn't. Ever so slowly, she backed up and turned around. We all stood silently until her taillights disappeared into the night.

"You'll be okay here?" Ruth asked.

"Yes," I said honestly. I appreciated the offer, but all I wanted was to be alone with Lacey. Brenna said she'd be letting the officers on shift know what had happened, but I sensed we'd be fine.

"You okay?" Lacey asked, taking my arm as we walked back to the house.

"More than. Apart from Shawneen, that was the best night ever. I want to have more big dinners. I want to invite everyone out—your whole family. Can we do that?"

"Of course we can. But right now, I'm so happy to have you to myself again."

I was glad I'd spent the afternoon in Lacey's bed when we climbed into mine together. I'd come down from the adrenaline rush of confronting Shawneen, but it left me wrung out. I didn't have anything to give Lacey. She pushed my shoulder, so she could spoon in behind me. Though I complied, I tipped my head back. "Is this an okay way to spend the night?"

"Of course. I couldn't be happier."

I drew her arm around my middle and thought of all I'd found in Quincy.

"What are you thinking?" She traced my hip with her wonderful fingers.

"That when I came to Quincy, I never expected to find a place where I fit. But I have. Not just here." I wiggled my tush into her hips. "Even though Charlie and Ruth went home tonight, I still feel like I found my spot."

"You're not worried about Shawneen?"

"Nope."

Her hand stilled.

"Well, I am worried she'll use your emotional attachment to that old car to manipulate you." She punched me lightly. "I mean it. Either let that car go or buy it from her if you care that much. You're not working on it for her anymore."

"Got it boss." She buried her head in my shoulders waiting for me to really answer her question.

"It's a lot to take in, all the stuff that Charlie never told me. But…I think we're getting to a place we'll be able to talk about it. It was so weird to see him here tonight. He was different, more like the dad I always wanted him to be. All those years I looked over at the trailer from my room, afraid of how quiet he was. I thought I didn't have any parents. I hated trying to explain to people who Ruth and Bo were, who the quiet cowboy in the corner was. Now I realize that I could have answered that I had three parents."

"Love does that."

"What?" I asked.

"Makes a family. There are so many different shapes, and if your family doesn't fit the picture, there's that fear that people won't understand. Joy is sure to face that when kids start asking her about her moms. You can help her explain that it doesn't matter what your family looks like as long as the people in that family love you."

"I wish someone had explained that to me when I was five."

"Me too," she said. I was glad she didn't add that I shouldn't have worried so much or should let it go now. She held on to me, and that was all I needed.

CHAPTER FORTY-FOUR

Madison

It would be so satisfying to say that when Shawneen left Hot Rocks that night, we watched the taillights disappear for the last time. But with her working down the street from the shop, we saw that Nova all the time. Occasionally we'd see her at the grocery, but she ignored us, and we did the same. You'd be surprised how little you can see of a person in a town as small as Quincy.

That didn't mean I gained much mental real estate—she still took up plenty of my brain space. Like the night a few weeks after my dinner party when I decided to surprise Lacey and take her out to dinner. She was finishing up her billing when I got there, a task I knew better than to interrupt, so I sat down on the porch with the current biography I was reading.

Across the street, Shawneen pulled into the restaurant parking lot. Though my head was inclined toward the book, I could see her clearly. She walked toward the building at a fast clip, only glancing at Rainbow Auto as she opened the door. Since she paused, I looked up. I couldn't read her expression as far away as she was, but I waved. As if trying to dodge a spell, she disappeared through the door.

My mind no longer on my book, I wondered what Lacey would say if I asked to walk across the street for dinner. I did love their broccoli and beef. But I knew what would happen if Shawneen were to serve us. I leaned against Lacey's house and shut my eyes, seeing her pause as she approached the table. I'd keep a hold of Lacey's hand. We'd sit on the same side of the booth.

She'd turn right around. In my mind I heard her arguing with her manager.

I will not stand by and tacitly condone their behavior by serving those people. Too vividly I remembered the icy tone she used when she talked to me now.

Because the world revolves around you, doesn't it, Shawneen?

I easily imagined her hateful gaze when she delivered our water and the force she would use when setting the glasses down.

Lacey would engage her in conversation about the Nova, ask how it was driving, suggest that she take the tan door to the body shop that had done such a good job on the Bug. I knew that it was killing her that Dennis had helped out by spray-painting it red, which made it look worse, but she had promised to let it go and so far had kept her mouth shut.

"You okay over here?" Lacey asked, sitting down next to me. Either I'd drifted more than I realized or she'd left her shop doors open and could see me watching Shawneen.

"Did you know Woodrow Wilson said that the one swimming against the stream knows the strength of it?"

"You just read that?"

"No. I was thinking about where I want to go for dinner."

"Are you the one swimming against the stream, or am I?"

"I'm the swimmer. Shawneen's the stream. What if I had my mouth set on Chinese?"

"Then I'd say let's go."

"Even though you know it would make her steaming mad?"

"I liked how Dani and Hope left when she came up to Hot Rocks spewing all that hateful stuff. She thrives on conflict, and if we avoid the restaurant where she happens to work, then she wins. If we go, we show her that we don't care and that her hateful words don't hurt us or change who we are."

We sat together for a few minutes as the truth in her words sunk in. I didn't want to give Shawneen power by avoiding her. I also didn't want to let her keep the lease on the space she had occupied for a very long time in my brain and heart. "What if I don't want the stress that would come from sitting there pretending her anger didn't hurt my feelings."

Lacey sagged next to me. "I'd be so relieved! I'd gear up for it if you had an investment, I promise, but pizza and beer sounds so much better to me!"

"Pizza and beer it is." My mind relieved of the worry of Shawneen, I remembered a message I was supposed to deliver. "Oh, I stopped by the post office on my way over. Nathan said he picked up…what was it? Some old car…"

"An Oldsmobile?"

"Maybe?"

"From the seventies?" Lacey sounded excited.

"How am I supposed to know?"

"You're the one who was talking to him!"

"And why in the world is he talking to me, the one who knows nothing about cars, instead of calling you?"

"That's the way it works in a small town. He's probably been meaning to let me know, but it took seeing you to remind him. He's been talking for a while about finding an Olds like the one he learned to drive on and restoring something like I did with the Beetle. Good for him. I'll give him a call."

She didn't move to get her phone or shut her shop. Instead, she leaned against me. We watched traffic go by, a fair number of drivers saw us sitting there and tooted their horns. We waved back, Lacey identifying the driver if I didn't recognize the vehicle.

"It's better than TV," I said.

Lacey laughed. "Back when I was little, we'd be driving my mom up the wall, and she'd tell us to sit on the porch and count cars. We couldn't come in until we'd seen ten cars the color she chose."

"That's not true. Why wouldn't she send you in the back where there's a fence?"

"Oh, she'd try that first. But we were loud, and she'd get tired of hollering at us through the greenhouse. We'd hear water hitting the glass as she tried to get our attention. We knew we pushed her too hard if she stormed out and marched us through to the front porch to count cars. Sometimes she'd say count to a hundred, but if she was really mad, she wouldn't let us come in until we'd counted twenty yellow ones. My brothers were sneaky though and would look for campers that had yellow logos painted on them. There were days we were still sitting out there when my dad got home."

"Would he be mad?"

"Nah. Most of the time, he'd join us and help finish up our count. He'd get us to confess all the trouble we'd gotten into while mom cooled down."

"Hearing you talk about your family is like learning a completely foreign culture."

"You sure you're up for hosting the Fourth of July festivities this year?"

"I'm sure," I said. I remembered that it was her family's favorite holiday and had spent the last week in a frenzy of buying all the supplies.

"Are Charlie and Ruth going to make it?"

"No. Ruth doesn't want to drive up on the holiday weekend, and Charlie doesn't trust anyone with the ranch yet. Besides, this is your holiday. I promised them they'd have us Thanksgiving weekend."

"I like the sound of that."

"Thanksgiving weekend?"

"Us. Now let's get us some food."

CHAPTER FORTY-FIVE

Madison

"You little stinker!" I swore, tearing after Bruno. I was certain I'd be able to catch an eight-year-old, but he easily left me in the dust, disappearing into the woods. "Who got into the silly string?" Hands on my knees, I stood there panting, swiping at the green strings that hung from my head, not registering how quiet it had become. The whole property was still.

I'd ordered a whole crate of the stuff since there were way too many trees on my property to do any fireworks. It was supposed to be a fun activity during the afternoon, and I'd had a plan. Being ambushed by an eight-year-old wasn't in it, and now I wondered if Lacey had set me up. Slowly I started backing up toward the house. They came from everywhere, behind trees and bushes, from every side, the house included, all of the silly string aimed at me. Where was Houdini when I needed him?

Lacey broke through the circle and handed me a couple of cans to defend myself.

"Sorry," she said without conviction. "We couldn't resist!" Trevor shifted his aim to his boys, winding both Bruno and Eric in a web of string, but Cal kept his aim on me. He had bigger cans of silly string, and he'd taped them together and rigged them somehow to shoot at the same time. With that setup in both hands, he had four lines of silly string going.

Both Iris and Lacey's sister, Chrystal, were trying to distract him, but he kept squirting like he planned to cover me completely.

I finally started hearing the hissing indicating the end of the can, a sound I'd never been so grateful to hear.

"This was the best idea ever!" one of Chrystal's kids said. Wesley, maybe. I still hadn't squared away the names of all the family I was meeting for the first time. All I knew was that they'd arrived wary and were all now smiling.

"Let's do it every year!" Trevor's Eric said.

"What do you think?" Lacey asked, helping me remove the mass of silly string that covered me.

"Will the cleanup keep them busy the rest of the afternoon?"

"It'll at least keep them outside," she commented as we watched them picking up longer strings in attempt to cover each other again.

"Hope you're not mad," Cal said, shaking his can, trying to get something more to squirt at me.

"Not at all," I said.

"Don't tell him that," Chrystal said, joining us. "It'll only encourage him."

"Whatever happened to the newbies being safe for a year?" Bennett said.

"I don't see why you're asking. You've never got anyone to bring home," Cal said.

"Neither do you, loser," Bennett shot back.

"Not true." Cal squirted air at his brother. "I have a girlfriend. She just couldn't make it today."

"She couldn't make bail?" Bennett saw Cal move before I did and was off running.

I was doing my best to keep up with their rapid-fire conversation and not worry about the boys running around in the woods.

"It's a lot to take in, isn't it?" I hadn't even seen Lacey's mom, Delphine come up beside us.

"Lacey tried to prepare me, but…" I shook my head.

"When Matt and I decided to have more than two, the idea was that they'd play with each other and keep each other occupied. I never thought that they'd try to rip each other apart."

Breathing hard, Bennett stopped next to us though he kept a wary eye on Cal who had stopped next to the bucket of drinks I'd put on ice. Cal pulled out a bottle of water and remained by the porch to drink it. Lacey poked me, and I realized I'd missed something.

"I'm sorry?" I said.

"My boys said that you named this place after a hot springs. Is it within walking distance?" Delphine asked.

"It's a little bit of a hike, but it's doable. The little kids might get tired on the way back, but I could see if Houdini is around."

"Houdini?" Delphine laughed.

"A horse. He came with the property but doesn't stay put."

"Perfect name."

In a flash, Cal was running again, this time with a bucket in his hands. Bennett grabbed me and spun me around using me as a shield. Cal didn't hesitate at all. I saw the ice water crest and hover in the air. My brain froze before it even hit me, just me, because Bennett had jumped out of harm's way.

"Calvin Melville McAlpine!" Delphine gasped as I stood there shocked and frozen. "Matt, get us some towels out here! Lots of them!" she called.

Lacey placed a hand on my shoulder. I was soaked head to toe, the tee cold and tight, and jeans shorts heavy on my hips. Water dripped from my short hair.

Chrystal hollered at her brother, but the way my ears rang, I only caught snippets. "…can't believe…idiot…" All the kids came running to see what the shouting was about. Cal yelling back, arms waving as he shouted like a child, "you're not my mom."

"Oh, If I were…"

"…don't even think…"

Goose bumps covered my body, and my teeth chattered.

"If Bennett hadn't…"

Lacey looked so worried, and I realized how I must have looked standing there dripping.

That idea kicked through the shock, and I couldn't help but laugh. I threw my head back and howled with laughter. The kids joined in first, and the adults, once they realized I really was laughing, joined in.

"Are you okay?" Lacey asked.

"I'm so sorry," Cal said. "That was totally meant for my idiot brother."

"You can't blame me!" Bennett exclaimed.

"Guys, chill," Lacey said, and I could hear that she was still worried about me. I was laughing so much that tears were rolling down my face. I couldn't control either one, the laughing or the tears, not to mention my shivering, and it felt so good. All that noise. All the chaos.

It felt like home.

It felt like family.

My own paradise.

Bella Books, Inc.

Women. Books. Even Better Together.

P.O. Box 10543
Tallahassee, FL 32302

Phone: 800-729-4992
www.bellabooks.com